LENORE'S LAST FUNERAL

LENORE'S LAST FUNERAL

J.M. DONELLAN

First published by Level Best Books 2023

This novel is entirely a work of fiction. The names, characters and incidents portrayed in it are the work of the author's imagination. Any resemblance to actual persons, living or dead, events or localities is entirely coincidental.

J.M. Donellan asserts the moral right to be identified as the author of this work.

Author Photo Credit: Dave Clarkey

First edition

ISBN: 978-1-68512-453-3

Cover art by Level Best Designs

This book was professionally typeset on Reedsy.
Find out more at reedsy.com

For Matilda, who changed everything.

Contents

Praise for Lenore's Last Funeral   iv

I   FOURTH BARDO

 1 WE ALL DIE (EXCEPT FOR YOU, APPARENTLY).   3
 2 ESCHATOLOGY   12
 3 RILEY   18
 4 POST-LIFE PROBLEMS   27
 5 FRANCIS BACON'S JUVENILIA   30
 6 ANGRY BETTY   35
 7 WHAT HAPPENS NEXT?   39
 8 CAN I HAVE HER SHOES?   43
 9 THE DEATH DOLLAR   48
10 DEATH, SEX, AND COFFEE   54
11 IMMOR(T)ALITY   62
12 THE GHOST DID IT   66
13 OUR LADY OF PERPETUAL SUCCOUR   71
14 ARE YOU DRACULA?   74
15 AN AVENGING ANGEL   80
16 NOT SIGN, SCION   86
17 WE WANT TO DEFEAT DEATH. TO LIVE FOR-
     EVER. HERE, HAVE A...   94
18 ETERNAL LIFE OR YOUR MONEY BACK!   105

II   FIFTH BARDO

19   AIN'T NO MOUNTAIN HIGH ENOUGH   113

20   WHY DON'T YOU START BY TELLING ME HOW
     YOU DIED?   117

21   OCKY'S RAZOR   122

22   PAINFULLY QUOTIDIAN   135

23   URBACH-WIETHE   141

24   I DO THIS IN SERVICE OF YOU   149

25   LET THE DEAD DIE   154

26   EDGAR ALLAN POPE   158

27   MASKS   163

28   VOMITING ON THE ASTRAL PLANE   167

29   BONE MUSIC   170

30   FAMOUS LAST WORDS   176

31   BLOOD   181

32   DEAD STARS   189

33   THE NEXT AND FINAL APOCALYPSE   193

34   TUN STATE   199

35   I LOVE THOSE EARRINGS! I'LL MAKE SURE
     YOU'RE BURIED IN THEM.   207

36   RED. VERY RED. EXTREMELY RED.   211

37   I'M IN THE DEATH BUSINESS   218

38   THE TAPE   223

39   VISUAL RATSAC   232

40   A SURPRISE CELEBRITY GUEST   236

41   ZOMBIES IN LOVE   240

42   RENA   243

43   ANTIQUARIAN FUTURE   252

44   USUALLY THERE'S A SEX SCENE OR A CHEER-
     ING CROWD?   257

III   SIXTH BARDO

45 AGATHOKAKOLOGICAL   265
46 THE WORLD'S MOST DEPRESSING SITCOM   268
47 AN EPHEMERAL SNEEZE OF PROGNOSTICATION   273
48 ECONOMICS IS TOTAL BULLSHIT   276
49 NERO, ASCENDANT   279

Acknowledgements   281
About the Author   282
Also by J.M. Donellan   283

Praise for Lenore's Last Funeral

"This captivating thriller will have you questioning everything you know about funerals. Like what exactly is a moirologist? Donellan blurs the line between literary and genre fiction in his portrayal of the human condition…A nice mix of the macabre and quirkiness, *Lenore's Last Funeral* is an intriguing look at mankind's mortality and the struggle to make sense of death."—Ivanka Fear, author of *Where is My Husband?*

Praise for previous books:

"Donellan gets readers to root for an unsavory lead in this funny, off-kilter thriller… The brisk plotting is enhanced by Archie's well-developed inner emotional life and Donellan's wry prose."—*Rumors of Her Death* reviewed in *Publisher's Weekly*.

"…cleverly crafted and overflowing with idiosyncratic characters and mordant humor."—*Killing Adonis* reviewed in *Kirkus Reviews* (starred review).

"*Killing Adonis* is the book that Agatha Christie and Tim Burton would have written together."—*Killing Adonis* reviewed by the NSW Writers' Centre

"Books like this are the reason I read."—*Zeb and the Great Ruckus* reviewed at Batch of Books

"Anecdotal and strange, he uses the language of an American comedian with a sort of British wit."—*A Beginner's Guide to Dying in India* reviewed in *Four Thousand Magazine*

I

FOURTH BARDO

1

WE ALL DIE (EXCEPT FOR YOU, APPARENTLY).

What Magnus lacked in a pulse, he certainly made up for in style. He was dressed in his favourite three-piece suit, hands folded beatifically across his chest, hair immaculately groomed, shoes polished to the point of reflectivity. He looked as though he was taking a cheeky coffin nap before heading out to a five-star gala.

Lenore gazed at his corpse, placed her palm delicately against his cheek. She dabbed at her tears, leaned in close, and whispered, "Thanks for the invite. The canapés are superb." She stood up and turned to see an elderly woman staring at her, face contorted in sympathy.

"I'm Maryanne. I don't believe I've had the pleasure," she said, holding out her hand. Her skin was blue-vein cheese wrapped in wax paper.

"I'm Jessica," Lenore replied, "Lovely to meet you, sorry it had to be under such…" she let her sentence trail off and wept, dabbing at her eyes again, as much in response to Maryanne's miasmic perfume as anything else.

Maryanne took Lenore's hand and patted it lightly. "How did you know Magnus?"

"I was one of his students. You?"

"He was my grandson."

"Magnus was a wonderful teacher."

"I'm sure he was." Maryanne gazed sorrowfully at Magnus.

Lenore took this as her cue and said, "I'm sorry, I should let you…"

Maryanne nodded, tears welling in her eyes as she turned and approached the coffin.

Lenore treated the other guests to her patented melancholic half-smile as she made her way back to the food table. She picked up a spring roll, dipped it in soy sauce, and had it halfway to her mouth when Simon hissed in her ear,

"I specifically told you *no food!*"

Lenore turned around and said, "But I've barely eaten since breakfast. I get very emotional when I'm hungry."

"It's a funeral. You are *supposed* to be emotional." He plucked the spring roll from her fingers and tossed it petulantly in the bin, then glowered at her and stormed away.

"I wish it was you in that casket," she grumbled. Lenore sat quietly in the corner, resisting the urge to check her phone. She studied the aged wooden floor underneath her feet.

A young girl clutching a plush tiger toy sat down unceremoniously next to her and fixed her with an unflinching gaze. "I'm Phoebe."

"Hello, Phoebe, my name's Jessica."

Phoebe gestured for Lenore to come closer. She leaned in as Phoebe whispered, "Don't be angry at Uncle Sime. He's just sad because Magnus got deaded." Phoebe pushed a spring roll wrapped in a paper towel into Lenore's hands and placed a conspiratorial finger to her lips.

Lenore smiled and hid the spring roll in her handbag. "Thanks, I'll save this for later," she said in a stage whisper.

Phoebe nodded, pleased. "Are you gonna die someday, too?"

"Yes, of course. Everyone dies eventually."

Phoebe shook her head, grinning. "Nuh-uh! Not me. I'm gonna move to Florida 'nstead."

"You sure about that? I've heard people say that's a fate worse than death."

"Florida is where Disney World is! I'm going to go on all the rides every day, all the time forever."

"Sounds like a brilliant plan."

"Yup!" a triumphant smile surged across Phoebe's face. She shoved a finger into her nose. "Do you gots kids?"

"Me? Oh, good lord, no."

Phoebe looked confused; her finger momentarily paused its burrowing. "How?"

"How…what?"

"How do you gots no kids?"

Lenore grimaced and said, "Wellll, when a man and a woman love each other very much—or at least enough to move in together even if marriage isn't quite on the table yet *despite* the fact that she's tried to tactfully hint at the subject *more* than once— and they don't want to be saddled with the myriad financial and emotional burdens of child-rearing, they can employ various methods of—"

"Are you worried they'll get deaded and you'll be sad?" Phoebe blinked at her, index finger resuming its excavation.

"We all get dead—ah, we all die. Except for you, apparently."

Phoebe nodded proudly. "Are you *scared* of being deaded?"

Lenore rubbed the ash diamond on her finger, gazed at the casket at the front of the chapel. "More than anything in the world. Intellectually, I know it's just the second law of thermodynamics—the arrow of time spares no one and all the rest of it—but when I think about the absence of my own consciousness, I start hyperventilating. I imagine my lifeless body buried beneath the earth, visited for a while by friends and family until eventually they go into the ground as well. No matter how much we exercise and meditate and diet, how kind or how cruel or generous or selfish we choose to be, we all end up the same: cold and forgotten.

"I know that when I'm dead, I'll no longer be able to experience the fear of death, but that doesn't do me any good right now, does it? I've had this debilitating phobia since I was a little girl, and I found out about what happened to my mother. I managed to suppress it all for a while, but it's all boiled back up to the surface since Quan died— which I can't help but feel responsible for because of various complex and possibly arcane reasons. And now, every time I experience the slightest shimmer of joy, the knowledge that I'm going to die swoops in and obliterates every shred of happiness from my system.

"I took this job because I thought it would help me confront my fear of death, force me to look it in the eye, and laugh. But really it's death that's laughing at me, at all of us…aaand I realise now that I probably shouldn't be saying all of this to a four-year-old child."

Phoebe stared at Lenore for a few seconds before saying, "And *three-quarters*."

"Three-quarters of what?"

"Of me! I'm not four. I'm four and *three-quarters*." She extracted her finger from her nose and wiped it on her frilly white dress.

"My apologies. Clearly, my age-estimating chronometer needs a little tweaking."

Phoebe shrugged and announced, "I gotta go poop," then slid off the pew and tottered towards the bathroom.

Lenore leant over her handbag, envying Phoebe's brazen disregard for social conventions, and quickly devoured the spring roll.

"*Jessica!*" snapped Simon.

She looked up at him and tried to smile without revealing that her mouth was filled with food.

"It's time for the ceremony. Hurry up and get outside."

She performed a two-fingered salute.

He rolled his eyes and turned his back to her.

She followed him out of the chapel, swallowing the last of her spring roll and dabbing at the non-existent tears in her eyes.

Outside, the guests were gathered in a semi-circle facing the unlit funeral pyre. The casket placed upon it was empty of course—state regulations strictly prohibited DIY cremation—but Magnus's will had insisted on this grandiose symbolic gesture. Lenore stood amongst the crowd, trying to avoid Simon's gaze. Wiry arms wrapped around her as a wrinkled face plunged into her shoulder, soaking it with tears. The elderly mourner looked up at her and murmured an indecipherable stream of grief-laden gibberish. Lenore placed her arm around the woman and patted her gently. "We're all going to miss him," she said.

Simon stood in front of the crowd and held his hand up for silence. "We are gathered here today to celebrate the life of our dearly departed Magnus. Each of you standing here is a testament to the great man he was, and how much he will be missed." The crowd murmured and sniffled in agreement. "As we explained at the start of the service, Magnus wanted a symbolic funeral pyre lit by an arrow. Always one for grand gestures, wasn't he? He has requested that his favourite pupil fire the flaming arrow. Jessica, if you would do the honours?" Simon collected the bow and arrow and held them out to Lenore.

The crowd turned to her, a sea of patient, red-rimmed eyes. She sighed deeply and whispered, "Are you *sure* about this? Wouldn't it be more appropriate for a family member to—"

"I'd barely know how to hold the bloody thing! I mean, look at these wheels. Since when do bows have *wheels*?" The crowd laughed as he poked at them, mystified.

"They're called cams."

"Right, exactly. Not at all my area of expertise."

Lenore offered a resigned nod and took the bow, strung the arrow. She placed its tip in the flaming brazier until it caught alight. She raised the bow, pulled back the string, and counted in slow, even breaths. She narrowed her eyes, let the target fill her vision, and listened to the sounds of the world fade to nothing. When the entirety of her existence was consumed by the target, she exhaled and released her fingers.

The crowd launched into an exultant cheer as the arrow soared through the air, but their jubilation nosedived into an anguished wail as it nicked the top of the pyre, then continued on, embedding itself in one of the catering tables. Cutlery and cupcakes were engulfed in flame, the sticky scent of burning sugar filled the air. One of the waiters ran to get an extinguisher as Lenore stared at the one tiny patch of the funeral pyre that had managed to catch fire. Everyone watched the flame's painfully gradual progress with horrified fascination. Lenore placed the bow on a nearby chair and walked briskly back inside the chapel. She slammed the bathroom door behind her and ran the taps for a while, staring into the mirror. She took off her glasses and gazed at her reflection. She looked gaunt and tired. Her head hurt. Her limbs felt weak and heavy. Lenore removed her gloves, took a moment to study the half-finished tattoo on her forearm. Her finger traced over the thick black lines of the raven's incomplete right wing. "I really ought to get around to finishing this wing of yours, otherwise you'll be doomed to fly in circles forever."

She took out her phone and wrote:

Just set a bunch of cupcakes on fire with an arrow. Hope your day is going better than mine.

She hit 'send' and waited for a reply. When none was forthcoming, she replaced her gloves and glasses, then exited and made a beeline for the coffee stand. She poured an espresso, then drained it and refilled it with one hand whilst grabbing a slice of cake with another. She bit in greedily, closing her eyes and exhaling with pleasure, her facade momentarily slipping under the weight of sugary bliss. When she opened her eyes, she found an irate, heavily made-up face staring directly at her. She matched the face to the photo in her dossier, snapped back into character, and said, "You must be Pauline. I've heard *so* much about you! You'll have to forgive my lack of decorum. Grief makes me hungry. I haven't been sleeping well since Magnus—"

"It's your fault he's dead," she snapped.

"I...don't see how?"

Pauline scoffed and said, "I'm *quite* sure that you do." She spoke with the cold, unflinching confidence of the resolutely irrational. "He. Died. Of. *Shame.*"

"I think you'll find the medical term is 'cardiac arrest.'"

Pauline leaned in close enough for Lenore to smell the cigarettes on her breath and seethed, "How long was it before you managed to steal him away?"

Lenore unleashed a tirade of internal profanities. There hadn't been anything in Magnus's file about an affair. "Magnus and I never slept together, I promise. I understand that you're upset, but yelling at me isn't going to bring him back."

Pauline's eyes seemed to vibrate with fury, "He always had a weird fetish for strange young *trollops*."

Lenore bit her lip, placed the cake and coffee back down on the table, then pressed her hands together and leaned into Pauline's ear, whispering, "Your husband has just died, so I am going to extend you the courtesy of assuming that you are mad with grief and politely refrain from grabbing the arrow I recently fired into a pile of cupcakes and ramming its lemon icing-encrusted point right into your withered, hate-filled heart."

Pauline yelped and drew her hand back to slap her, but was prevented by Simon's grip on her wrist as he hissed, "Pauline. You're embarrassing yourself. And there's been more than enough embarrassment today." He shot an angry glare at Lenore and said, "This woman didn't sleep with Magnus. She's never even met him."

Pauline's eyes rapidly transitioned from baleful to bewildered to broken, as though she were performing an ocular illustration of the emotional spectrum. "But, why is she—"

Simon grabbed her gently by the shoulders, turned her around, and explained, "Magnus's students hated him. I couldn't convince any of them to show up today. That archery academy was his entire life, and *not one* of his students or staff liked him enough to come and pay their respects. Do you realise how embarrassing that is? So, I had to hire Lenore. She's a...professional."

"A prostitute?"

"A professional mourner. Or moirologist, if you prefer the technical term," said Lenore.

Pauline deflated and murmured, "I'm so sorry. So you're not some chea—"

"It's fine, you're emotional. It's perfectly understan—"

"You're just a *vampire*." Pauline picked up the cake on the table and hurled it at Lenore, striking her square in the face before storming away. Lenore sighed as clumps ran down her dress and onto the floor.

Simon called out to one of the catering staff and pointed at the mess on the carpet, then grabbed a fistful of paper towels and led Lenore towards the bathroom.

Lenore pushed the bathroom door open. Simon followed behind her, locking the door. She glared at him and said, "I assume you're aware this is the ladies' bathroom?"

"Just trying to make sure no one witnesses this whole debacle. Also, I need to have a word in private. I can turn and face the wall or something if you like?"

"It's fine." She moistened the paper towels, wiped at the smears of chocolate on her face and dress. "Good thing I wore black, huh?"

Simon responded with a bitter snort. "The file you gave me didn't mention anything about Magnus having an affair."

"I didn't know about it! I couldn't even guess who his mistress actually was. Maybe it was all in Pauline's head. Hard to say. She's always been a few sandwiches short of a picnic. Then again, Magnus was very secretive. I've only just found out he had $26,000 worth of credit card debt and a shed filled with a prodigious fetish porn collection. I did not expect disposing of seventeen boxes of skin mags to be part of the funeral duties."

"Would it help if I told you that's surprisingly common?"

"It would not." Simon leaned back against the wall, gazed at the fluttering fluorescent light. "What Pauline said to you, I have to sincerely apologise on her behalf. She's a bit…what's the polite way to say 'sustained purely by unbridled hate and vitriol?'"

Lenore wiped away the last of the cake and dumped the paper towels in the bin. "We'll call it even, given my little mistake out there."

"How the hell could you miss at that range?"

"*Technically,* I didn't miss. And besides, you only paid for two archery lessons. It's not as easy as it looks. In any case, we should probably get back out there." She turned to see Simon with his head buried in his hands, dissolving into a series of arrhythmic sobs. She slid her arm around his shoulder and said, "Let it out. Take it from an expert, the crying helps."

"I'm so embarrassed. I never cry in front of people."

She handed him some paper towels, and he blew his nose. "Nothing embarrassing about it. Let those tears flow. You'll feel much better."

Simon regarded her with a grateful half-smile. "I'm so sorry. You shouldn't have to deal with this."

She patted him reassuringly on the shoulder. "It's alright, all part of the job."

2

ESCHATOLOGY

The ground was covered with a macabre confetti of corpses. In every direction, limbs were splayed, unseeing eyes stared at a dull grey sky, foetus-pink tongues lolled from open mouths. The only sound was the raven cawing above them, its voice uncannily loud amongst the quiet of the killing field. Darius had been dead for only a few minutes, but it was already eyeing him as a particular favourite amongst the smorgasbord of carrion. It cocked its head and dropped to the ground next to his feet, pecked experimentally at his boots, then jumped on top of his face.

"Look at them. A legion of empty vessels that once held radiant souls. Bleeding chunks of flesh that were once fathers, mothers, lovers, dreamers." The stranger's voice cut through the air, his arms outstretched to the heavens in a manner that he reasoned to look triumphant and regal but was actually a little ridiculous, to be perfectly honest.

"We shall pray for them," said his companion. "The tears and supplications of the bereaved will reverberate throughout the heavens." She fell to her knees and buried her head in her hands.

He placed his hand on her shoulder and said, "Your tears are wasted, sister. Death has them now. Sorrow shall not restore them. The fifth age is in its twilight, the time for us to bring the end of eshka…um, esh-ack, ahhhh…fuck. Jason, how do you say this word again?"

"Eschatology," said Jason, dropping his headphones from around his neck and restraining the urge to leap from behind the camera and strangle Kyle right in front of the entire cast and crew.

"Riiiiight. Got it! Esky-lolly-greens."

"It's pronounced es-*kuh*-tol-*uh*-jee."

"That's what I said, exactology. What is that, Hebrew?"

Jason blinked, rubbed his beard in the way he always did when he was irritated, and said, "Let's take five. Can someone go over the script with Kyle? Preferably someone who knows how to read at a sixth-grade level." The cast and crew scattered towards the craft services table, eager to avoid Jason's rancorous gaze.

Darius sat up and stretched, his vertebrae cracking like Lego pieces snapping together.

"Hey, you. The one the bird likes, what's your name again? Laurence? Zhao? Timothy?"

"Darius?" he said his own name like it was a question, as though he'd be happy to change it to something else if that was Jason's preference.

"Right. I knew it was something with, y'know, vowels. C'mere a sec."

Darius walked over, attracting the envious glares of the other background actors. "Good work keeping it together when the raven jumped on you. Those things are blade-mouthed, feathery harbingers of death. I fucking *hate* birds. Y'know that old line, 'never work with children or animals'?"

"Yes?"

"They should add Kyle fucking Abrams to that list. Never work with children, animals, or childish animals like Kyle Abrams. I can't believe the studio cast that insufferable hack. His popularity is testimony to the death of modern cinema, amirite?" Kyle's cinematic history featured a plethora of films co-starring rapper/actors, model/actors, viral video star/actors, and once, an anthropomorphised CGI version of a Japanese erotic massage toy. Essentially a 78-minute exercise in product placement, *Most Excellent Intimate Relaxation Aide and Foolish American Tourist Vs. The Zombie Yakuza* currently held duel records for being one of the worst-reviewed films of all time and one of the most popular choices for cult cinema midnight screenings. It was a sort of Japanese heir to Tommy Wiseau's *The Room*, only with less angst and more dance scenes. "Anyways, keep up the good work. Might see if I can find a few more lines for ya. Sound good?"

"Y-yes?"

"Cool. Alright, well, we've just had another set of rewrites sent through. I've never seen so many fucking rewrites. If I make it to the end of the week without blowing my brains out, I'll get Chantelle to hook you up. Can you go over to her now and let her know I've said that? I've had a lot of coffee today. I might forget we've had this conversation. Especially after the Hemingwayesque quantity of liquor I plan to down once we wrap for the day." Jason walked away without saying goodbye, leaving Darius a quivering mess.

He fell into a chair as his legs liquified underneath him.

"Did you get offered actual lines, you lucky bastard?" said Tabresh, taking a seat beside him. "Damn it, why didn't that stupid bird jump on *my* face? You know it did a couple of episodes of *Game of Thrones*? Fucking raven has a better resumé than I do. And did Jason say something about *more* rewrites? I thought we'd be wrapped months ago. My wife keeps complaining I'm too bony. Says it's like having sex with a sack of coat hangers. I can't wait til we're done. I keep dreaming of food."

"Me too. Yesterday, I stood staring in the window of a Sushi train until the shopkeeper chased me away. This weight maintenance clause is ridiculous. We're probably shaving years off our lives. What the hell are we even doing here?"

"We're doing what we do best, my friend, absolutely *nothing*!" Tabresh laughed, then patted his stomach and said, "When this is finally over, I'm going to eat pizza every day for a month. You ever hear of a production going two *years* over schedule? I mean, what the hell is this, *Apocalypse Now*?"

"I heard a rumour that we aren't even shooting a commercial release film."

Tabresh's water bottle paused halfway to his mouth. "You mean it's going straight to Netflix or something?"

"No, like it could be political propaganda, or the longest and most expensive ad campaign ever made. Naomi reckons the whole thing is actually just footage for a video game."

"I wish they'd let us see the script. Do you know anyone who's read it in its entirety?"

Darius shook his head. "I need to take a leak. I've been holding on for an hour." He stood up and took a single step towards the bathroom as Jason's artery-rupturing roar cut through the set. "I will fucking *eviscerate* you; I will *defenestrate* you; I will *lobotomise* you!" Jason was talking to a tall, grey-suited man Darius had seen on set a few times before. He had the confident gait of someone who would be more likely to know the asking price for a bakery than the loaves of bread it sold. The suit placed his hand gently on Jason's back and attempted to lead him away from the set. Jason slapped it away, and the suit held his hands up defensively.

Darius crept towards the bathroom, which was conveniently behind where the two men were arguing. He slipped inside and stood on his tiptoes next to the window.

"Jason, you really don't need to make such a scene." The suit's voice was blood on a birthday cake.

"I *do* need to make a scene. That's my fucking job, Csaba. I'm a director. I make scenes."

"And that is what we want you to do. Just a little differently, okay pal?"

"Don't call me 'pal'. I can't work like this. You have no respect for the artistic process!"

"I can assure you that's not true. Although, if I could explain via one of my favourite musical anecdotes—"

"For fuck's sake, I've got to shoot three scenes before—"

"The song 'Respect' was originally written and recorded by Otis Redding in 1965. In his version, it's a desperate plea from an oft-wounded man to his beloved, telling her that she can do whatever she wants, as long as she gives him a little 'respect' when he comes home."

"I don't have time for—"

"But when Aretha Franklin covered it, she made it her own, transformed it into the declaration of a powerful woman demanding that her man treat her with the respect that she deserves at all times. Same source material, two very different visions and versions."

"Look, I can see what you're getting to, but can we—"

"Let me cut to the chase. That's a directorial analogy for you right there."

"You're lucky to have me around, you know that? I'm a fucking visionary. You couldn't do what I do if you had a hundred lifetimes to try." This was a histrionically hyperbolic statement. Jason Banderfield's cinematic CV was less than luminary. His specialty was high-octane, low-quality summer fodder featuring large-chested women brandishing firearms alongside muscle-bound men driving cars off cliffs. He was most infamous for his adaptation of *Macbeth* featuring a cast of porn stars. One critic had notoriously called it 'a film that will make your eyeballs want to commit seppuku.'

Csaba smiled cheerily and said, "A hundred lifetimes? I should be so lucky. All I'm asking you to do—in *this* lifetime—is shoot the new scenes and take the extra wad of money we want to throw at you. I know for a fact that this bonus alone is three times what you got paid to direct *The Waiting Void.*"

"How do you know what I got paid?" Csaba snorted a laugh and ignored the question.

"If you don't want to continue with us, that's fine. We'll get someone else."

"This project is already on its third director, two years behind schedule, and thirteen million dollars over budget. You really think changing captains again is a smart move?"

"Well, I'm not the creative talent. I'd like you to keep wearing the captain's hat, provided you can weather the storm and keep the ship on course through rocky waters without succumbing to the lure of the sirens— whoops! I think the maritime metaphor got away from me there. Point is: get the rewrites done before the ceremony or fuck off into the sunset. Okay, bud? I'll need your answer by the end of the day and—ohhhhhh, cinnamon buns! Good thing it's my cheat day!" Csaba laughed and walked off towards craft services, leaving Jason to fire off a prolific barrage of profanity.

Darius stepped away from the window and examined himself in the mirror. Even without the grime and make-up, he looked like a zombie: skeletal, wan, bleary-eyed. Pretending to be dead ten hours a day was taking its toll.

Chantelle made the call to return to set. Darius sighed and prepared to become a corpse again.

3

RILEY

Lenore stared out the car window, her head a dizzy mix of caffeine, confusion, and exhaustion. Double bookings were always challenging. Some days, she had to act like a wailing maniac in the morning and a stoic mute in the afternoon. This morning, she'd been an archer, yesterday the aggrieved lover of an expert in Norwegian folklore. It had been a strange afternoon, trying to feign an acceptable knowledge of troll taxonomy and pronounce words like *jötnar*. Still, it had provided her with some fun conversation material in the unlikely event of her attending a dinner party in the near future.

"You going to a funeral?" the driver asked.

"Second one today."

"I'm sorry to hear that."

"It's okay, it's just for work."

The driver's face crinkled with surprise in the rearview mirror. "You a funeral director or something?"

"Or something." Her phone bleeped with a message from Darius. She made a mental note to call him after work. She was about to turn it off when it bleeped again, this time with a message from her employer, Threnody Grief Services. She didn't have time to read the entire lengthy diatribe, but the gist of it was she could expect her bookings to terminate completely if her client reviews continued to mention things like 'unreliable', 'distracted,' and 'ate the last cupcake, right in front of my crying three-year-old daughter.' They'd already knocked her back to just a couple of gigs a week after the infamous 'eating of the absurdly realistic wax fruit' incident. Her bank account had been haemorrhaging for months. Any further damage and it would be deader than the occupant of the coffin she was about to meet.

The car pulled into the driveway.

"You have a little..." the driver gestured at her collar where a few obstinate cake crumbs were still lingering.

She brushed them off and stepped out of the car. Her dossier for this booking had been sparse. She was hoping it would be a simple sit-n'-sob gig. After the morning she'd had, this would certainly be a welcome reprieve.

Lenore entered the twin open doors. Thick with ornate woodwork, they looked like they'd been specifically built to withstand a proletariat uprising. She took a moment to admire the foyer as she entered, a gigantic chandelier suspended above her, its shards reflecting fractured light around the room. The staircase was covered in a thick red rug that resembled the tongue of some regal giant. She whistled in admiration, then snapped her hand to her mouth. Two seconds through the door, and she'd already let her veil slip. She closed her eyes, ran back over her cover story (distant, out-of-town relative working as a part-time graphic designer), set her face in an appropriately sombre expression, and stepped through the door of the chapel.

It was as grand as the rest of the house: carved oak pews, Art Deco roof, stained glass windows. It was also completely empty. Lenore walked down the aisle, her footsteps echoing cavernously on the aged wooden floor. She sat in the fifth row (her favoured position—front row implied immediate family, back row distant acquaintance). She turned her phone on, double-checked the time, and turned it off again. Lenore stared ahead with her practiced forlorn expression as she held the memory of Quan in her mind's eye, picturing the grey pre-dawn light playing over his face as she stirred into wakefulness, whispered good morning, and placed her arms around him. Outside, the garbage truck clashed and clanged, the faint stench of refuse wafting through the half-open window. His skin had been so cold.

Footsteps echoed through the chapel. She turned to see an elderly woman, white hair exploding out around her tiny black fascinator, feet and cane moving in an uneven scattering of triplets. Lenore greeted her with a sorrowful half-smile; she nodded at her and took a seat a few rows behind. Slightly relieved, Lenore returned her gaze to the front of the chapel and waited. For a few minutes, the only sound was the elderly woman's quiet wheezing.

Finally, the priest entered and approached the lectern with long, even strides. He glanced out at the almost empty chapel and cleared his throat. He appeared to be barely out of his teens. His oversized robes made him look gawkish rather than pious. He coughed, examined his notes, drank from his water bottle, examined his notes again, and looked up at the crowd as though his brief act of stalling would've allowed time for dozens more guests to arrive. "Well, ah, I suppose we'd best get started, shall we?"

Lenore looked around the chapel again. It was, of course, perfectly normal in her line of work to be one of only a handful of attendees, but making up half of the audience was a new and entirely uncomfortable experience.

"We have gathered here today to celebrate the life of Elliott Brindle, a man who—"

"Excuse me, dear?"

The priest looked up from his notes. "Yes, ma'am?"

"Did you say 'Elliott Brindle'?" asked the elderly woman, her voice echoing throughout the near-empty chapel.

"Y-yes?" the priest replied.

"Oh. Dear me."

"Is there, ah, a problem?"

"I'm here for Agnes Yates?"

The priest stared at her like a troll frozen in sunlight. Finally, he stirred back into motion and shuffled through his papers. "Let's see, Agnes, Agnes… Here we are. I knew it was…yes, this is it. Agnes's service is tomorrow."

"Tomorrow?"

"Yes."

"Not today?"

"That's right."

She laughed. Lenore turned to look at her as she shook her head and tapped the pew with her cane. "What a silly mistake. I've gotten myself all muddled up again. Happens a lot these days. See you tomorrow then!" She looked at Lenore. "Have a lovely service dear. Sorry for your loss." She rose slowly to her feet and hobbled down the hall. When the last of her footsteps had faded, Lenore returned her gaze to the priest and waited for him to continue.

"Ah, I guess we should..." the priest waved his hand in the air and swallowed. "Look, I'll be honest with you. I'm new at this. This is only my second eulogy, and the first one didn't go very well. It was an open casket funeral, like this one, and I tripped and bumped someone and, well, we don't need to go into details. But suffice to say, cleaning coffee from a burial suit is a lot more complicated than you might think." He laughed timorously and said, "Gosh, I just hate funerals, don't you?"

She nodded and searched for something to say, wishing she could accelerate time through sheer force of will.

"I'm Peter, by the way. I figure we should introduce ourselves given that, you know..." he waved his hand at the empty pews.

"Mallory."

"Hi Mallory, were you and Elliott, ah, close?"

"Not really, I'm afraid. He was my second uncle, once removed. It's been years since I've seen him."

"Oh gosh. That is, to be honest, a *huge* relief. I really didn't have much to go on for this one. Please forgive me if the eulogy's a bit, ah...I didn't really have any stories from family or anything to work with, so I had to do my research on... well, you'll see. Anyway, best get on with it." He gulped at his water and said, "We are gathered here today to celebrate the life of Elliott Brindle, loving husband, successful businessman, and CEO of Amrita Industries. Elliott's father was an engineer of some renown, and his mother a history teacher. Elliott showed an early interest in finance and politics and once wrote a letter to the prime minister outlining several suggestions on economic policy. He was the youngest person to ever receive an official response from the prime minister's office, citation needed."

Peter's face flushed a deep red. He locked eyes with Lenore, then looked back down at his notes and murmured. "I, ah, ignore that bit." He turned to the open coffin behind him and said, "I, ah, rather feel like switching places with you right now, Elliott."

Elliott maintained a resolute silence.

* * *

After five of the most awkward minutes of her entire life, the eulogy finally finished, and Peter played a crackling funeral hymn over the chapel's antiquated speakers.

Our souls are gathered now to him
Who doth absolve us of our sins

The empty chapel was one of the saddest sights she'd ever seen, and as someone who attended funerals professionally, that was saying something. Lenore had a legion of questions marching through her brain, but for the moment, she just wanted to endure the rest of the ceremony and go home.

Heaven's gate is now flung open
No more pain, just calm devotion

Catholic hymns were the worst. Lenore had attended funerals in dozens of different religious traditions, each with their own foibles and charms, but at least most of them had half-decent music. Catholic elegies sounded like they'd been designed as auditory torment.

Though your earthly vessel is destroyed
Now you revel in the saviour's joy
Though your earthly vessel is destroyed
Now you revel in the saviour's joy
Though your earthly vessel is destroyed
Now you revel in the saviour's jooooooooooooooy!

HEL-LO, *faithful listener! Welcome to writing inspiring Eulogies! Congratulations on taking the first step towards creating—*

Peter leaped out of his seat and ripped the stereo plug out of the wall, shot her a look of apology, and murmured, "Well, I'll um…let you say your goodbyes." He scampered off, and Lenore laughed to herself, then took a moment to enjoy the silence.

She stood up and walked towards Elliott. It was strangely comforting to be alone with the deceased without having to worry about maintaining a facade. She peeked inside the coffin. The dossier photo of Elliott Brindle had been classically cold and professional, all stark lighting and sharpened edges. Here, he looked calm, peaceful, avuncular. Crow's feet gathered at his eyes, a network of well-worn wrinkles ran across his face. "Hi, Elliott," she said quietly. "Sorry about the eulogy. I'm sure you were a nice guy, citation needed."

She ran her hand along the edge of the coffin. It was an imported ivory and gold model, heinously expensive. The bizarre posthumous vanity of deluxe coffins never ceased to amaze her. But then, the very same vanity kept her employed, so she could hardly complain. "Mind telling me what I'm doing here?" she asked. Elliott was predictably taciturn. She placed her palm against his cheek, one of her favoured gestures. "Goodbye, Elliott, I hope you—"

The motion was subtle, but unquestionably, irrevocably, immutably *there*. She snapped her hand back and glanced around the room for some external source of movement, a fleeting minor earthquake perhaps, but there was nothing. She leaned in close to him and touched his cheek again. There.

Again. And again. And again. A regular, rhythmic pulse. She placed her fingers against his neck but found no movement. She leaned in close against his cheek and realised it wasn't a pulse, but a tick.

Tick.

Tick.

Tick.

It was coming from his mouth. Lenore glanced around the room, hesitated, then pried his jaw slowly open. A glint of gold peeked out from between his teeth. She considered talking to Peter but reasoned that he might not be the best source of advice. Curiosity quickly pummelled all other considerations into submission. She pulled his mouth carefully open, reached in, and grabbed the tiny gold fob watch. She removed tissues from her handbag, cleaned and inspected it.

It was beautifully made, accompanied by a resplendent gold chain, and covered in elegant filigree. She popped the cover open. The watch face was marked with Roman numerals, the second hand ticked in slow, steady increments. On the inside cover was the engraving:

Riley

Lenore stared at the name for a moment, then closed the watch and held it in her palm, glancing from it to Elliott's open mouth and back again. Inspecting the watch was one thing, but keeping it would qualify as grave robbing. She stared at his open mouth.

Tick.

Tick.

Tick.

"Lenore Lyn?" She convulsed with surprise, dropping the watch into her handbag by what she would later swear was pure accident and spinning around to face the speaker.

He was uncommonly short—perhaps a hair's breadth over five feet—with a peanut butter-brown beard cascading down his chin. He was dressed in a close-fitting black suit. Heavy silver rings adorned his fingers. He was carrying a briefcase that looked comically large in comparison to his stature.

"Actually, my name's Mallory," she said.

"S'awright love, you can dispense with the charades and chicanery. My employer's the one who hired you. You wanna go chat somewhere a smidge less sepulchral?" He gestured towards the foyer, and she followed him. He sat on a red-cushioned antique couch and waved his hand at the armchair opposite. "Please, have a seat." She did so, wondering if there was any chance he could hear the quiet ticking of the fob watch in her bag. He removed a small file and placed it on the table, then sat back and said,

"People call me Ocky."

"That's an unusual name."

"Didn't say it was my name. I said it's what people call me."

"I'm Len—"

"Lenore Lyn, professional moirologist. I'd never heard of that before yesterday, y'know? Always nice to learn something new. Enjoy the service?"

"Enjoy is not the word I'd use."

"Yeah. Too right. Anyways, best get on with it. I've gotta pick my daughter up from her jujitsu class in half an hour, and if I'm late, I'll never hear the bleedin' end of it. You got kids?" Lenore shook her head, eyes locked on the file.

"The light of my life and the bane of my existence, those two." He sighed, stabbed a finger at the folder. "Everything you need to know should be in here."

"Everything I need to know about...?"

"23 Mondegreen Avenue."

"Which is?"

"Yours."

Lenore opened the folder and stared at the deed bearing her name in formal, flowing font. "I don't understand."

"Amrita Industries—my employer—was part-founded by Elliott Brindle, who some time ago left the company for a variety of reasons which are both abstruse and irrelevant to the matter at hand, and passed his portion of control to the other proprietor, Mr Adami. His will, which I am currently tasked with administrating, was written many a moon ago, and for reasons which are beyond my comprehension, and—to be perfectly fucken' frank—sphere of interest, states that his extensive estate be divided amongst a variety of charitable organisations, with the exception of his personal residence."

"23 Mondegreen Avenue is his home?"

"Was. Now it's yours."

"But why—"

"This is going to go a *lot* faster if you quit interrupting." He checked his watch, swore quietly. "Due to the fact that Mr Brindle has no surviving kith nor kin—"

"The priest said he was married?"

"She's dead. Well, sort of. Deadish."

She opened her mouth to ask the obvious question, but Ocky silenced her with the kind of glare that suggested consequences of an extremely dire nature. "I have mere seconds remaining before I need to take my leave, so you'll forgive me for shuffling things along here. The home is bequeathed according to a clause in his will which states that it should be given to the first person who turned up to his funeral."

"Why would he—"

"I believe it's some sort of posthumous humour. Just between you and me, rumour has it, he was a touch barmy towards the end there. His will also stated that Mr Adami be denied access to his funeral service." This time, Ocky raised his hand to silence her question before the first syllable had emancipated itself from her lips. "Bad blood, time-honoured feud of Shakespearean proportions. Complex and, more to the point, none of your damn business. To continue, Amrita has an almost alarmingly generous and complex post-life care program for its employees."

"What do you mean 'post-life'?"

"It includes the hiring of one professional mourner. Thus, you are here, and I am here explaining this to you, and 23 Mondegreen Ave is now yours, and I..." he glanced at his watch again, "...am about to have my ear chewed off by the angriest adolescent on God's green." He snapped his briefcase shut, stood up, and tossed a set of keys on the table.

"But what am I supposed to do with it?"

"Live in it, rent it out, turn it into a wax museum. I ain't gonna tell you how to live your life." He waved over his shoulder as he departed. "It's been a pleasure, love. All the best." He walked out the front door, stepped into his car, and drove off towards the storm clouds gathering on the horizon.

Lenore placed her handbag on the table in front of her and picked up the keys. From inside the black Italian leather, she could barely make out a quiet

Tick.

Tick.

Tick.

4

POST-LIFE PROBLEMS

Orin had been dead for three weeks and still hadn't figured out how to play *Red House*. For years, he'd been promising himself, 'When I finally have more time, I am going to learn how to play that song.' Now that he was dead, he had a literal eternity to play with, but little interruptions kept getting in his way. This morning, for instance, he'd been planning to redecorate his sepulchre only to find that a small family of possums had nested in the back-right corner. He'd searched around for something to remove them with, eventually finding an old blanket in a dumpster near the church. Trying hard not to think about the origins of the various stains populating its surface, he lugged it back along the street to the graveyard, tremendously grateful for his invisibility. He quietly draped it over the possums, pulled the corners quickly together, and then dragged the kicking, screaming mess out into the daylight. He hurled it away from him towards the nearest tree and ran quickly in the other direction as they emerged. He wasn't sure if possums could get rabies, or the recently deceased for that matter, but he certainly wasn't keen to find out.

Once the possum fiasco was dealt with, he sat down, tuned the rusty strings of his guitar, and consulted the Jimi Hendrix tab book. It was one of the few meagre possessions he kept in his tomb. He also had a sleeping bag, a few sets of clothes, his diary, and a pile of tattered sci-fi novels. Orin strummed experimentally on the opening chord and fumbled through the first verse. The strings sounded awful. He tried to ignore their inferior quality and push through, but he felt like he was spitting on Hendrix's tomb with his appalling rendition. He put the guitar down and sighed, which was really just an affectation now he no longer needed to breathe. Orin wondered what the hell he was going to do with the rest of his afterlife. He'd thought about trying to do something important, like tracking down erroneously acquitted murderers and haunting them into confessing their sins. But he wasn't much of a detective, and without being able to access the internet, he'd be practically useless.

He decided to go for a walk to clear his head. Before his death, Orin had never been very contemplative. He'd made his way through life in much the same way as a leaf carried along a raging river. This shift to endless serenity was proving to be a difficult adjustment. He was forever reaching for the pocket where his phone had once resided, or mentally scrolling through the catalogue of upcoming meetings that no longer existed. Orin whistled to himself as he strolled amongst the tombstones and wondered if it was anyone's birthday at the office today. Birthdays were good. There was always cake on birthdays.

In life, he hadn't spent much time in cemeteries. He hadn't been to a funeral since he was a child, and he was surprised at how much individualistic flair the graves had. They had sculptures and poems and photographs and flower beds. His favourite, however, was a simple grave decorated with a collection of tiny plastic dinosaurs. He knelt down and examined stegosauruses and pterodactyls and plesiosaurs, marvelling at the fact that they were made from plastic refined from oil made from dead dinosaurs. The essence of a dead thing transmogrified into a cartoonish self-representation.

He drew himself back up and watched as a young woman placed flowers on a nearby grave, tears running down her face as she uttered a staccato stream of apologies and adoration. Since dying, he'd become fascinated with the candour and kindness that people seemed to reserve for the ears of the departed. All throughout the cemetery, notes of grief and love and regret blended together into a grand, elaborate requiem. The words Orin's family had said after his own death had been heartbreaking. The thought of his parents' faces made his head sting with tiny hot spears. It had also been the first time he'd seen Wanda since she left. Watching her hold Adrian's hand as she wiped tears away had been nothing short of torturous. He banished the memory and headed out the front gate of the cemetery. He strolled down to the river's edge and spent some time skimming rocks. He imagined once he'd been practicing for a few years, he'd be brilliant. After a good century, he'd probably be better than anyone alive. For now, though, he sucked. The rocks clipped the water once, twice if he was lucky, and then plunged beneath the murky brown surface.

A car rolled down the quiet street, stopping in front of the abandoned house with the gigantic green fence. Orin had toyed with the idea of exploring it a few times, but he wasn't much of a climber. He also wasn't sure what would happen if he broke his legs, but he assumed that finding a doctor specialising in treating the recently deceased would be no easy task. A young woman stepped out of the back seat. She was short, thirty-something, dressed in black, elegant dark glasses framing her eyes. She was the kind of pretty that would've made Orin break out in a sweat in his pre-death existence. He watched as the car slipped away, and she stood staring motionless at the front gate for a full minute. Eventually, she pulled a small gold watch out of her bag and clipped it open, stared at it for a second, then put it away again and removed a set of keys. She inserted them into the lock and froze.

Her hand dropped away, leaving the keys dangling idly in the lock as she stared silently at the door again. Orin nearly yelped with excitement. This was by far the most interesting thing that had happened in his entire post-life. She took a phone out of her bag and dialled. He couldn't make out her words from his spot by the river. After a minute, she hung up, took a moment to steel herself, then turned the keys and slipped inside. If Orin's heart had still been working, it would've been running at two hundred beats a minute. He crept towards the gate.

She'd left it ever so slightly open.

5

FRANCIS BACON'S JUVENILIA

Darius hadn't picked up. Audrey hadn't picked up. It was times like this—staring at the gigantic dilapidated house she'd inherited from a dead stranger—that Lenore regretted her dedication to what she termed 'social minimalism.' She had to begrudgingly admit that a slightly expanded social circle would not be without its benefits. She opened the door and was immediately lambasted with the scent of mildew and wet socks. Not a great omen.

She stepped over the threshold and yelped in shock. The entire front room was a chaotic mess of mattresses, magazines, books, and broken toys. Cobwebs and dust coated every surface. The walls were covered in mould and cracks. A scuttling sound emanated from beneath a pile of magazines. Lenore desperately hoped the creature she heard scurrying off into a wall cavity was something adorable and reticent rather than verminous and pestilent. Her phone rang in her handbag, and she nearly dropped it in surprise. "Hi, Audrey."

"Hey, I can't talk for long. I have a client with me. Everything cool?"

"I would say that everything is the diametric opposite of 'cool' at this point."

"Is it your dad?"

"No, I was at work today and—"

"Did you get accused of being someone's mistress again?"

"Well, yes, actually, but that's not—"

"Hang on a sec. Listen to me, you vermicular, repulsive *cretin*! If you aren't done in the next ten minutes, I will punish you in ways that would make Dante recoil in horror! What? No, not Dante the Mexican rapper, Dante the poet. He wrote *The Inferno*? How fucking *stupid* are you? Sorry Len, what were you saying?"

"I appear to have inherited a house."

"..."

"Hello?"

"I heard you. Just processing."

"Yes. I'm here now. It's very…Tim Burton."

"Well, that is something. Did you— ugh. Hold on. *The same one we used last time, you wretch!* I'm so sorry. I really should deal with this mess. I'm almost finished. Text me the address, and I'll come straight over, okay?"

"Thanks, Audrey."

"No worries, hun, have fun exploring. I said *clockwise,* you pathetic, prattling pig!"

The call ended.

Lenore sent Audrey the address, hung her handbag on the hook on the back of the door, and stepped into the front room, careful to avoid a tiny box of ball bearings at the entrance. She flicked the light switch with the back of her hand in case the wiring was faulty. The lights didn't so much brighten the room as cast it in a hazy nicotine yellow, but at least the power worked. There was a walking cane—inexplicably topped with a duck's head—leaning against the wall. She picked it up and tapped at various boxes, checking they weren't filled with rats or possums or hobgoblins.

Thunder rumbled outside. The rain would break at any moment now. Lenore was about to let her fear pummel her curiosity into submission when she glimpsed the painting hanging on the wall. She approached it slowly, as though it would leap out and bite her. It depicted the very room in which she now stood, albeit far less laden with junk and detritus. The faded pink couch in front of her—covered in boxes of Christmas decorations and old electronics—was portrayed in the painting in vibrant red. Seated on the left was Elliott Brindle. The painting had obviously been commissioned some time ago. He looked much younger. Elliott was grinning, dressed in casual summer attire. He had his arm around a beautiful dark-haired woman, some years younger. She had broad shoulders and a bright smile and was holding a blanket-wrapped bundle in her arms.

Lenore stared at the painting for several minutes. She heard shuffling from the wall cavity and tried to ignore it as she studied every aspect of the painting's composition and execution. Once, years ago, Quan had taken her over to his friend Alexa's place, and they'd all dropped acid. While the others had run around the house yelling and throwing cornflakes, she'd sat in a quiet room and stared at one of Alexa's paintings depicting a green-eyed woman with velvety antlers sprouting from her jet-black hair. She'd spoken to the painting for hours, told it her deepest fears and secret desires. She'd convinced herself that the voice of some omniscient shaman was speaking to her. In the morning, groggy and bleary-eyed, she'd gone back to the painting to find it was merely one of Alexa's jejune self-portraits and felt thoroughly foolish. But as she stared at the picture of Elliott and his family, she felt much the same as she had that night, as though there were voices reaching out to her from the paints and pigments. She grabbed at the painting, flipped it over, checked its lining, patted the wall behind it in search of irregularities. Nothing.

Lenore placed the painting back on the wall and took a photo. Outside, the light was fading. She didn't want to stay here too long after dark, even with Audrey around. Lenore opened the oak double doors at the end of the room, coughing and spluttering as a cloud of dust descended on her. The doors opened into the kitchen, which held an even more impressive array of hoarded miscellany than the front lounge room. She walked through the kitchen, trying to convince herself that the tiny ripples of movement she caught in her peripheral vision were just her imagination, and stepped on the deck outside. The wood felt worryingly soft underneath her feet, but the vines from the tree that leaned against the house had become so entwined with its structure that their thick brown roots had nearly supplanted the need for the deck's rotting struts.

The garden below was a thick, verdant jungle of trees and shrubs and a bush turkey mound the size of a sedan. It was both inviting and terrifying, as though nature had decided to make an angry annexation of this one tiny corner of the suburbs. However, by far, the most interesting thing in the garden was the compact corrugated iron roof shed in the back corner. In this one section of the garden, the trees and shrubs had been cleared, evidently to aid the efficiency of the solar panel on the roof. The shed was covered in vines, and the windows were boarded up.

Lenore was beginning to mull over the multitudinous possibilities of its contents (munitions storage, corpse freezer, sex dungeon) when the sound of the front door creaking open cut through her musings. She darted behind a wall as the sound of ball bearings bouncing and rolling all over the floor filled the house. She searched for the closest object that could potentially be employed as a weapon and settled on a gigantic pair of secateurs she found on top of an old rusty barbecue. "Who's there?" she called out, immediately cursing her own stupidity. What self-respecting axe murderer would identify themselves upon request? A demonic shriek cut through the air, followed by the frantic scrambling of an indeterminable number of feet. She ran towards the sound to see a possum scurrying over the fence with a terrifyingly large feral cat in pursuit. The floor was covered in ball bearings, blood, and fur. It looked like a piece of Francis Bacon's juvenilia.

"Len?" She looked up to see Audrey in the gateway. In the twilight, she could just make out the expression on her face: a confused blend of intrigue and terror. "Have you inherited a house built on an ancient burial ground or something? This place looks like the set of one of Darius's films."

Lenore shook her head and dropped the secateurs, then ran to Audrey and wrapped her in a hug.

"Hey. Nice to see you. You going to show me what you got here?"

"Would you hate me if I suggested we come back tomorrow instead? This place is quite unsettling. I'm worried the eyes in the paintings are going to follow me around the room."

"This place, weird? The one you inherited from a dead stranger that's filled with boxes of junk and covered in blood and ball bearings? I never would have guessed."

"Believe me, I'm as shocked as you are. Could you give me a ride home?"

"Only if you promise to tell me what in the *seven circles of hell* is going on here."

"I will, just let me grab my handbag." Lenore ran back inside, grabbed it, and locked the door behind her. "How was work?" Audrey rolled her eyes,

"Not great. I was in the middle of a session when we spoke. Two seconds after I hung up, my client's girlfriend burst in and started screaming. It was a nightmare. Let's talk about your thing. Begin at the beginning."

"I set a table on fire today. With an arrow."

Audrey laughed, "Sounds like something you'd do."

Lenore left the gate swinging behind her. Orin emerged from the shadows of the garden where he'd watched the girl with the glasses appear on the balcony. He listened to the sound of the car disappearing and set about the busy task of exploring.

6

ANGRY BETTY

Lenore said goodbye to Audrey and stepped out into the pouring rain, trotting quickly down the driveway of her apartment block, past the heinously ugly garden gnome that stood in the front courtyard. Angry Betty was smoking on her deck. She regarded Lenore with silent, eldritch rancour. Lenore ignored her and entered the foyer, checked her mailbox (empty), stomped up the stairwell (pungent), and stepped into her apartment (chaotic).

She slumped onto her couch and stared at the cobweb of cracks on the ancient ceiling. The ticking of the fob watch was barely discernible in her handbag. She took it out, ran her fingers over the filigree, and put it away. She stood up and boiled the kettle. Upstairs, Angry Betty was banging pots and pans as though she were maladroitly auditioning for a street percussion band. Lenore stared at the photo of Quan on her kitchen bench. He'd always hated having his picture taken. He liked to joke it was because he was in witness protection. She'd managed to snap this one at a party while he'd been distracted by the snacks table, the camera catching him as he gained awareness of its presence. He was caught at the precise moment that his irritation transitioned into amusement, his mouth filled with half-chewed Cheetos.

The kettle screeched, earning angry thumps from the floor above. Lenore turned it off, and Angry Betty resumed whatever cacophonous cooking activity she'd been engaged in, either unaware or unconcerned with the irony of asking for silence immediately before smashing steel against the stove. "I hope you die in a fire," murmured Lenore as she poured her tea and sat down on the balcony, staring out at the early evening activity outside. People were coming home from the pub, work, afternoon picnics, study. She envied their pleasant banality. Lenore placed her mug on the table and tossed her newly acquired keys from one hand to another. The image of the Brindle family portrait burned into her brain. Obviously, the woman in the painting must've been Elliott's partner, and the child was theirs. Was Riley his wife, his child, or someone else?

There was something about their house that was simultaneously intriguing and terrifying. She'd been relieved to make her escape, and yet the moment Audrey's car had pulled away, she'd felt the urge to turn around. She could feel the need to explore its anarchic nooks gnawing at her. Lenore took out her phone and searched for 'Elliott Brindle', finding the same Wikipedia page that the priest had used to write his eulogy. She trawled for other sources. The only images of him were the professional photo shoots that had been used for press releases. Slick, sterile, and utterly devoid of character. He could've been any rich white man to have ever run a company.

Upstairs, Angry Betty was running a bath, the banging of the pipes drowning out the sound of the wind and rain outside. Lenore groaned with irritation and kept searching. His various social media profiles were clinically tailored: commentary on market developments, bland holiday greetings, cookie-cutter post-catastrophe commiserations of 'thoughts and prayers.' It was the kind of anodyne content that had obviously been written by a PR rep. Her high school graphing calculator had more personality. It took her a moment to realise that the most recent post was five years old.

She searched again, attempting to avoid sites connected with the business world. She scrolled past the Financial Review, CNN, the *Sydney Morning Herald* and was about to give up when she chanced upon the somewhat disconcertingly titled *enlightenedandheightened.com*. She opened the page and immediately recoiled at the garish green title font. It looked as though it had been designed by a colourblind twelve-year-old after six cans of Red

Bull. The bulk of the text was IN CAPS and employed FAR TOO MANY EXCLAMATION MARKS!!!!!!!!!! None of this was exactly confidence building. Lenore scanned past hyperbolic titles that blatantly disregarded both veracity and consistent capitalisation such as *The reptilian Agenda: Trump is One of them!!!!!*, *Bildeberg Group: Hilary Clinton sacrifices Human babies!!!!* and *Chemtrails continue unabated: READ the Truth HERE!!!*

Lenore could almost hear the frantic nail-biting and delirious murmuring that doubtlessly accompanied the composition of posts like this. She navigated to the specific entry featuring Brindle's name and arrived at a page detailing suspected members of the global conspiracy. She found a blurry black and white photo depicting Elliott between two figures, both faces turned away from the camera and cast in shadow. They were all smiling resplendently. It was the first time she'd seen his face display anything but Swiss neutrality.

She saved the photo and zoomed in. The magnification helped a little, but also exacerbated the pixelation. The figure on the left was possibly the same woman as in the painting. The man to his right was slightly more discernible but unfamiliar. The text beneath the photo read ELLIOTT BRINDLE STANDING WITH TWO UNIDENTIFIED MEMBERS OF THE ILLUMINATI, POSSIBLE REPTILIANS!!! IF YOU KNOW WHO THEY ARE PLEASE EMAIL ME!!!

Not wildly illuminating, but still, it was—to quote Audrey—'better than a kick in the snatch.' She slurped the last of her tea and slumped off to the bathroom to brush her teeth. The screeching of the pipes above continued unabated.

Lenore stripped down to her underwear, turned out the lights, and flicked on the fan. She picked up her phone and wrote:

Today has been surreal. I'll tell you all about it when I see you, but you're going to need to drastically recalibrate your idea of 'strange' before I tell you the whole story.

Sleep well.

XO

She hit send, then put in her earbuds and played a Nina Simone mixtape that Quan had made for her. Lenore closed her eyes and surrendered to sleep.

7

WHAT HAPPENS NEXT?

The moon was a bright white pancake set upon a tablecloth of stars. It illuminated Orin's pale skin to the point of near-translucence. He brewed himself a cup of tea, not to drink, but just to watch the steam rise. He'd loved drinking tea in life, and he couldn't quite break the habit in death, despite being unable to taste anything anymore. He hummed quietly to himself and thought about the girl with the glasses, wondering what she'd been doing in this house, if she was the new owner, when she might return. He'd been enjoying solitude thus far, but he couldn't deny the fact that loneliness had begun to quietly gnaw at the periphery of his consciousness. He sat on the back verandah, listening to the late-night quiet. Since transitioning to a primarily night-time existence, he'd come to view the world as a sort of timeshare between diurnal and nocturnal creatures. This time of night, the only sounds were possums and the occasional taxi or truck driver. Despite sharing the same physical space, they were inhabiting different worlds. He thought often of the time some years ago when he'd gone to check the mail and his neighbour—home sick with the flu—poked his head out the door and said in confused irritation,

"Who're those guys in high-vis vests doing all that lawn mowing?"

"The maintenance crew," replied Orin. His neighbour looked at him like he'd just said they were Santa's elves and slammed the door shut. Apparently, he'd believed that the apartment block lawns magically attended to themselves. It had never occurred to him that actual working human beings performed the maintenance work while he was away at the office.

Orin was posthumously discovering that the whole world was compartmentalised like this. There were beautiful people who would insist that 'you can make anything happen with a smile!' which was partially true, provided that smile was Hollywood-white and perched upon a magazine-worthy face. Rich people who would sagely advise the less fiscally fortunate to 'work harder and get a high-paying job!' Healthy people who would advise friends with depression or chronic fatigue to 'Meditate! Eat Well! Try Yoga!' as though this would provide a complete panacea for complex neurological and physiological conditions.

In life, Orin had been more lonely than loved, more cynical than optimistic, and not so much 'outdoorsy' as 'behind-closed-doorsy'. He was trying to figure out where he would fit into his new world, or underworld, as the case may be. He didn't like the term 'undead' as it grouped him with vampires and zombies, and they were a) unpleasant and b) non-existent. He decided to distract himself with television, something he'd done often before his death but never since. The dusty screen sprung to life, bathing the room in flickering blue light. It was a reality TV show about people who were hoping to meet their true love by being blindfolded in front of a camera. How odd that someone would employ the same methodology as a terrorist filming a propaganda video in the pursuit of true romance. The music swelled. They cut between an array of soft-lensed interviews of family and friends making their various prognostications, and at long last, the blindfold was removed. The two would-be lovers stared at one another, eyes wide with shock as the narrator's silken voice announced, 'What happens next? Find out…after the break!' The television cut away to a series of commercials that diabolically alternated between calorific snack foods and soporific weight loss products.

Orin turned the TV off and hummed to himself as he walked through the darkness of the old house. The black mould covering the walls produced a comparatively pleasant aromatic distraction from the scent of his decaying flesh. The subdued late-night soundscape was ruptured by the screeching of the front gate's hinges. Orin jumped up, spilling the tea on himself.

He yelped before remembering that his nerves were essentially a series of severed phone lines, their messages of pain and sensation forever unanswered by his brain. He brushed the tea off his arm and crept to the front of the house; his heart—were it still functioning—would have been pounding like a drum circle at a folk festival.

He pressed his nose to the glass and watched the gate swing open. She was standing there in the light of the moon, her face obscured by the twin cascades of her long, dark hair. For a while, she stood still, staring at the house. Orin's mouth parted into a grin. She brushed her hair behind her ears, and he nearly stumbled backwards with shock. The girl in front of him was not the girl with the glasses at all. Her face was difficult to discern in the half-light of the moon, but it was certainly not the one he had seen earlier. There was something odd about her skin. It was waxy, bizarrely wrinkled, almost reptilian. He ducked behind the wall before slapping his forehead and remembering that he was invisible in any case. This was one of the strangest days of his post-life.

"Hello?" she said. Her voice was hoarse and high-pitched. She sounded like a chronic smoker who'd inhaled a lungful of helium. Orin stepped back to the window and looked outside; the girl was right there on the front deck. She raised her hand and waved at him. Orin froze, afraid for the first time since his death. After a pregnant pause, he waved in return. She smiled, creating undulations in the complex network of wrinkles blanketing her face. Now that she was closer, he could see that she was quite young, perhaps only a teenager. Despite the unusual wrinkled patterning of her skin, her eyes had the bright and playful luminescence of youth. There was something else there as well, or perhaps an absence of something. Orin's fear metastasised into full-blown terror for reasons he could not consciously articulate.

"Is this Claire and Elliott Brindle's house?"

Orin tipped his head and considered the question. The girl with the glasses had been called 'Len' by her tall friend with the tattoos. He assumed this was a nickname, but it couldn't possibly be a derivation of 'Claire.' He shook his head, still too dumbfounded to be able to speak.

The lizard-skinned girl nodded in thanks, pulled her hoodie over her head, and walked back out the front gate, slamming it closed behind her.

Orin slumped against the wall and slid down to the floor. A small furry something rustled amongst the piles of boxes. This house was far too strange and macabre. He'd have to go back to sleeping in the cemetery.

8

CAN I HAVE HER SHOES?

enore was wrenched from sleep by a single drop of water striking her neatly in the middle of the forehead. She snapped her eyes open. They took a few seconds to adjust to the dark and confirm the spider web of cracks that had appeared in her ceiling was not a hallucination. Water dripped from a dozen different points. Tiny puddles collected on her dresser, the floor, inside her shoes.

Her head still dizzy with sleep, Lenore took a moment to take all of this in before klaxons began screaming through her re-emerging consciousness. Another droplet struck her in the chest. She yanked her earbuds out, grabbed her phone, and jumped from the bed. She pulled on the bathrobe hanging on the door, picked up her handbag, and ran outside screaming. She was barely out the front door when the roof crumbled with a fatalistic yawn as it released a biblical deluge. Lenore stared transfixed as water lapped against her ankles and a gilded clawfoot bath plunged through the vacant air that had— until very recently— been occupied by her beloved Art Deco ceiling. The bath landed neatly on her bed, crushing it, and settling right where she'd been sleeping moments earlier. Angry Betty lay back in the bath, head resting on her chest. Aside from the nudity and soap bubbles, she looked for all the world like she was taking a pleasant Sunday afternoon nap.

* * *

Lenore watched the paramedics wheel a black leather bag containing the formerly living flesh of Angry Betty into the back of the ambulance.

One of them stopped to ask her a few questions, his voice sounding distant and faded. "Do you know if she has any living relatives?"

"I don't know. No one ever came to visit her. I didn't even know her real name."

"Had she been unwell lately?"

"Huh? Not sure. She moaned and yelled a lot. But I think she was mostly screaming at quiz shows."

"Do you have somewhere you can stay?"

"Yes. My brother is coming to pick me up."

"Do you mind if we get your contact details, just in case there's any follow-up we need to do?"

"Hrm?"

"Your contact information, may I have it please?"

"Oh, I'm sorry, but I'm not really looking for a relationship right now." The paramedic stared at her blankly as Lenore's mouth and brain reconnected after a brief separation. She slapped her hand to her mouth and yelped, "I'm sorry. That's not what I meant."

He laughed, handed her a notepad and pen, and said, "It's fine, you're obviously pretty shaken up. It's not even the weirdest thing I've had someone say to me. The other day we were picking up this heart attack victim, and as we were zipping her up, her neighbour leans in the apartment door and says, 'Can I have her shoes?' We looked at her, horrified, and she rolled her eyes and said, 'Well, she's obviously not going to use them anymore.' Death makes people crazy."

"*Life* makes people crazy. Death makes them honest."

The paramedic smiled and said, "That's cute. You make that up?"

She shrugged. "I guess." Lenore scribbled her information on his notepad.

"You should stay out of the apartment until it's been properly cleaned. It's structurally unsound, plus there's all kinds of bacteria rolling around in there. I hope you've got a good landlord. And insurance."

Lenore nodded. She had neither. She watched the ambulance pull away and stood on the footpath, staring at nothing for a while. A car drove past. The driver flicked a cigarette that sailed through the air and landed in Lenore's hair. She tore it out, screeching as the singeing smell flooded her nostrils. The car sped away but then sat idling at the red light at the end of her street. Perhaps because her inhibitions had been violently eroded by a combined near-death and near-to-death experience, perhaps because it was way too early in the morning to put up with people hurling abuse from cars, Lenore had a flash of vengeful inspiration.

She grabbed the hideous garden gnome that Angry Betty had placed in the front courtyard and ran towards the car, her bare feet slapping the concrete. The driver didn't even notice Lenore approaching until she let cry a primal scream, eyes lit with furious glee, garden gnome raised high above her head like an executioner's axe. The light switched to green, and the driver slammed his foot on the accelerator just as Lenore hurled the gnome at the back window. She watched as time slowed to a sedate crawl, the gnome sailing through the air with all the grace of an Olympic diver. The car pulled away, and for one hideous nanosecond, it appeared as though the gnome's kamikaze attack would end in failure. But a speeding cyclist cutting in front of the driver forced him to slam the brakes, spinning the wheel as hard as he could, turning his side window to face the gnome, resulting in a catastrophic collision.

Plaster and glass exploded in a cosmic collection of shards and shrapnel. Lenore watched them rain down onto the footpath as the driver stared at her in silent horror. She watched as his expression transitioned from awed to confused to vengeful. He pulled the handbrake, killed the engine, and opened the door. The adrenaline pounding through her system had imbued her with a temporary mad courage, but she was still keenly aware that she was only slightly less fragile than the naked, elderly body that had recently invaded her apartment.

"You fucken' *bitch.*" The driver pointed at her, his finger a digital declaration of war. He strode towards her with purposeful steps, only to find his progress blocked by the arrival of a familiar beaten-up green Mazda. Lenore yanked the passenger door open and jumped inside. The

Mazda took off with tyres screeching like rubber banshees.

* * *

It was only after a protracted explanation, a forty-five-minute long shower, and an ill-fitting change of clothes that Lenore realised she'd left her handbag on the grass forecourt at her apartment complex. Darius spent the entire length of the journey haranguing her for being so careless and proclaiming that it would almost certainly have been taken by now. Fortunately, Lenore had managed to drop it so that it was obscured by both her front fence and an unwieldy shrub (although a bush turkey had given it a good pecking).

They drove to the nearby K-mart to acquire toiletries, shoes, and a few sets of the cheapest clothes on offer. Lenore piled the bags into the boot saying, "There goes this week's pay. At least I won't have to pay rent for a while." They climbed into the car.

Darius looked at her and asked, "Are you sure you still want to visit Dad today? If I'd just had the same couple of days as you, I'd want to lie around and do nothing for a week. That said, I do that professionally, so…"

"I'm fine. Well, not fine. But if I sit around and actually process what's happened to me recently, I might go certifiably insane, so it's probably best to keep moving. When are you going to finish that absurd film anyway? I'm worried about you having to stay so thin for so long. What if you get carried away on a strong summer breeze?"

"I don't know. The schedule keeps changing. Along with the director."

"Your film goes through directors like Elizabeth Taylor went through husbands."

"I know, but I've never done a film like this. I feel like it could be something really iconic."

"Perhaps. Although you did say that about *Kraken 3: The Final Krakening*."

"The world wasn't quite ready for that one, but I thought I put in a good performance."

"You were certainly the best 'beach-goer devoured by kraken #5' I've ever seen."

"Not all of us can get paid to pretend to care about dead rich people, Lennie."

Lenore shrugged. "You get paid to pretend to be dead. I get paid to pretend to care about the dead. Wouldn't Mum be proud?"

Darius shot her a disparaging glare. "That's not funny."

She frowned and stared contritely at the floor. "Apologies, I'm not thinking straight. Still pretty shaken up." She reached into her handbag and held the fob watch tight between her fingers. Its gentle ticking had become oddly comforting.

9

THE DEATH DOLLAR

"Morning, Darius, Lenore." Ray greeted them with a firm handshake. He had a smattering of something that could have been banana purée, vomit, or vomited banana purée on his scrubs.

"You saving that for later?" asked Lenore, nodding at it.

He frowned, grabbed a tissue from the reception desk, and wiped it off. "Occupational hazard. How are you both?"

Darius tilted his head towards Lenore and said, "This one attacked a guy with a garden gnome this morning."

Ray raised an eyebrow and looked at her, awaiting an explanation.

"Oh, come on, we've all done it. No need to talk about it all day. How's Dad?"

"Richard's…good." Darius and Lenore looked at each other. "No, I mean, don't worry. It's nothing serious. But his memory's definitely not getting any better. He's forgetting me more often than he used to."

"You do have a very forgettable face," said Lenore.

Ray gave her a mock-wounded look and continued, "He still has mostly good days. But his bad days are becoming a lot more frequent. I just want you to be prepared. He's also growing increasingly fixated with his…project." Lenore stared at the floor. "I honestly can't say if that's helping or making things worse. I can't even remember the title. Something about

48

the interconnectivity of—"

"*The Death Dollar: A Study Of The Interconnectivity Of The Economics of Mortality, Late Stage Capitalism, Entropic Systems, and the Alteration and Augmentation Of Human Life.*" Lenore extolled the verbose title with a weary resignation.

Ray smiled and said, "Yes. That one."

"He goes on about it, doesn't he?" Lenore sighed. "We call it 'The Death Dollar theorem. Or 'advanced D & D.' That's a nerd reference to—"

Ray held up his hand, "I spent my high school years as a thief class elf named El-shanarr. You don't have to explain *Dungeons & Dragons* to me."

Lenore raised an eyebrow at him.

He shrugged, then asked, "You understand any of it?" Lenore and Darius both shook their heads. Ray smiled and said, "I oughta get on with my rounds. Lemme know if you need anything."

They thanked him and continued down the hall, passing a series of rooms housing men and women watching TV, reading, staring vacantly out the window. He was seated in his red leather chair, notebook and pen in hand, floor carpeted with scattered pages forming a tapestry of scrawled notes and diagrams. He had three screens connected to his antiquated, wheezing PC that displayed a stream of ever-changing matrices and indices. He was murmuring excitedly to himself, tapping his pen on the arm of the chair. Lenore knocked on the open door. He turned around, greeting her with a broad, sandy-toothed grin. He jumped out of his seat and said, "My beautiful Christine! You've come back to me!"

Lenore's heart sank, and she murmured, "No, Dad. Christine's dead, remember? I'm your daughter, Lenore?"

He stopped, sadness colouring his face, and covered his mouth with a trembling hand. He reached out, his fingers gently touching her cheeks, ears, and chin before finally pinching her nose and blowing a raspberry, proclaiming, "Bloody hell, Len, I know it's you. I was just mucking around. I'm not completely mad. Yet."

"Dad, that is *not* funny," Darius groaned.

Richard laughed and grabbed them both in a bony hug, then muttered, "If an old man can't mess around with his kids, what the hell is he supposed to do with his time? Sit down, sit down…ah, here let me clear some space for you. Been busy with the Work, you know." He waved his hand expansively around the room. "Made some good progress this week. I've been working on the chapter examining correlations between colony collapse disorder and the destabilisation of the Dow Jones. I'm also looking into this Google sub-company called Calico, you know, the one I told you about that has the ultimate aim of curing death. They've been very secretive over the last few years, but lately, there have been some very inter-est-ing developments. The world's largest company aiming to actually bring an end to death. It's like the Epic of Gilgamesh rewritten by *Forbes* magazine." He snatched up pictures of a bull and a bear, both covered in masses of red markings. "And think about this. We always talk about bull and bear markets, right? Or companies talk about competitors, survival of the fittest, paralleling social Darwinism with economy, which I mean, it's a logical fallacy, not only because—"

"'Social Darwinism is a corruption of the basic principles of Darwin's ideas,'" quoted Darius, settling in to endure his father's familiar diatribe.

"Ex-*act*-ly! The idea of 'fittest' equating to the 'most aggressive' is a classically Western capitalist logical fallacy. In a drought, or famine, or any kind of extreme conditions, it's the predators and large animals that die out first. I mean, you don't, you don't exactly see—"

"'T-Rexes and saber tooth tigers running around the place these days, do you'?" quoted Lenore, flipping through an old *National Geographic*.

"Precisely, it's the small, agile creatures that require minimal calorie consumption who survive. And what's more, are more likely to have superior adaptation mechanisms in place. I've also been researching *Turritopsis dohrnii*, known as the immortal jellyfish." Lenore and Darius looked up, this part was new to them. "This tiny, miraculous little creature can revert to polyp stage an *infinite* number of times. It is, in a very real sense, biologically immortal. In an enclosed environment with a regular food source, this creature would never die."

"So why aren't the oceans—"

Richard silenced Lenore's question with an exultant yelp and said,

"Swarming with tiny jellyfish? Beeeeecause, they are tiny and weak. Lots of things eat them. Immortality is their only defence mechanism. Sounds sort of like a Wu-Tang lyric, doesn't it?" Richard's children stared at him with wide eyes. "I'm discovering lots of new music in my free time. The GZA has some excellent references to quantum physics, and much of their lyrical content references the feudal nature of modern economies, particularly in relation to sub-legal narcotic distribution. In any case, you have the immortal jellyfish, but there are also creatures with profound longevity, like the tuatara and some species of tortoise, and then there's the toughest animal on earth: the tardigrade. You ever seen those things?"

"Yes. Most people call them water bears," said Lenore.

"Right. They're tiny, about the size of a dust-mite, but in-*des*-tructible! They can survive extreme heat, cold, pressure, the only known living thing that can survive in the vacuum of space. The ultimate survivalists, but importantly, their survival mechanism isn't based on strength. It's their ability to enter this extreme hibernation. The obvious parallel in economic terms is that market survival may not ultimately depend on expansion, but suspension. I've been monitoring a slew of major companies who seem to be entering a state of caretaking, as though they're preparing for… you know you don't exactly make me feel thrilled when I see your eyes glaze over like that."

Lenore shrugged and said, "You know the way you feel when I start talking about guitar rigs and amp settings?"

"Why talk about it? Just make the sounds you want and get on with it."

"Exactly. That's how I feel when you talk about the Work."

He threw his hands up and sighed. "Ungrateful brats, the both of you. Sometimes, I wonder why I even brought you into the world."

"I'm pretty sure Mum did the hard yards on that front," scoffed Darius.

Lenore stared at the floor. "We should talk about something else."

"Okay, fine. How's work?"

"A bird landed on my face, and I didn't flinch, so the director said he's going to hook me up with a small speaking part."

"I did a double shift yesterday. Shot a flaming arrow at the first. At the second, I was the only one there, and the guy left me his house in his will. The whole thing's rather peculiar. I might just try and sell it."

Richard nodded, took a long slurp from his tea, placed it back on its saucer and said, "I know my work on the Death Dollar is at least in part to blame for you both ending up in the jobs you have. I know I told you 'death is a futureproof industry.' But I don't understand either of your jobs *at all*. Whatever happened to having a job like 'teacher,' 'carpenter', 'lawyer'? One word, everything you need to know. You know Jeanine told me her granddaughter is a 'data systems analyst consultant?' Hector has a son who's a 'behavioural design implementation strategist.' What does that even mean? Four words. Is that a job title or a haiku?" He sighed, exasperated. "Anyway, I'm going off on one of my rants again. Let's talk about something less controversial. Like, when the hell are you gonna produce some grandkids? I'm gettin' old, in case you hadn't noticed. Wouldn't mind meeting them before you put me in a box and argue over the inheritance. You know I'm the *only* guy on this whole floor without grandkids! Harry has *thirteen*."

"Would it be unreasonable to ask for at least a three-month grace period between the death of my boyfriend and you nagging me to produce spawn despite the fact I've *repeatedly* told you I don't want to have children?" she snapped.

His face fell, and he murmured, "I'm sorry, Len, I wasn't thinking. You know I was very fond of Quan."

He rubbed her shoulder affectionately, then whipped around to face Darius. "But you have no excuse."

"Dad, cut him some slack. He looks like off-brand Skeletor."

Darius raised his middle finger at her. "I *have* to stay this skinny. It's in my contract. Plus, that doesn't even make sense. Skeletor had a six-pack." They laughed and lapsed into silence.

Richard wobbled, held the wall for balance, and looked up at Lenore. "Christine?" he said, rubbing at his forehead, hand gently trembling.

Lenore groaned, "Dad, please. Twice a month is too often; twice a day is unbearable. I haven't even told you about my ceiling collapsing—"

"Christine, I've missed you so much." Tears pooled in his red-rimmed eyes, and Lenore fell into silence. He threw his arms around her neck, and Lenore patted him gently on the back as he sobbed into her shoulder.

53

10

DEATH, SEX, AND COFFEE

Lenore sat on the park bench, watching an elderly woman feeding a murder of crows with her granddaughter. The tiny blonde girl in light-up shoes threw bits of bread and clapped delightedly when the black-winged bastions of death obligingly consumed it. Her grandmother beamed proudly, murmuring encouragement.

"They do that every week," said Ray, taking a seat beside her. "They've actually brought more crows to the area. They dig up the bins, scatter chip packets all over the place. I gotta clean my car twice as often because they keep shitting on it. We've asked them to stop, and Mary always says, 'Yes, yes, of course, dear. Sorry to make trouble.' But she forgets, her granddaughter comes to visit, and off they go. Throwing food to the feathery vermin."

Lenore said nothing for a while, then turned to him and replied, "You really need to work on your pick-up lines."

He laughed and said, "You never explained why you have that half-finished crow on your arm."

"It's a raven. And no, I didn't."

Ray waited for her to continue, but when she said nothing further, he asked, "How was Richard today? Did he remember you?"

"For a while. Then he thought I was Mum again."

"That must be hard." Lenore nodded.

"It is. Also painful. Also confusing. My fault for killing her, I guess."

Ray looked at her, then back at the crows. "I guess I'm not the only one who needs to work on my pick-up lines."

She punched him in the arm and said, "Come on, you've got me for a couple of hours, then I need to get on with hiring someone to clean this weird and potentially haunted house I've inherited."

* * *

The painting was enormous. It covered the entire wall in an abstract array of reds and pinks. It was the kind of innocuous non-art that hoteliers would put in the front lobby of their three-star chain hotel. Ray was naked save for a towel around his waist, wreathed in the steam of the shower he'd just exited. Between the steam and the canvas, it was unclear if this was a new residence or the one he currently occupied. Ray chatted convivially to whoever was in the room with him, but was brutally silenced by the slicing of his throat. A sanguine stream flicked across the room, a new shade of red merging with the crimson-coated canvas.

* * *

"You're always so quiet after," he said as he placed the mug of coffee in front of her. He was wearing Spiderman boxers; she couldn't decide if this was adorable or deplorable.

She shrugged. "What's there to talk about? It's sex, not a book club."

He smiled and sat down opposite her. "So, I was thinking—"

"You really ought to stick to your strengths."

"Not funny," he said, throwing a sugar cube at her face. "I was thinking we could—"

"No."

"Do me a favour and let me finish."

"I'm doing you a favour by not allowing you to start. I like you, Ray, but it's too soon. Quan's only been gone a few weeks. I feel like a trollop as it is. Besides, I'm not sure that we're compatible."

"'Trollop'? Who the hell says 'trollop' anymore?"

"You'd be surprised."

"I know you're still in mourning, but I'm not asking you to move in with me. We can take it slow."

"We've been over this. You're nice, this is nice, the sex is…better than nice. But you should be with someone who's going to commit. Someone without so much emotional baggage she has to get an extra allowance at the airport."

He frowned and muttered, "That's a poorly constructed analogy," as he slurped his coffee.

"Don't slurp your coffee just to annoy me."

"I'm *not* doing it just to annoy you. This is how I like to drink my coffee. Watch." He slurped greedily and smacked his lips with satisfaction. "Ah. Delicious and noisy."

"Don't be so passive-aggressive. Even if I wasn't in mourning, I've…got a lot going on right now."

Ray scoffed and shook his head. "Right."

"What?"

"That's *such* a bullshit line. It's something women always say when they can't articulate their feelings properly."

Lenore placed her mug on the table and fixed him with a challenging glare. He slurped again, his gaze unflinching. Lenore inhaled and said, "When Darius was born, it nearly killed my mum—"

"You've already told me this story. Also, are you even remotely familiar with the concept of segueing?"

"I haven't told you— or almost anyone else— the whole story. I'm about to share an intimate and unquestionably strange secret with you. I hope you appreciate what that means." He nodded, gestured for her to go on. "She saw the light at the end of the tunnel, but felt herself being pulled back to the world; she made it back into the land of the living. Afterwards, she was filled with a sort of awe at the tiny creature she'd created, but she entered a chronic postpartum depression. Mum was a coroner, so she always had a morbid professional fascination with death, but she became obsessed with mortality. It didn't help that our house was filled with all this macabre iconography, Dad's notes and diagrams, her research texts. It became the only thing she'd talk about: the Tibetan concept of the Bardo state, Zoroastrian sky burials, Hindu rebirth cycles, and especially her own death. She'd told him, 'I've seen it, Richard. I'm going to die in a car crash. I don't want anything fancy for my funeral,' and then the next week, she'd say, 'I'm going to drown. It will be a calm, natural death. Please don't cry for me.' This went on and on. She saw her death in increasingly unusual circumstances: plane crash, fire, lightning strike, terrorist attack.

"It drove Dad crazy; he insisted that she see a therapist, but she told him, 'Why bother? By the time we have a half a dozen sessions I'll be on my way out. It would be rude to inconvenience them like that.' He was starting to reach his wit's end when they found out she was pregnant with me. For a while, the excitement took her mind off things. He thought she'd moved on.

"Then, one morning, he's rummaging around in some boxes looking for spare light bulbs, and he finds her diary. For the last few weeks, all she's been writing about is her death, but this time, she's fixed on how it's going to end: on the table in the delivery room, with me being cut free from her stomach. She describes every detail: the doctors, the time of day, the nurse's harsh northern accent. He confronts her about it, and she shuts down, refuses to talk about it."

Lenore stared into the inky black well of her coffee. "A few months later, they're approaching the scheduled delivery date, but, classic me, I decide to show up egregiously early. They rush to the hospital, but there's a fucking football game on, traffic is gridlocked. Things go bad quickly. By the time they get to the hospital, Mum's already in serious trouble. They did what they could, but they lost her, just like she said they would. She was thirty-three when she died, same age I am now. Can't tell you how much that's been playing on my mind lately." She stirred her teaspoon in her cup, not so much to dissolve the sugar as to hear the sound. "They cut me from the belly of a dead woman. Life born from death."

"I don't mind you telling me this whole story again, but none of this is new to me."

She nodded and said, "This bit will be. Just a heads up; it's going to get weird."

"As opposed to the quotidian tale it's been thus far?"

She ignored his comment and continued, "My first boyfriend, Mark, and I were together for a year before we slept together. I thought he was the one. The naïveté of youth, right? The first few fumbling encounters under the sheets weren't particularly earth-shattering. The sex was brief, sweaty, awkward."

"Sounds familiar."

"After we'd tried it a few times and we had a better understanding of each other's bodies, I climaxed, and before I could even process the rush of pleasure and release I felt the vision flooding my brain, swallowing all my other thoughts. I watched this blurry, hallucinatory scene unfold where Mark—he must've been fifty, maybe sixty—was walking in the woods with someone I felt to be his wife. A snake leapt out of nowhere and dug its fangs into his leg. He dropped to the ground. His face turned purple, and she screamed, calling for help, but they were alone in the middle of nowhere. It wasn't long before the light faded from his eyes."

She watched Ray turning the information over in his head and could almost hear his neural gears grinding. "You're telling me you had an *orgasm-induced* hallucination?"

"Not hallucination." Ray put his coffee down, arched an eyebrow.

"Come on, you're saying that—"

"It makes a strange kind of sense, I think, the moment of death revealed during the act that creates life. You've probably heard people calling the orgasm *la petite mort; that's* French for 'the little death.' It's a reference to the idea that the transcendence which occurs during orgasm is similar to the transcendence of death. Once upon a time, we believed that each orgasm expended a tiny amount of 'life force' or chi or élan vital or whatever you want to call it. The visions kept coming—don't even *think* about making the awful joke I can see brewing behind your gorgeous brown eyes. Every time I slept with someone, well, at least the ones who knew what they were doing, I saw a vision of their death. Cancer. Suicide. Heart attack. Melanoma. Electrocution. Car crash. Drowning."

"Wait, how many guys have you—"

"Not even remotely the point. But each of them seemed to be in the mid to distant future, decades at least. I always assumed it was a pathological condition, a legacy of Mum's death."

"Like an epigenetic inheritance of her trauma?"

"Perhaps a combination of epigenetic inheritance and emotional trauma from Dad finally telling me the whole story when I was a teenager. The first time I slept with Quan, it was different. He didn't appear to have aged much at all, no greying or receding hair, or crow's feet, or scars. And I saw him sleeping. It looked quiet, peaceful."

"What did he say when you told him what you saw?"

She cast her eyes down at the table.

"You didn't tell him?"

"Every guy I've ever told this story to said I was crazy and either broke up with me or insisted I see a psychologist. Which I tried, by the way, to no avail. I knew Quan was someone I could see myself falling in love with. I didn't want to ruin it. It killed my libido. We had a lot of arguments about why I was never 'in the mood', even though I was more than happy to—"

Ray waved his hand, grimaced. "I'm not the type for retrospective jealousy, but there's no need to go into detail."

"That's fair; you get the idea in any case. Quan resented me for never wanting to have sex. I had a guilt complex about not telling him that I'd seen his death, or at least thought I had. I kept telling myself, 'it's a delusion; none of the men you've ever been with have died.' Then, finally, I woke up. Everything was exactly the way I'd seen it: the pre-dawn light outside, the sound of the garbage truck on the street, his old Radiohead hoodie slung over the back of the chair. And him. Silent. Breathless. Still."

Ray didn't say anything for a while, then he got up and refilled their cups, fixed Lenore with a thoughtful but skeptical gaze. "I appreciate you sharing your story with me."

She stared into his eyes for a few seconds, then said, "You sound like a therapist. I knew I shouldn't have told you."

"Just because I don't necessarily *believe* the particulars of—"

"It's not about belief. I'm recounting events, not asking you to sign an affidavit saying you agree with my conclusion."

He pondered this, sipped his coffee.

"It's strange. I get that. But is it any stranger than the fact that we know exactly the way the universe is going to end? If the final pages of this universe have already been immutably inscribed, doesn't it make sense that it might be possible to take a sneak peek at the ending of the little footnotes of our lives?"

"What do you mean 'we know how the universe is going to end'?"

"Heat death."

He looked at her like she was speaking ancient Macedonian.

"Sometimes I forget other people didn't grow up in a house obsessed with endings and epitaphs. The laws of thermodynamics dictate that over time, energy will be exchanged and transformed into a state where it can no longer achieve exchange or transformation. Eventually, the universe will become filled with black holes, cool to near absolute zero, and everything will be perfect, quiet chaos. The end."

"That's…pretty grim."

She shrugged. "None of us will be here to see it. Fun fact: Ludwig Boltzmann, who discovered the equation for entropy—essentially the underlying cause of the inevitable path to the universe's eventual destruction—hanged himself. They used the equation as his epitaph: $s = k. \log W$."

"Not exactly poetic."

"Depends on what kind of poetry you're into."

Ray stared into the swirling black void in his cup, imagining stars collapsing, galaxies drifting apart, light fading into infinite, immaculate oblivion. "You've got a real knack for killing the mood."

"I shouldn't have said anything."

"I was kidding, it's fine—"

"You should find yourself someone less, I don't know, morbidly oracular." She stood up to leave, and he grabbed her arm gently and said,

"But what if 'morbidly oracular' is my type?"

She fixed him with twin retinal lasers.

"No, come on, I'm kidding. Sit down and finish your coffee, at least. You've got to give me a little time to soak all that in."

She acquiesced, sat back down.

"Besides, now I have to ask the obvious question."

"Please don't."

"Come on, if you were me, wouldn't you want to know?"

She rolled her eyes and said, "Of course I would." Lenore rotated her cup on the table and mumbled. "Just...promise me you won't do any redecorating."

11

IMMOR(T)ALITY

Darius savoured each slow bite of his apple, the only food he would consume for the next six hours. He rolled his neck, swung his arms, stretched. Pretending to be dead was surprisingly taxing work. He'd started inventing games he could play while he lay for hours beneath his fellow background actors, soaked in the stench of dirt and sweat. He made lists of increasing complexity; authors (alphabetical, Austen to Zamyatin); albums (chronological, Miles Davis to Kendrick Lamar); countries (ascending number of syllables, Fiji to the Democratic Republic of the Congo). He knew Tabresh sometimes snuck an earbud into his ear and listened to podcasts, but he'd heard of extras being fired for a lot less. He gulped down a cup of water, almost choking when Kyle slapped him on the back.

"Whoa, dude, slow down. It's not a boat race."

Darius recoiled, both from the force of the slap and the sheer wonder of the implausibly famous actor deigning to talk to him. "Boat race?"

"Yeah, man, you know, where you slam a beer, and then the next person slams a beer down the line until you're all finished?"

"Why's it called a boat race?"

Kyle shrugged and said, "Because people play it on boats I guess? I've only ever played it on yachts. And once in a hot air balloon." He was giggling incessantly, his eyes were glazed and red-rimmed, which explained his flouting of the conventional social chasm between leads and extras. Kyle picked up a donut and looked at Darius through the hole in the middle. "Heyyyyyy. I can seeee you!"

Darius laughed nervously and said, "Yeah, you can. Hey Kyle, do you think you could help me out with something?"

Kyle munched on the Donut and said, "Sure, bro, lay it on me."

"Jason said he'd try and get me some lines, but I'm a bit scared to remind him because he's been pretty angry of late. "

Kyle laughed and said, "You chasing lines?"

"Yeah?"

"Sure thing, man, I've got some prim-o ye-yo in my trailer; I'll hook you uuuuuuuup!"

"No, I mean lines in the film."

Kyle laughed, spilling chunks of donut on the ground in front of him, "Right right right. I was just kidding. Yeah, no problem. You can have my lines if you want 'em. Who wrote this fucking thing anyway, it's like, 'incongruent,' 'eschatology'? Is this even *English*?"

Darius nodded and summoned the courage to continue, "It's about the ending of everything. The apocalypse. So, my name's Darius, if you wouldn't mind double-checking with Jason?"

"Darren. Got it."

"Darius."

"Sorry. Okay, no problemo, Derek."

"*Darius.*"

"Riiiiiiight." Kyle laughed and sucked loudly at the chocolate icing on his fingers. Darius stared at him, incomprehensibly jealous of his ability to ingest mountains of junk food whilst maintaining an Adonis-like physique. Kyle glanced conspiratorially around the set, grabbed Darius in a headlock, and pulled him in close. The other background actors regarded him with fervent envy. "Devon, can I tell you something?"

"It's Darius, and yes." He leaned in extra close to his ear and whispered, "I'm not going to have an ending. *I'm never going to die.*"

Darius let the words sink in, reminding himself that Kyle was both stupidly high and highly stupid. "What do you mean?"

"I'm not even getting paid for this film! I mean, fuck I've got, like, fifty million in the bank already. Or, wait, is it billion? Lots of zeroes, anyway. My accountant said I'm all gravy. What the hell do I need money for? I'm doing this film in exchange for immorality."

"Ah, do you mean *immortality?*"

"Yeah, that one." Kyle grinned at him, placed his fingers to his lips, and said, "Ssssssshhhhh.' Don't tell anyone, though. It's a big secret. Also don't tell anyone I'm stoned. It helps me remember my, you know, ahhhh..."

"Lines?"

"Exactly. Listen, man, I may be dumb, but I'm not, like, *stupid.* Look at this face. This face is my fucking meal ticket. I'm a good actor, but I'm not great, you know?"

"Hey now, that's...not...true..."

"Nonono s'okay, I know what I am. I'm *cool* with it. BUT, look at, like, Steven Seagal, one of the great actors of his generation, right?" Darius resisted the urge to vehemently disagree. "He was it. A-list. He was everywhere. But now, he's like, pretty fat, you know? And he's doing limited-release B-grade films and shit? I don't want to get like that. This face." He gestured to it like a prosecutor pointing an accusatory finger at a witness. "Is gonna get *wrinkles.* S'gonna get OLD man. I can't be having' that. But I don't wanna go full James Dean, either, you know? I mean, I'm fuckin' scared of death." He paused and stared at Darius with disarming sincerity and said, "But no matter how much money I make or how many models I bang or how many cars I own or how much blow I snort or how many tropical islands I visit or how many—"

"Yeah, I get it. No matter what you do, you'll still die eventually."

"Right?"

Darius nodded. It was the first point he'd completely understood and agreed with so far.

"Right, you get me Declan. You *see* me, don't you? You see my *soul.*"

"How exactly are you going to become immortal?"

Kyle shook his head and placed his fingers to his lips, but then raised both his hands, holding up six fingers.

"Six?"

He nodded, giggling idiotically, "That's right, son."

"Six what?"

"Kyle. My third favourite star." Csaba reached his arm around Kyle's neck affectionately, no easy feat given that he was at least six inches shorter.

"Third? Who's—"

"Right behind Ursa Major and Sirius A," Csaba interrupted, before unleashing an avuncular laugh.

Kyle frowned and said, "I don't get it."

Csaba winked at Darius and said, "It's an astronomy joke. Wrong crowd, obviously. This gigantic chunk of talent isn't hassling you, is he pal?"

Chantelle called everyone back to positions. Darius shook his head and said, "Oh no. Not at all, it's a pleasure to—"

"Mind if I steal him away for a minute?"

"Of course."

Kyle flicked him a wave goodbye and said, "Later, Danielle."

Darius watched the two of them walk away and murmured, "Great, there goes the man who could change my life forever, and he can't even remember my name. Or gender." Darius grabbed the last macaroon, opened his mouth, and watched in horror as the crow swooped over, plucked it from his fingers, shat on his shoulder, and flew off back to its handler. The handler yelled a half-hearted apology and then took the bird back to its trailer, its gigantic, luxury trailer.

"Ok, crew, let's fucking shoot this bitch!" yelled Jason.

Not for the first time, Darius mulled over the dark humour of this sentence's unintended double entendre. He grabbed a handful of paper towels, wiped the shit from his shoulder, and lay back down in the dirt, dreaming of immortality.

12

THE GHOST DID IT

"**I**f you two don't cut it out back there, I will throw your iPads in the toilet!" Audrey screeched. Her girls were pawing at each other and shrieking like creatures from Grecian myth.

"Patti bited me!"

"It's 'bit,' Janis, 'Patti bit me.' Patti, don't bite."

"I didn't, I didn't she's *lyyyyyyying!*"

"I *saw* you do it. She has bite marks on her arm."

"Nuh-uh."

"Are you saying Mummy is a liar?"

"No!"

"Are you saying I'm imagining the bite marks on her arm?"

"No…"

"Then how did they get there?"

Patti paused, considered the question, and replied, "Auntie Lenore did it."

Lenore laughed, impressed and terrified by her commitment to the lie in the face of overwhelming evidence. She could make a great politician someday.

"Really? Auntie Len leaned back from the front seat and bit Janis, all without Mummy noticing?"

"Yup." Patti sounded pleased with herself, obviously missing the scorn in her mother's voice.

"If you're gonna lie, at least try and make it plausible."

They pulled in front of the house and parked the car. Lenore unloaded the box of tea and snacks as Audrey grabbed the bag of cleaning supplies. The twins tumbled out of the back seat, immediately spilling a slew of soft toys and plastic gewgaws onto the footpath. They seemed to manifest mess and chaos around them, as though it were a superpower.

Lenore eased the gate open.

Janis and Patti latched onto her legs, shouting, "Robot legs robot legs!"

She unlocked the door, put her box down, and obliged, making mechanical hydraulic noises as she raised and lowered the girls, gripping tightly at her calves.

The girls screamed with delight for a few steps and dismounted, eyes wide with wonder. "Is this Dracula's house?" asked Janis. "It smells like wet cats and dry poop."

"That's a very creative description, but no. This is my new house. Apparently." The girls tore off down the hallway. "Are you sure it's safe for them to be here?" she asked Audrey. "There's mould and junk all over the place."

"It's fine. Their after-school care centre is practically a biohazard zone. They have the immune systems of a field-hardened epidemiologist. And it's kinda nice to know that they can run riot and not actually mess the place up any worse than it already is," said Audrey, inspecting a box filled with vintage dolls. "Hey, these are cool."

"They're yours if you want them. Honestly, Aud, how are you still *alive*? I couldn't survive a weekend with two kids," she shrugged and said, "Once you give up sleep and any sense of self-identity, it ain't so bad. At least Pete has them half the time. When he fucking shows up." She sniffed and scowled, "Janis wasn't wrong about the smell, though. You going to hire professional cleaners?"

"I'll have to. I figure I'll borrow some money from Dad, then pay him back with money from the sale of the house. But before I sell it, I need to find out who they are." She pointed to the painting of Elliott and his secret family.

Audrey considered the painting and asked, "You thought of hiring a private detective?"

"Maybe. Think that'd work?" Audrey shrugged.

"Dunno, but it'd probably be more efficient than a Google search. Maybe—holy crap, is this a *laserdisc*? Remember these things?" She picked up one of the pizza-sized discs and flung it across the room like a frisbee.

"You are supposed to be *helping*."

"I *am* helping. Look, I helpfully started a helpful new pile for all the helpful laserdiscs."

Lenore rolled her eyes and stared at the painting, then made her way to the front-facing bedroom. The door opened with a rusty hair metal shriek. It was slightly less cluttered with detritus than the lounge room, but still chaotic enough to give an interior designer a panic attack. She closed the door and turned to see a painting leaning against the wall. She placed it on a nearby desk and sat down on the bed to examine it. Like the painting in the living room, it depicted the Brindle family. But in this image, they were standing in the room she now inhabited, and the child was a little older, no longer a baby but a toddler in a dress. She stared at Elliott and his wife, each of her tiny hands clasped in theirs. Lenore leaned in close to examine the face. The artist had depicted her gazing down, long fringe covering her face. Not very useful. She snapped a photo and moved on to the bathroom.

It was pleasantly free of boxes and miscellany, but not-so-pleasantly coated in a remarkably varied palette of black to green mould. Downstairs, she heard something smash, followed by Patti screaming, "We didn't do it, Mummy, it was a ghost."

Audrey groaned and yelled, "It's okay, Len, it was just a crappy old vase. Sorry." before unleashing a matriarchal tirade.

Lenore continued her explorations in the master bedroom. It opened onto a private deck with a breath-abducting view of the tree canopy above. The bulk of the room was occupied by a king-size four-poster bed. The curtains surrounding it were tied back, but a thick mass of cobwebs was doing a thoroughly adequate job of standing in their place. This room, like the others, was filled with bibelots and curios. On the antique vanity was a minuscule militia of mythical creatures: basilisks, dragons, unicorns, nyads and dryads, dragons, phoenixes, mermaids and sirens, centaurs and minotaurs. Lenore picked up the basilisk—one of her personal favourites—and placed it in her breast pocket. She made a habit of always wearing clothes equipped with pockets, something that was irritatingly difficult to acquire in women's clothing, and it was moments like these that validated her predilection for sartorial storage.

The mirror in the vanity was cracked, representing the room in fractured chaos. She leaned in and examined her reflection. She looked skeletal, frail. Black bags hung under her eyes. She reached her hand to her face. The smell of Ray's cologne was still thick on her fingers. Lenore searched for another painting but found only boxes of books with obscure titles (*Parallel System Synthesis In Primate Hierarchies, Do Not Go Gently: Signs And Portents In The Work Of Dylan Thomas*) and bags of extravagant clothing (feather boas, fascinators, corsets, tailcoats). She was about to leave when a thought struck her.

She turned to the bed, got down on her knees and peered underneath. Her lips peeled back into a grin. Lenore pulled the painting out and used it to push back the thick mass of cobwebs, then placed it on the bed. Again, the Brindles stared back at her, standing in a tidier, brighter, incarnation of that same room. The unknown girl was a little older— perhaps eight years old—her head turned away from the painter, face obscured by fringe and shadow. But now Lenore could see there was something odd about her skin. It resembled paper that had been scrunched up and smoothed out again.

Audrey's phone rang, Lenore heard her ordering the girls to stay outside and be quiet before taking the call. "This had better be good, you vile, vacuous vermin!" Audrey paced back and forth, the voice on the other end tinny and inaudible. "If your account isn't sorted by the end of the day, I am going to hang you out to dry. Do you hear me, you loathsome, lecherous loser?"

Lenore made her way downstairs. Audrey greeted her with an apologetic look and mouthed, 'Five minutes, sorry, hun.' Lenore waved the apology away and entered the first room next to the stairs. She froze, soaking up the strange spectacle in front of her, then gently closed the door. She stood in the centre of an empty, pristine, ethereally white room. Her footsteps echoed across the wooden floor. The only markings were a series of measurements marked in pencil against the doorframe, reaching from Lenore's knee to the final one at roughly shoulder height. She placed her palm against the wood— a formerly living thing that had begun as a seed, fallen into the earth, yearned for the sun, reached out roots and shoots, hosted bugs and birds in its branches, fed animals with its leaves, ascended into the forest canopy, lived and grown through long winters, scorching summers, violent storms, until finally, after hundreds of earthly laps around the sun a chainsaw wielded by a tiny bipedal mammal—a fraction of its age and mass—had brought the ancient tree crashing to the ground. It had been sliced up, transported, and transformed into pieces of this house. The bones of a dead thing used to build a home for imperious primates. As though in response to her musings, the house creaked and groaned with the rising morning heat.

She turned around. Hanging on the door she'd closed was another painting. This time, Elliott and his partner were nowhere to be seen. The image showed their daughter standing alone in the garden outside, framed in a verdant network of vines and trees. She stared directly out from the painting as though she were about to leap free of its frame. She looked around ten years old in stature, but her skin—clearer in this picture than the last—was oddly aged and wrinkled, almost reptilian. Strange as this was, the most striking thing about her was her eyes. Whereas a child of her age normally projected a pyrotechnic blend of joy and curiosity, she possessed the formidable, focused gaze of a Zen master. Her fierce blue eyes contrasted starkly against the absurd pink frilliness of her Pumpkin Patch dress.

Lenore was so hypnotised that it took her a minute to even notice the name inscribed in the centre of the frame beneath:

Riley.

13

OUR LADY OF PERPETUAL SUCCOUR

Orin rose from his sleeping bag, stretched, and performed his morning self-confidence-building mantra (*I am a confident, successful, creative individual. I am a confident, successful, creative individual*). It hadn't worked for him in life, but he was sanguine that death would be an entirely different matter. When he'd finished his mantra, he strummed his guitar (he'd broken the high 'B' string the previous day, so his chords were awkward and incomplete) and thought about the lizard-skinned girl. He'd always imagined death would be peaceful, but it was turning out to be far more challenging than the monotone dirge of his previous existence.

The lizard girl had seen him. This meant either she was, like him, something supernatural and/or post-life, or his invisibility was losing its efficacy. If the latter was the case, he might be able to visit his parents. He pondered this for a moment, then felt an immediate full-frontal assault of anxiety. He placed his hand on the ground to push himself up and felt a scrap of rusty metal sink into his skin.

He pulled it out and tossed it aside, grateful to no longer feel pain but irritated by the inconvenience of the wound. His tomb was sadly bereft of first-aid supplies. He tore a strip off one of his shirts and wrapped it around

71

his hand, then decided it was time to return to the house by the river. He whistled to himself as he walked, studying the expressions of the people who passed him. They all seemed oblivious to his existence, their attention focused on yelling at their phones or their dogs or their children. This was a relief. It appeared his invisibility was selective, for the moment at least. Orin arrived in front of the church and stopped.

He had always been fascinated by the name of this particular religious institution: Our Lady of Perpetual Succour. It was a radiant blend of atavistic and ridiculous. On a whim, he entered, walked to the front of the chapel, and sat on the front pew. The cross before him depicted Christ's head hung bloody and defeated, his stomach rippling with calendar-model abs. Orin wondered how he'd had found the time in his busy messianic schedule for crunches and push-ups. Christ on the cross looked like he'd been a Christ who was fond of CrossFit.

"Hi, Jesus. It's me, Orin. But, ah, you know that, obviously. If you exist. Which I don't really think you do. Although I am here talking, so I guess… that's proof that I think there might be a chance? Or maybe I'm simply hedging my bets. Engaging in a diversified ontological portfolio." Jesus remained silent. "Um. I guess I'd like some advice? I seem to be dead, which is fine, you know. I'm not complaining or anything. I mean, everyone who's ever lived has died, or is going to. It's just, I'm not sure what to do next? Should I be haunting criminals, rescuing kittens, atoning for my sins? I still feel pretty guilty about that time I ate all the chocolates from my school's fundraising supplies and never told anyone about it."

Jesus was not forthcoming with either recommendations nor condemnations. "And there's this girl… I guess a lot of people come to you looking for dating advice. Although you died a bachelor, and your mum was allegedly a virgin, so I'm not sure you're the best source, no offense. What I'm saying is, if she's the one I'm supposed to help, could you give me a sign?"

Outside, a motorcycle barrelled past, filling the air with the angry roar of its engine. Jesus was conversely quiet. Orin stood up to leave, his footsteps quick and light on the aged wooden floor. Just as he reached the exit, a gust of wind howled through the open doors, shaking the windows and wall hangings. Orin turned around, desperately searching for a bible opened to a relevant page or a fallen candlestick pointed in the direction of some miraculous clue, but all he found was a pile of scattered pamphlets advertising Tuesday night computer lessons for the elderly. He attempted to interpret this as something personally significant, but the purple-haired woman with coke-bottle glasses staring into the monitor with a confident grin really didn't seem relevant. He sighed, threw Jesus a desultory wave, and continued towards the house.

14

ARE YOU DRACULA?

O rin entered through the front gate, made his way down the side of the house towards the semi-subterranean lower level and searched for an open window. He was hoping to avoid breaking anything to gain entry, although given the state the house was in, a broken window would hardly have attracted notice. He found a window on the lower level that was jammed open with a small wooden wedge. It was narrow, but Orin judged himself to be barely slender enough to slip through it. He pushed it open, rested it on its upper latch, and maladroitly manoeuvred himself up into the slender opening. He managed to make it halfway before becoming stuck, performing a series of inelegant contortions until he wrestled himself free and popped through onto the tiles of the bathroom floor.

He opened the door and walked down the hall. The house had an almost palpable atmosphere of patient expectation, as though it had filled its lungs and was waiting to exhale. He inspected the first room past the bathroom. It was curiously empty, painted in a luminous white. There were no features or furnishings save for a painting of a girl with scaly, reptilian skin. The plaque below read 'Riley.' Theories and speculations cavorted through his mind, but he was distracted by the arrival of a car pulling into the street outside.

This room being utterly bereft of hiding places, he vaulted into the downstairs lounge room, hurriedly opened a cupboard, emptied it of its contents (inexplicably—a withered pot plant seated on a broken wooden chair), and jumped inside. He heard the gate opening and the sound of several voices clamouring through the house, at least two of them appeared to be children. The hurried thundering of feet across the floor quickly confirmed this. Orin listened to the two girls running down the stairs, laughing and chattering. It was difficult to make out over the children's excited chatter, but he was tentatively convinced that one of the two voices upstairs belonged to Len, the girl with the glasses. His heart performed an exultant skyward vault.

The two girls ran into the living room. From the sound of it, they had found the broken train set that had been lying on the floor.

"Cooooooool! It's a choo-choo train!"

"Trains don't go choo-choo dumb-butt. They're 'lectric now!"

"In real life, but this one is an olden days train. Look, it's got a chimney. I'm going to be the driver!"

"I'm gonna be the driver!"

"Nuh-uh, you can be this ugly girl with pigtails and we'll tie you to the tracks and then the train comes at you like 'choo-choo!' and then the villain that's tied you there says 'Moo-ha-ha. Now you will be runned over by my train. Serves you right for eating my dinosaur spaghetti!'"

"Okay. Then she can break free and zap him with laser vision! Pew pew pew!"

Orin listened to the sounds of colliding trains and nefarious villains and silently willed the girls to find another room to play in so that he could hear Len's voice. He was so focused on telepathically transmitting his request for them to depart that he failed to notice the spider that dropped from the ceiling of the cupboard and began quietly gallivanting along his shoulders. When it reached the skin of his neck, however, the touch of its tiny furry feet sent electric shockwaves of fear and revulsion hurtling through his body. He was not enjoying the return of fear. He'd been quite fine without it since his death, and its reappearance was extremely unwelcome.

He threw the door open, swatting and flailing. He watched the spider fly off his shoulder, land in a corner, and scuttle beneath an old leather couch. The twins were staring at him with mouths agape. It appeared his invisibility had once again forsaken him, just as he'd feared it would. For a few bemused moments, no one said anything.

Finally, the one on the left said, "Are you Dracula?"

He shook his head, placed his finger to his lips, and whispered, "Shhh. I'm a friend of Len's."

"You mean Auntie Lenore?" said the one on the right.

"Yes. Lenore." He savoured the sound of her name on his tongue, but then directed his focus on managing the minor crisis at hand. "I'm her friend, and…we're playing a game of hide and seek. Do you want to play?" The girls rolled their eyes with the preternatural coordination that is typical of twins, and the one on the left said,

"Hide and seek is for *babies.* We are *five.*"

"And a *half.*"

"Yeah. And a half."

"Ah, right. Well, um, you have to keep it a secret because…"

"Why are you so white? Are you a ghost?"

Orin thought for a moment. It occurred to him that perhaps the two children had not yet learned to filter the supernatural in the same manner as adults. This might also explain the girl who had seen him last night, who was also well short of adulthood. He remembered an incident his uncle had told him about that had occurred during a visit to India. He'd been at the top of a castle in Rajasthan, gazing out at a river below, when he'd seen a shadowy black shape playing in the water. At first, he'd convinced himself it was a morbidly obese woman swimming in a burqa. It was only after a few minutes that he realised he was witnessing the gleeful frolicking of a baby elephant. He'd never seen one in the wild, and the strangeness of seeing the enormous creature romping like a puppy had been so great that he'd filtered it into a more plausible and anthropocentric spectacle.

Perhaps this is what the girls were experiencing, having not yet learned to properly process the unknown through the filter of the mundane. They were still of the age when they believed in the corporeal existence of Santa

Claus and the Tooth Fairy. To them, reality was an elastic concept that could be gleefully jammed into any available explanatory crack, crevice, and crevasse.

Orin smiled broadly and said, "Yes. I am a ghost." It was at least a half-truth, after all. "And I don't want to scare Lenore or—" he made an educated guess, "—your mother. Can you keep a secret?" They nodded. "I've been sent to help protect Lenore."

"Like a guardian angel?"

"Yes. Except a ghost."

"A guardian…ghost?"

Orin was pleased with how well his fabulation was evolving.

The twins exchanged a series of near-telepathic twitches and micro-expressions, then nodded. The one on the left leaned towards him, he bent down, and she whispered, "We'll keep the secret. But only if you're a *good* ghost, 'kay?"

"Of course."

The other one leaned in and said, "Yeah, if you're a bad ghost, we'll summon a nether demon to devour your soul and repeatedly dis-em-bowel you from now until the sun turns cold."

"That's…remarkably specific."

She nodded, pleased with herself, and said, "I learned it from *The Mighty Wizards of Malkir*. That's a show about wizards who are mighty."

"And they live in Malkir," added the other one.

"It's a deal. I'll be good, or a demon will repeatedly disembowel me."

"Until the sun grows cold."

"Got it. Okay, well, I'm going to go back to hiding in this cupboard now…"

The two girls waved goodbye. He opened the cupboard, only to find that the spider had returned to its favoured hiding place; he yelped and jumped backwards, knocking over a vase from a nearby table. It shattered in a storm of blue and white porcelain. The twins glared at him, and he whispered, "Ah, it's a test. Of your promise. If you can keep quiet I'll…show you where the secret treasure is."

The girls looked at each other with greedy excitement and nodded, then shoved him into the cupboard and closed the doors behind him.

Footsteps stomped down the stairs, and Audrey's furious voice filled the room, "Are you *kidding* me?!? I leave you alone for *five minutes!*"

"It was an accident," they implored.

"Not good enough. I told you if you break anything, no iPads for one week. So this is what's going to—"

"The ghost did it," yelped Janis, her fragile resolve broken by the draconian threat of deprived digital recreation.

Audrey groaned and began, "Mummy *told you* that—" Her phone rang, and she snorted angrily, then banished the girls outside and answered. "This had better be good, you vile, vacuous vermin!"

Orin listened in silent terror as she described a series of medieval tortures to the poor soul on the other end. He heard Lenore making her way down the stairs and opening one of the bedroom doors. He kept his hand clasped tight over his mouth, his faith in his imperceptibility now thoroughly shaken.

"Mummy!" The twins squealed in unison. "We found an ice princess in the shed!"

"Yeah, she's sleeping or dead or frozen like a necromancer's winter minion."

Audrey finished up her call and yelled, "Has your dad been letting you watch *Wizards of Malkir* again?" There was an awkward pause, followed by,

"...no? It doesn't matter. Come see. Come see!"

Orin listened to the sound of her footsteps, followed by a nightmarish scream and the pounding of feet. "Len! There's a fucking *corpse* in that shed!"

"A *what?!?*"

"I need to get my girls out of here. You gotta call the cops, immediately."

"God, Audrey, I had no idea. I am so, so sorry."

"It's fine," Audrey replied in a tone that implied the exact opposite. "Girls. Car, now!"

"But Muuuuum!"

"I'm counting down. Five, four—"

Orin listened to the sounds of tiny feet racing down the hall, up the stairs, and out the gate. Audrey's car revved and accelerated away. It was a few minutes before he heard Lenore's slow, deliberate steps down the hallway. He heard the shed door creaking open, Lenore's terrified scream, the pounding of feet, the slamming of the door.

Orin emerged and crept down the hall. He was consumed by a quiet, pulsing fear. This was, of course, thoroughly irrational. Given that he was already dead, he had no need to be afraid of threats to his life. If anything, a dead body was a kindred spirit. Nonetheless, as the leaves crunched beneath his feet and he approached the shed, he felt pure, undiluted terror rampaging through his system. He stood at the door, steeled himself, and pushed it open.

It was filled on one side with the usual shed accoutrements—gardening tools, a workbench, a couple of old chairs—but the other side was immaculately clean and uncluttered. A series of wires ran towards the coffin-shaped box that occupied roughly half the floor space. It emitted a quiet, refrigeratoresque hum. Orin inched forward, the cold blue light from the box spilling onto the walls and ceiling. He leaned in close enough to peer at the glass window opening at the coffin's head. There, just as the girls had claimed, was an ice princess.

Or possibly a dead body.

15

AN AVENGING ANGEL

Darius walked between the rows of trailers, searching for Kyle's. It wasn't hard to find, given that it was twice the size of anything else on the lot. The music blaring from inside was distorted but familiar. He stood listening for a few minutes, trying to place it. When he finally matched the melody against the catalogues of his memory, his head spun with disbelief. He held his fist hovering over the door, bit his lip, and knocked.

"Come in!"

Darius eased the door open. "Heeeeey, buddy." He winced at the stupidity of the words vomiting out of his mouth.

"Darius, have a seat man." The interior of Kyle's trailer featured gilded crushed velvet couches, marble-topped benches, a carved mahogany dresser, and a chandelier the size of a pregnant porpoise. "Yeah, yeah, I know. I'm seeing this interior designer. She had it all done for me. Bit much if you ask me, but whatevs." On the bench sat a large tank filled with sand, rocks, and what appeared to be a diminutive dinosaur.

Darius leaned in and inspected it.

"His name's Nero. He's a tuatara from New Zealand. Csaba got him for me. He said they're special because they have three eyes, but the third one's, like, invisible or something." Kyle sat with his laptop open, script laid out in an anarchic pile on the table.

Darius approached slowly, taking a tentative seat next to one of the world's most famous people. When his heart finally stopped pounding, he asked, "Are you listening to Bach?"

"Yeah. You a fan?"

"Are you *kidding* me? I wrote my undergrad thesis on the Goldberg Variations."

"You studied music? That's cool."

"Yeah, I started off with composition, then changed to ethnomusicology."

"But you're a…background actor?"

"…yeah."

"Nothing to be ashamed of."

"I…didn't say anything about being ashamed?"

"Oh, right. My bad. Anyway, I know classical music is supposed to be for old people and nerds, but it helps me memorise the scripts, you know? I know everyone thinks I'm an uncultured moron—"

"Hey. That's…not…true…" The words tumbled limply out of Darius's mouth.

"C'mon man, I know what they say about me. But it's hard, you know? I had my first lead role when I was ten, and haven't stopped working since. I had on-set tutors, but I mostly bribed them to let me get away with not working. They were pretty useless anyway. Most of them tried to use me to get into acting, except Mrs. Polmotti. She just wanted to fool around." Darius recoiled. Kyle waved his hand and said, "Oh no, it's cool. That was when I was older." He was halfway through exhaling with relief when Kyle continued, "I was, like, fourteen, and she was pretty hot, so it wasn't gross or anything. Besides, we only made it to second and a half base."

"That's still *very* worrying, have—"

"So I never had much of an education. And once I was mega-rich, taking time out from being in movies seemed boring and pointless. I mean, I can read, I can count, but I basically only had a ninth-grade education. I figured getting into classical music would be the easiest way to become cultured, just throw some music on while working out or having sex or whatever? But I found I really liked it. When I listen to Bach or Beethoven or Vivaldi, I close my eyes, and I see a world of sound, harmonies, and melodies. It's like the entire cosmos contained in a few minutes of sound."

Darius nodded in bemused agreement and glanced at the fabled script in front of him.

Kyle clocked his gaze and said, "Ah, you're not supposed to look at that. I mean, you seem cool, but we had a reporter from Scriptpeek sniffing around the lot the other day. Chantelle and Csaba are seriously worried about leaks, so…" Kyle gathered up the pages and turned them face down.

"Sorry. I didn't mean to look."

"All good in the hood. What did you want to see me about anyways?"

"I wanted to say thanks for hooking me up with those lines. I know you probably have six personal assistants and a butler, but if you ever need a favour, I'm in your debt."

Kyle grinned and said, "That's cool of you, man. There's a lot of take, take, take in this job, you know? You get rich, people turn into fucking vampires. You hang out with someone, think they like you as a person, and then it turns out that they just want you to donate to their political campaign or their insurrectionist militia or whatever. It sucks."

"Did you say 'militia'?"

"Yeah. People can be such jerks. They see you as this handsome, famous, charismatic, multi-talented, sexually athletic, award-winning ATM, you feel me?" Kyle ran a hand through his short black hair with a petulant grunt. "First-world problems, I guess. Hey, so I've just had more fucking rewrites handed to me this morning. If you wanna help me run some lines, that'd be cool."

"Of course."

Kyle beamed and slapped him on the back, briefly knocking the wind out of him. "Sweet. Okay, soooo…" he shuffled through the mass of papers, extracted one, and threw it on the table. "…in this scene, I've recently found out that my sister is dead, and I have to tell our father. You want to play his part?"

"Sure."

"Okay. Here goes." Kyle closed his eyes, murmured, *"red leather yellow leather red leather yellow leather big black bugs bleed black blood,"* then exhaled, opened his eyes, and said, "Father?"

"Hang on, where's my…okay, got it." Darius cleared his throat and raised his hand in a regal greeting. "Enter, it's been a hundred cycles since I saw you lastly!"

"Father, I express sadfeel because I bring malnews."

"Onebreath, eldest progeny. I shall make the holosphere stopsound. Sorry, can we stop for a second?"

"What's up, hombre?"

"Why do these characters sound like an internet translation of a Lithuanian kids' show?"

"Right. Should've explained that. This scene is from the third act. It's set in the 23rd century."

"It jumps *two centuries?*"

"Yeah, but that's a big secret."

"But you're playing the same character, with the same dad?"

"Yeah, it's weird, but trust me, it'll make sense when you see it. Basically—"

Kyle's phone rang. He paused the music and answered. "Hey Csabs. Sure, that shouldn't be a problem. Email it through to me." He mouthed 'Two minutes.' and went outside, closing the door behind him.

Darius sat in the grandiloquent surrounds, staring at the hypnotic spectacle of the light refracted through the chandelier. He glanced at the script, reached out to it, then drew his hand back. Nero stared at him with rancorous reptilian eyes. Darius reached out again, peeked, put the paper back down. Kyle's computer blipped with a notification. Darius glanced at the screen, and his curiosity for the script was instantly obliterated by the video's thumbnail image. He pressed play. The video was grainy and dark. The camera panned slowly across a wide-open space filled with what at first appeared to be oversized test tubes lit by cold blue light. A quiet hum filled the air, like the warm feedback of a vintage amp. As the camera moved towards the centre of the space, Darius realized they weren't test tubes at all, but cryonic suspension chambers. Each of them held a frozen body, icicles encrusting lips and eyelashes.

The camera tracked along the length of the space, revealing it to be a large warehouse. There were hundreds of bodies inside, each of them still and silent. Right at the far end of the warehouse, there was the faint glimmer of candlelight. The camera held the shot for an uncomfortably long time. There was a barely perceptible rhythmic noise in the background. He turned the volume up and placed his ear against the speaker. It was thick and static, but it sounded like it could be the rumble of industrial machinery, or possibly some kind of chant. He heard feet clanging on the trailer steps and quickly closed the video, then buried his eyes in the page he'd been rehearsing with Kyle.

The door swung open, and Chantelle entered. "Darius."

"Chantelle."

"You're here because…?"

"I was helping Kyle run his lines."

"His lines." He felt himself depleting beneath the intensity of her choleric gaze. "The lines you have been explicitly and repeatedly told you are not so much to glance at under *any* circumstances?"

"I didn't mean to—"

"I'm going to have you hung, drawn, and quartered." She stepped closer. Darius withered, his heart pounding. "I'm going to—"

Kyle leaned his head in the door, phone held to his chest, and said, "Chantelle, leave him alone, okay? I asked him to help. He's pretty good, too. You should give him more lines." He disappeared. Chantelle and Darius stared at each other.

Darius felt like her gaze was slowly melting his internal organs.

She sat down next to him, snapped the computer shut, and folded her black-nail polished fingers over one another. "That true? You any good?"

"I, ah, I mean, I like to think so." The faint hint of a smile flickered across her face.

"Am I making you nervous?"

"What, you mean, because of the threats of violence and those eyes that could probably burn through six-inch steel?" She glowered at him. "They're beautiful eyes. Eyes of an angel. An avenging angel. One of the tough ones with a flaming sword."

"You think I have beautiful eyes?"

"Yes?"

"Why are you saying that like it's a question?"

"I'm not. You do. Have them."

She laughed and leaned back. "How has a tremulous little thing like you managed to make it in this industry?"

"'Make it' is something of a stretch."

Her expression softened slightly into a taut smile. "I should've been back on set six and a half minutes ago. Better get back to Captain Trust Fund and the talentless hacks brigade. Keep Kyle on his lines. I'll throw you a bonus if you can make sure he knows all the rewrites by the end of the week. How's 5k sound?"

"Yesitwouldbemypleasurethankyousomuch!"

She shot him a condescending pout and placed her hand against his cheek. "Oh honey, you really are a sweet little thing, aren't you? Chin up, you're playing with the big boys now." She squeezed his jaw in her hands. "And if you hear anything about the Sixth Sun, you keep your skinny little face shut."

"What's the Sixth Sun?"

She patted his cheek and said, "The thing you need to keep your face shut about. Be a good boy. Everything will be sunshine and puppy dogs. Make me angry, it'll be more like *Reservoir Dogs*. Ciao." She slammed the door, and Darius slumped into the couch, staring at the light reflecting in the chandelier. His phone buzzed with a message from Lenore. He opened it and looked at the image she'd sent, then opened the computer, stared at the video file, and back at Lenore's message again. His eyes darted between two screens displaying images of frozen faces entombed in cold blue coffins.

16

NOT SIGN, SCION

I t was times like this Lenore wished she smoked. She already had the phantom limb of the addiction, occasionally reaching into her handbag, fidgeting, staring longingly at people as they lit up. She thirsted for a vice that she understood—intellectually if not experientially—to be blissful in the short term and terminally corrosive in the long term. Sort of like the human condition, she mused as she stared at the river and pulled at the grass. It had been ten minutes since she'd found the body and for reasons she couldn't quite fathom she hadn't yet called the police. She'd grown up in a house filled with books about Aztec burial rituals, embalming, autopsies, the Bardo Thodol, The Egyptian Book of the Dead, and depictions of every death deity from Ankou to Yama. If anyone should have been prepared for finding a corpse, it should have been her.

And yet.

Lenore felt a tightness in her chest. Her breath sped up. Her head felt light and buoyant. She stared up at the radiant blue sky. At least it was a lovely day to be having a panic attack. She squeezed her eyes shut and attempted to calm herself, trying to name the beast that was attacking her. *It's not real; it's just a panic attack. It's not real; it's just a panic attack.* She ran through the mantra, listening to her breath, listening to the water, drawing focus to the sun on her skin, the grass beneath her bare feet.

Her pulse began to slow and steady. She exhaled and eased her eyes gently open, only to be greeted by the face of a homeless man staring at her. She yelped and scampered backwards, then said, "Sorry, you scared the hell out of me. I know I probably looked like I needed help, but it was only a panic attack. It's fine. I'm fine. Um, how are you?"

He stared at her, his eyes wide in amazement, hand clasped over his mouth. His skin was the colour of teeth.

"Do you need money? I have some…actually, I left my purse inside."

He continued staring.

"Do you speak English? I know some Cantonese, but I'm guessing that's not going to be much use to you?"

"You can…see me?" he said, voice drenched in astonishment.

"Well, yes. You're right there. Unless, of course, you're a panic-induced hallucination. Which isn't completely out of the question."

His clothes were ragged and filled with holes, his hair incongruently groomed into a neat sideways part.

"Although if I was going to hallucinate anyone, I'd prefer it to be Idris Elba."

He sat down opposite her. "You can *see* me!" he repeated.

"I'm fairly certain we already covered that. Listen, I've had a really rough day and, well, I'm sure your life's no picnic…although I suppose you probably do eat the majority of your meals outside, so it might be fairly picnicky in that respect, but—"

"My name is Orin," he interrupted her, holding out his hand. She shook it and said,

"Lenore."

"Len-*ore*. *Len*-ore," he repeated, moving the sounds around in his mouth as though savouring a meal. "You have a beautiful name. Are you some kind of necromancer?"

"I don't recall any recent romancing of necks, no."

"Not '*neck* romancer,' 'necromancer.' A sorcerer who raises the dead?"

She shook her head.

"I'm sorry. I must sound quite mad."

"Actually, you're surprisingly articulate for a homeless guy."

"What do you know about the art of prognostication?"

She tensed, looked away. "Odd question to ask a stranger, don't you think?"

"So, not 'nothing' then?" he was alarmingly eager. He glanced at the raven on her arm. "It's not a coincidence, is it? You wearing the mark of an emblem of the netherworld? Albeit an unfinished one."

"It's kind of a long story."

"I imagine it is! And I look forward to hearing it, although perhaps we should start with basic introductions."

"You mean like hometown, age, star sign? I don't really go in for astrology. My life is chaotic enough as it is. I don't need to subscribe to the belief that distant clusters of burning gas are meddling with me on a day-to-day basis."

"I was thinking more along the lines of sharing preternatural abilities? Clairaudience, claircognizance, clairgustance, clairolfaction, clairsentience, clairvoyance—

"I don't have any of those 'Claires' as far as I know. Could—"

Orin ignored her interruption as he ticked off his supernatural checklist on his fingers, his speech increasing speed and volume as he continued. "Psychoscopy, psychokinesis, pyrokinesis, postcognition, precognition—"

"I'm starting to get a really bad headache, if that's anything?"

"—prophetic dreams or visions, possibly induced by intense neurological activity such as seizures, extreme pain or even org—"

"Orin!" She snapped her fingers in front of his face, startling him out of his supernatural taxonomic queries.

"Yes?"

"This is officially the strangest introductory conversation I've ever had. And I'm afraid I've no idea what you're talking about."

Orin studied her face. Her voice wavered as she spoke. She pushed her palms against her thighs. How curious; her mannerisms were nearly identical to Wanda's on the day she'd sworn she definitely, certainly, *absolutely* wasn't seeing anyone else. He wondered what Adrian and Wanda were up to these days. "My apologies. I know this must seem extremely odd. It's just that ever since I died, I've been—"

"'Ever since you died'? I can assume you mean that in some extravagant hyperbolic sense, like when I told everyone that a piece of me 'died' when the White Stripes broke up?"

"No. I mean it in the most literal sense. I died a few weeks ago. Since then, I've been wandering the earth, trying to discover my post-life purpose. Attempting to actualise my potential as—ugh, did I just say 'actualise my potential'? How repulsive. I spent way too much of my life being forced to watch motivational speeches."

"You were *forced* to watch motivational speeches?"

"Tragically, yes. They were terribly depressing."

"You know, Orin, there was a moment, I believe it was maybe four or five seconds ago, when I thought to myself, 'this conversation can't possibly get any weirder.'"

"Yes, I suppose that must've sounded very odd. But look, we can talk about my life later. Right now, we need to talk about my death."

Lenore buried her head in her hands and groaned.

"Are you alright, Lenore?"

"No, I am not alright. I just found a dead…ah, battery. In my car. So I have that problem to deal with. And now I'm having a conversation with a crazy homeless man who, I mean, I apologise I don't mean to stigmatise your mental illness or your situation, especially given the current housing crisis—"

"I'm not homeless."

"Well, that's good to hear."

"I live in a crypt on the hill over there."

She stared at him with a look that she normally reserved exclusively for wild-eyed proselytisers of trickle-down economics. "That's swell. That's tippity-top. In any case, I suppose I should get back to my various crises. You have a nice life. Or death, as the case may be." She stood up to leave.

He jumped up and grabbed her by the wrist.

She yanked her arm away and yelled, "Do *not* touch me!" Then spun around and stormed back towards the house.

"I'm sorry," he called out after her. "I've barely spoken to anyone else besides the lizard-skinned girl in weeks and—"

She turned and said, "Did you say 'lizard-skinned' girl?"

"Yes. She was one of the few people I've met since my death who was able to see me."

"Where did you see her?"

His eyes darted upwards, and he cleared his throat and replied, "Just… around here. In this sort of…general area."

"In this 'sort of general area'?"

"…yes?"

"Can you take me to her?"

"Definitely. At least, I think so. Probably. I can help you find her. She's like us."

"How?"

"She's a scion of death."

Lenore stared at him. "What do you mean 'sign of death'?"

"No, not 'sign,' *scion*. S-c-i-o-n. As in child, descendant, progeny. We're *connected*." He gripped her shoulders and stared at her with unsettling intensity.

She pushed his arms away, noting the bloody makeshift bandage on his hand. "You'd better come inside. We've got a lot to talk about."

Orin's pale face illuminated as he yelped, "You believe me?"

"I would rate my current levels of credulity at somewhere between 'faked moon landing' and 'Elvis alive and well in rural Wisconsin.' But I would very much appreciate the opportunity to place all the crazy you're throwing at me in a box so I can codify it later. Care to join me for a cup of tea?"

"Oh, I don't drink tea anymore, but I still enjoy watching the steam rise." He registered the expression on her face and said, "That didn't exactly nudge your 'levels of credulity' in a northerly direction, did it?"

She opened her mouth to reply but was interrupted by a large truck speeding down the hill, sending tremors running through the ground beneath them. It pulled up in front of the Brindle house, and a team of overall-clad workers piled out, unloading power tools and industrial cleaning supplies. They streamed in through Lenore's front gate with military efficiency.

"Why are all those cleaners going into your house?" asked Orin.

Lenore shot him a confused glare. "How did you know that's my—"

They were again interrupted, this time by a red sedan blasting The Supremes' "Stop! In The Name of Love." It screeched to a halt behind the van, and a short man in a suit and sunglasses popped out, whistling. He waved to the workers and announced, "And a very good morning to you all! I hope you're ready to turn this 'fixer-upper' into an 'all-fixed-up'." He tossed a set of keys to a portly man carrying a paint tin and said, "Tell you what, Eduardo, I'll make you and the team a deal. Finish by five, and the knockoff beers and pizzas are on me. And by knock-off, I mean 'end of day' not 'inferior facsimile.' Let's get to it."

Lenore turned to Orin and said, "You saw that too, right? I'm not hallucinating?"

"I did, but it would be remiss of me to not point out that according to your own theory, I myself might be a hallucination and, therefore, not the ideal source of verification for—"

She clutched at her temple and groaned. "It's been a rough day. As in, sandpaper rubbed on nether regions rough. I think I might need to postpone our tête-à-tête until tomorrow."

"Are you sure you don't want me to stay and help?"

"By doing what? Rattling chains and going 'woooooooo'?"

"I see your point. Tomorrow then. I shall very much look forward to it."

"Yes. It'll be, you know, a thing." Lenore raced across the road towards the man in the suit, who greeted her with a friendly wave and held out his hand in greeting. She stared at it for a few moments. He coughed, glancing at his hand, hovering expectantly. She relented and allowed him to clasp her fingers in the zealous shake of a real estate agent on inspection day. When he released it, she took a step back, drinking in the sound of the prodigious activity bustling all around her: drills, hammers, the clatter of tins and tools. It was an appropriate soundtrack to the chaos inside her skull.

"Lenore, I presume. *So* glad to finally make your acquaintance. Here, I have a present for you." He reached into the passenger side of his car, removed a cactus, and held it out to her.

She examined it as though it might contain explosives. "Right. Thank you. I should mention I have *quite* a few questions."

He laughed and clasped his hands together. "I should imagine you do, fire away!"

"Who are you? Who are these people? Why are you here? Why do you have keys to this house? Why do *I* have keys to this house? How do you know my name? Did you know Elliott? Who was Elliott, and why did you give me a cactus?"

"That is quite a quiver of queries, Ms Lyn! Let's start with the easy ones first. I made a copy of the keys before my associate handed you the originals. Your name was on the employment contract for the funeral, and my name is Csaba Adami, CEO, of Amrita Industries." He placed a splayed-fingered hand on his chest.

She copied the gesture and said, "Lenore Lyn, normal human person."

Csaba laughed and continued, "The cactus is a traditional housewarming gift. I know, I know, it's somewhat kitsch, but I do *so* love the cactus as a symbol of survival and endurance. Not to mention its hallucinogenic properties! Business on the outside, psychedelics on the inside, much like many of my colleagues."

Lenore looked at Csaba, then the cactus, then back at Csaba again. Over the last couple of days, her confusion had become so constant it was beginning to replace her baseline state, but this was nevertheless a definite peak. He swept his hands around at the bustle of oompa-loopaian activity around them.

"And *this* is a tragically belated gift for my dearly departed friend. Even though the benefits shall fall to his heir—who by a series of convoluted legal intricacies turns out to be you—I feel like I owe him a grand gesture, if only to honour his memory."

"A gift in the form of a cleaning militia?"

"Very amusing. Yes, I know this is something of a surprise, but I assume it's a welcome one?"

Lenore ran a rapid series of risk/benefit calculations and asked, "Could you, by any chance, get them to stay very entirely and completely out of the shed?"

Csaba raised an eyebrow. "Something private in there?"

She rubbed the back of her neck and glanced at her shoes, an affectation she often employed at funerals when attempting to exaggerate awkwardness, then leaned in close and whispered, "Elliott left behind a rather prolific collection of, let's call them 'Men's Interest' magazines. I'd rather you let me dispose of them discreetly."

Csaba chortled gleefully. "Elliott, you saucy son-of-a-bitch!" He placed two fingers in his mouth and whistled. The cleaning militia froze immediately. "Attention everyone! This is the lovely Lenore. You are to treat her every command as though it were my own. She has requested that the shed be declared off-limits. We all clear on that?" There was a chorus of murmured assent. "Marvellous, as you were." The cacophony of cleaning resumed. Csaba turned back to her and winked. "We'll stay out of the shed and clean everything else until it looks—as my mother would say—good enough for the Queen on her birthday. Now then, you and I have a great deal to discuss!"

"Indeed we do. Can I make you a cup of coffee?"

"Oh, I stay well away from caffeine. Although I'd take some jasmine tea if you have it." Lenore gestured towards the door and said, "Welcome to my humble and soon-to-be-not=rat-infested abode."

17

WE WANT TO DEFEAT DEATH. TO LIVE FOREVER. HERE, HAVE A BROCHURE!

Lenore studied Csaba as he sipped his tea and smacked his lips in satisfaction. In her years as a moirologist, she'd developed a finely tuned set of emotional heuristics. She could spot a reformed alcoholic at fifty paces, identify a closet BDSM practitioner within a couple of sentences, pick a moon landing truther out of a crowded room. Csaba, however, represented a significant challenge to her operating system.

His car was almost aggressively humble, but his watch was a work of art. His suit was a basic grey, no fancy cufflinks or ornamentation, but his nails were finely manicured. He laughed with the jolly manner of a shopping centre Santa Claus, tempered with the vocabulary and cadence of an English professor. He caught Lenore's gaze and said, "I'm sorry, is the watch distracting you? I realise it's ridiculously rococo, but it was a gift from Elliott."

"You must've been very close."

He nodded, the sound of hammering filled the air between them. They looked at each other for a few seconds until the worst of it was over. "Once upon a time, we were, yes. In recent years…" He stared into his teacup,

94

stirred it gently with his spoon. "When I was a child, back in Hungary, my mother would make a pot of jasmine tea every day. My brothers and I would sit and listen to the radio, and once the pot was finished we'd clean and cook until my father came home and beat us all within an inch of our lives. Strange how something so simple as a pot of tea can come to represent the very idea of tranquillity." He sipped, placed the cup back down, turned his phone off. "Please don't think I'm being arrogant when I tell you that I usually don't turn this thing off for anything besides funerals and coronations."

"You go to a lot of coronations?"

"Yes," he said brightly, as though she'd asked him if he enjoyed cheese. "Now you have my complete attention."

Lenore recalled the old cliché about unexpected gifts and equine dentistry, but thus far the gentleman in front of her represented her only viable lead. "Tell me about Elliott. How did you first meet?"

Csaba nodded and said, "I met Elliott in the summer of 1984. We ran a four-man crew. There was me, Elliott, Jimmy the Shoe, Mickey three-fingers…" He grinned at her. "I'm kidding. Just a little humour to break the tension."

Lenore smiled obligingly.

"Sorry. I don't deal well with death. My therapist says I have a pathological incapacity to deal with my own mortality coupled with overdriven paranoia and a curious predilection to divulge personal information. But the PI I hired to check her out told me she lives alone with three cats. So what would she know?"

Lenore maintained a resolutely unimpressed expression.

Csaba slapped his hand and said, "Mea culpa, bad Csaba. Elliott and I met when I first came to this country, as a young teenager. My mother managed to smuggle our family out of Hungary in the thick of night, we fled to the airport with the last of our money and came here to stay with my auntie.

"Mum knew no one in the whole country. She spent every minute either working or looking after us. Her one reprieve was our weekly visit to the local church. I *hated* church. The joyless hymns, the cold rituals, the snotty blonde kids who made fun of my English. But as a business model?

The church was fa-scin-at-ing. Low overheads, tax exemption, a zealously dedicated customer base, it was a veritable monument to capitalism! Every week I'd watch in wonder as fistfuls of cash dropped into the collection plate."

An electric sander swallowed everything in its roar. Csaba rolled his eyes, stood up, and walked down the hall. The sound ceased. He re-entered the room and said, "Apologies, I've told them to lay off the power tools until we've finished our chat. Where were we?"

"You were talking about your time in church?"

"Ah, yes. People forget that there's a scene in the bible where Jesus overthrows the tables of the money lenders outside of the church and *beats them with whips*. I think he'd be quite surprised by the megalithic commercial enterprise his little spiritual start-up has become. Elliott hated church as much as I did. We became friends when we found out we shared a fondness for hiding in the parking lot to smoke and figure out arcane methods of coercing the vending machine into dispensing free snacks. We became quickly inseparable. When we finished school, his uncle got us both jobs in his bank.

"We worked our way up the ranks and eventually procured a loan for our first business venture: air conditioning. It had just started to proliferate to homes and businesses, so there was installation, maintenance, repair, and a boom industry. It was a veritable *cold*-mine. The business practically ran itself. After growing up in a poor, hard-working family, I felt unfathomably guilty for making so much money from such little effort. I put on weight, and my doctor recommended I take up regular physical activity. I thought Latin dancing might be fun. I was the first to arrive, and the moment I saw Rena..." He threw his fingers wide open, miming an explosion. "*Instant* connection, sparks flying like we were a pair of Tesla coils. I was the first one there, she looked me up and down and said, 'You danced much before?' I shook my head. She leaned in close and said, 'Well, I'm going to teach you. And you better listen good, because the way a man dances tells you the way he makes love.' She moved in a couple of months later."

He poured another cup of tea. Lenore glanced at the wedding ring on his hand. "Elliot met his beloved Claire a few months after Rena moved in with me. She was working as a waitress in a cocktail bar, like in that song, you know? They used to think that was so funny, they played that thing all the time. It was disgusting and adorable, the way love usually is. You ever been in love?"

Lenore glanced at the half-finished raven on her wrist. "We're not here to talk about me."

"I'll take that as a 'yes'. In any case, we all got married on the same weekend. Rena and I Friday, Elliott, and Claire Saturday. For the next few years, everything was magical. We ate, we drank, and were merry. Life was as close to perfect as it could be." He paused, massaged his temple with his fingers. "You can probably guess this story is about to take a dark turn." He picked up the cactus he'd given her, examined it as he spoke. "We all made the decision to forgo having children. Life was perfect, why change anything? It was a bold decision to make, quite frowned upon back in those days."

"Still is. I told someone the other day I wasn't planning to have kids, and she looked at me as though I'd invited her to take part in a ritual sacrifice."

"Ritual sacrifice. That's funny. So there we were: wealthy, accomplished, in love. No one gets to be that happy. It defies the very nature of the universe."

"What happened?"

Csaba said nothing for a while. He poured himself another cup of tea, offered the pot to Lenore. She shook her head. "Rena ate well, exercised regularly, drank in moderation, meditated, never smoked. She should've lived to a hundred." Lenore looked away. She'd heard this story innumerable times. "She had hypertrophic cardiomyopathy, a heart problem. It can remain cruelly undetected right up to the moment it kills, as was the case with Rena. She dropped dead in the middle of a class, right in the centre of the dance floor, like the lyrics of some awful end-of-disco-era song." He stared out the window. "Do you mind if I ask how old you are, Lenore?"

"Thirty-three."

"Your messianic year."

"Sure, if you want to get philosophical."

"I usually do. You look so much younger; what's your secret?"

"Strict diet of unicorn blood and phoenix eggs."

Csaba smiled, "Rena would've loved you. She was twenty-nine when she died, even younger than you are now. It broke us. All three of us: Claire, Elliott, and I. We were utterly devastated. I tried everything. Therapy, drinking, drugs. Elliott became obsessed with the fear of losing Claire. He kept saying to me, 'I couldn't handle it. I couldn't go on.' Have you ever lost anyone close to you?"

"Death practically has a customer rewards card with my name on it."

"I'm genuinely sorry to hear that. I can see you, and I have a lot in common. It weighs heavily on you too, doesn't it, the fear of death?"

"I don't feel comfortable—"

He waved his hand and said, "I apologise. Elliott's passing has left me quite shaken. Let's continue. After Rena's death, I vowed to bring the full force of our formidable resources to bear to ensure that we could solve the last great problem: immortality."

Lenore turned the word over in her head a few times to check she'd heard it correctly. "I'm sorry, did you say 'immortality'?"

"Transhumanism, immortality, eternal life, post-mortality transformational systems. There are many names for the one thing that humans of every culture and creed have been striving for ever since the evolution of consciousness made us aware of our own impermanence. The story of the human species is little more than a ceaseless battle against death in which we have lost every single round, until now. We want to defeat death. To live forever. Here, have a brochure!"

He reached into his pocket, whipped one out, and handed it to Lenore, then leaned back into his seat with a grin. "We already have hundreds of very happy customers!"

Lenore examined the uncomfortably upbeat copy,

Here at Amrita Industries, we're travelling into the bold new frontier of permanent existence. Joy, prosperity, and a functioning life vessel forever, that's OUR promise to YOU! Utilising a complex blend of cutting-edge cryonic and medical therapies, we are turning the impossible into the achievable, TODAY!

"Cryogenics, is this for real?"

Csaba made a pained expression and corrected: "*Cryonics*. Cryogenics is the study of the production and behaviour of materials at extreme low temperatures, cryonics is the art of preserving human life. We offer a unique blend of cryonic solutions alongside cutting-edge in-house medical research to ensure that we can not only preserve our clients, but restore and augment them once it's time for them to be awakened. The future is bright. It is radiant. It is *resplendent*."

She placed the brochure back on the table, resisting the urge to run to the bathroom to wash her hands.

Csaba grinned at her like a father who'd just presented a picture of his eldest child in a graduation gown. "I realise it's a lot to take in. I often forget that public acceptance of cryonic technologies is so backward. But you know, there was a time, not so long ago, when people treated the automobile as a hostile, dangerous intrusion into their lives. Now, they are fundamental to our daily existence."

"I'm not sure there's a direct parallel between my rusty Toyota and snap-freezing human beings."

He winced at her phrasing. "I'd thank you to not use such disparaging language."

Lenore glanced at the brochure again. "Why isn't Elliott—"

"One of our VIP customers?" Csaba sighed, leaned forward, and looked directly at her. "We had a falling out. A disagreement that could not be mediated. He disavowed himself from the organisation we'd built together. You'll forgive me for not going into details."

"How long ago?"

Csaba rubbed his forehead, "Do you know, I think I've been saying 'ten years ago' for the last five years? So I suppose it must've been fifteen. God, the things we said to each other. It's always the ones you love that hurt you the most." He poured the last of the tea, watched the drops spill into the cup, and held the empty teapot in the air. After a few seconds, he placed it back down and stared into the cup. "I loved that man, I loved him as much as it is possible for one human being to love another. It wasn't a sexual thing. I loved his *soul*. The very essence of him. In a just world, the four of us would have embraced the bright new future with open arms for all of eternity. But it's not a just world, is it?"

"I'm not sure that 'we didn't get to live forever' is the same thing as injustice."

He snorted and raised an eyebrow. Downstairs, someone switched on a steam cleaner. Csaba raised his voice over the rumbling and said, "I have to sternly disagree with you there. I think it is the most heinous injustice there is. One which I aim to correct." He looked at her. "I can see I'm giving you a lot to take in. I'll try and stick to the point. After our falling out, barely a word passed between us for years. I wrote, called, sent gifts, everything. There was never any response.

"I didn't know where they'd gone. They were wealthy and well-connected, it wasn't hard for them to disappear. Then finally, one day—must've been three years ago—he sent me a message stating that Claire was dangerously ill. He said that he still didn't want to have anything to do with me, but that, as a mark of respect for our former friendship he thought I had a right to know. Naturally, I tried to find them, to offer what help I could, to pay for treatment, organise doctors, cleaning services, food deliveries, therapists, but I received no reply."

Csaba removed an embroidered silk handkerchief from his pocket, dabbed at his eyes, and said, "It was only through Claire's illness that I was able to find them again. Turns out they'd never even left town. Amazing how easy it is to stay hidden when you have infinite funds for delivery services and rarely leave the house. But when Claire became ill, they started ordering specialty items that were relatively easy to trace."

"Chemotherapy treatments?"

Csaba recoiled in disgust. "Nothing so vulgar. The nuclear option, in every sense of the term. No, they ordered the components for the cryonic dewar that Claire's sleeping in outside."

Lenore froze and glanced at the door, adrenaline surging through her veins. He reached out a hand and placed it gently on hers; she snatched it away.

"Please, I wanted to be able to fully explain myself before I told you I knew. You poor thing, it must've been terrifying to think you'd found a cadaver in your own backyard! I can assure you she's not dead, merely hibernating."

"I'm afraid you and all of science may slightly disagree on that matter."

He flashed her a condescending smile. "I'll forgive your impudence in light of your distress. But I beg you, let me help. Elliott wanted her resting here out of mere spite. Our facility is the best equipped in the entire world for her needs. Without a trained technician to constantly monitor her, she'll die—permanently."

"Strange to hear temporal modality applied to the word 'die.'"

"I'm trying to do the right thing here. If we don't move her to our facility, I'll have to dispatch a team of technicians to live in the residence on a rotating basis, which I imagine you'd rather avoid. Please, let me help her. Despite the distance between us over these years, Claire is still one of the most important people in the world to me. Our address is right there on the brochure. We'll have her relocated and set up in a couple of hours. You can come right over and visit her if you like. And if you change your mind, we can always bring her back."

Lenore stared at him as she listened to scraping and raking and painting and stomping and nailing. She examined the lounge room and was unable to disguise her awe. She'd been so entranced by their conversation that she'd barely even looked up at what the team of cleaners and laborers had been doing. The place looked borderline inhabitable. "Many hands, light work, huh?" she whispered.

Csaba swept his hands around the partially transformed living room as he stood up and clapped theatrically. "Great work, team, the lady is pleased. I think a few industrious workers might be getting a little something extra come bonus time." They thanked Csaba and Lenore, then resumed working at amphetimesque speed. He sat back down and said, "We're doing what we can here; let us use our hands to ease your burden with Claire as well. You've only been caught up in this by sheer circumstance. I loved Elliott, but *man,* could he hold a grudge! Even if it meant harming himself and Claire in the process. It's clear from the state of this house that he'd been living the last few years in a state of crippling isolation and depression. The fact that he insisted on his service being in the Catholic tradition—the faith in which he was raised but utterly abhorred—speaks volumes about the extent of his mental deterioration. I assure you that if he'd been of sound mind, then he would have insisted on our caring for Claire. I'm happy for you to have executive control over all decisions if you so choose. But remember, she's a stranger to you. To me, she is an old, dear friend."

She is the body *of an old dear friend*, thought Lenore.

"You can drop in anytime. I'll give you a personal tour. That's a treat I usually reserve for heads of state."

"You have many of those touring your facility?"

Csaba grinned, "If you drew a Venn diagram of the attendees of the last G8 summit and our future clients, it'd be a circle."

"Fine. You can take the body."

He cleared his throat and regarded her with those luminous blue eyes. "I would *sincerely* request that we do not refer to her 'body'. Her name is Claire."

"Understood."

He clapped his hands together. "Excellent! Shall we shake on it?" He extended his hand and shook with a firm, gentlemanly grip, then leaned over the railing of the verandah and called out, "Sandra, she's given the go-ahead. Could you grab the rest of the relocation team and ready the transportation dewar? That older model she's in looks like it might be beyond saving. Thanking you!" He beamed at Lenore and said, "Would you be so kind as to give me a moment? I have a few things to organise."

"Sure."

Lenore walked to the bathroom, now resplendently white and clean, thick with the smell of bleach. She listened to the sounds of dozens of workers scurrying like worker ants around the home that she now owned. Her phone buzzed. Darius had replied to her message.

I'll call you after work.

Been a very strange day.

We need to talk. URGENTLY.

Lenore stared at the white walls. As she allowed herself a moment free from stimulus, the typhoon in her mind quelled to a gentle breeze, and she realised she'd forgotten to ask Csaba the most important question of all. She washed her hands and opened the door. Csaba grinned at her as he yammered rapidly into his phone, placed it to his shoulder, and mouthed 'Sorry. Give me five minutes.' Lenore sat down and watched as a team of workers looking like underdressed pallbearers carried Claire in her refrigerated coffin.

She stared at her still, cold face, wondering if those eyes ever really would open again. If an organism as simple and insignificant as a tardigrade could revive from complete stasis, why not a person? Csaba paced back and forth, waving his hands around like a conductor as he spoke. He turned to her, rolled his eyes, and made a 'talk-talk-talk' gesture with his free hand. She smiled and watched the birds outside.

Csaba hung up and sat down. "Sorry, that was the Prince of Monaco. He wants us to set up one of our facilities over there, but it's never straightforward with him. I always have to go through a whole litany of 'hello' and 'how are you?' before getting to the meat of things."

"Princes can be tiresome that way."

Csaba grinned at her. "Not afraid to speak your mind, are you?" She shrugged. He cocked his head and asked, "Do you mind if I ask you how you came to be in your particularly unusual line of work?"

"My father always said that 'death is the only industry that is truly future proof.' I suppose the two of you would disagree on that."

"Indeed we would. But the ability to disagree amicably is the mark of an evolved society." Csaba spoke as though he had swallowed a book of platitudes. His phone emitted a tiny bleep. He checked it and said. "I must apologise. I have a flight this afternoon. I've only a little more time to spare. If you have any burning questions, it would be a good idea to get them out of the way now?"

Lenore nodded. "Yes. Good plan. And thank you for being so helpful so far."

He waved her apology away and said, "Think nothing of it." His fingers tapped and swiped at the screen. Any one of these subtle gestures could cause hirings and firings, promotions and humiliations, merges and purges.

"One question before you go: what can you tell me about Riley?"

Csaba's fingers froze. A recalcitrant smile crawled across his face. "Ri-ley?" He forced each syllable from his lips as though passing linguistic kidney stones. "Was she a maid or something?"

"No, she was their daughter."

The phone dropped from his hand. It bounced three times on the floor before landing face up, a network of fissures freshly opened on its surface. He snatched it up and yelled, "Everybody, out. Now! This fucking instant!" The workers dropped their brooms and paint brushes and hammers and scampered out the door. Csaba and Lenore stared at each other. The house felt eerily quiet in the sudden absence of furious cleaning and repair. Csaba cleared his throat, composed himself, and sat back down. "I need to be absolutely clear about this. It is imperative that you tell me everything you know about Riley. *Everything.*"

18

ETERNAL LIFE OR YOUR MONEY BACK!

Nero edged up to the glass of his tank and watched as Kyle yawned and stretched his arms above his head. He displayed the kind of muscle tone that made Darius feel as though he should be classified as his own species; *Homo perfecta*, or perhaps *Homo makemefeelinferia*. Kyle sighed with gratification, tossed the script on the table, and opened a beer. "I think I'm done with the script for today."

"Of course. I should get going." He held out his hand and said, "Kyle, I want to sincerely thank you for this opportunity."

Kyle slapped his hand away and laughed. "Dude, it's not a job interview. Although, I've never had a job interview so I'm not really sure what they're like. You can hang out if you want. Wanna watch a movie or order takeout or something?"

"Hang…out?"

"Yeah. You know. Two people, in the same room, sharing an activity?"

"But…with me?"

Kyle laughed, "Yeah, that'd be the general idea."

"Don't you have friends with their own clothing lines and perfumes to hang out with?"

Kyle rolled his eyes and said, "Sure. But I'm sick of hanging out with richos."

"Richos?"

"Yeah, richos, rich people. You know, the other day, I was talking to Adam Palmer—"

"Adam Palmer? *The* Adam Palmer? Adam Palmer of Adam Palmer & the Palm Readers Adam Palmer?"

"Quit saying Adam Palmer. Yeah, so, we're talking, and I realised a few minutes in, this guy does not ask questions. *At all.* He went for thirty minutes without asking a *single* question of anyone. Not 'how's the family?', 'how's the shoot going?', 'where did you get that outfit?', just statements, opinions, anecdotes. And then, after half an hour of talking about nothing but himself, he hits me up for a favour, wants me to help get one of his boring songs in this astronaut movie I'm doing with Common, Ice-T, and 50 Cent. I'm going to be the only lead with an actual name for a name. Point being,; I'm sick of celebrities. I'm quite happy to hang out with a normo for once."

"A 'normo'?"

"I didn't mean it as an insult."

"It's fine. I think I can live with 'normo.' I've been called worse things in my life."

Kyle slapped his back, sending seismic waves through his barely 50kg frame and possibly dislodging a few internal organs. "Cool! Hey, what did Chantelle talk to you about?"

"We mostly talked about the film. A bit. Sort of." Darius stared at Kyle's hypnotically gorgeous face. It was offensively lacking in flaws, as though it had been designed by a classical Greek sculptor after a heroic dose of MDMA. "Actually, do you mind if I ask you, what exactly is this film about? I know it's supposed to be a big secret, but I've spent two years of my life starving myself for this thing, and I don't even know what it is?"

Kyle bit his lip and waggled his head back and forth, considering the question. "Sorry, man, I don't think I can tell you. Non-disclosure agreement and all that. My lawyers would *kill* me. 'Do what your lawyer tells you'; Patrick Wilton taught me that."

"Isn't he in prison?"

"Yeah, because he didn't listen to his lawyer." Kyle glanced at the script scattered on the table, then up at Darius, then back at the script. "Buuuuuuut, what say I *accidentally* leave my computer open with some rushes, and you *accidentally* press play and *accidentally* watch them, then it wouldn't technically be my fault, right?"

"You don't have to…" Kyle shook his head and said,

"It'll be our little secret." Kyle clicked at the mousepad, then grabbed his phone and said,

"You got any food stuff? Gluten-free dairy free GMO-free vegan kosher macrobiotic fruitarian raw food Atkins paleo—"

"I'm supposed to be on this ultra-low calorie diet because of this stupid job, but after today, who the hell cares? Anything but human flesh is fine by me."

Kyle shook his head in disbelief. "Normos are *the best*." He spun the computer around and said in *sotto voce*: "Well, friend! I am going *outside* now to order some food, and then perhaps I shall take a nice relaxing stroll for five to ten minutes. See you shortly." Then didn't so much wink as smash two eyelids together before exiting.

Darius's finger hovered over the space bar for one, two, three seconds. He hit play.

The camera gazes directly down at the earth below, slowly descending. There is a gathering of people, tiny dots moving on a green field surrounded by grey rectangles. It could almost be an eighties 8-bit video game. Blackness fills the screen, disappears, fills it again. A raven sweeps into view, caws ominously, follows the camera's journey as it slowly descends.

We see that the gathering is in fact a funeral. A floral wreath lays upon an oaken coffin encircled by mourners. We are now close enough to hear their tears, lamentations, and the droning eulogy of the priest,

"We commend her into your care, O lord, and ask that you would number her amongst your most favoured, for she has lived a pure and virtuous existence in this world, and we pray that she shall do so in the next..."

As his ashen voice continues, the camera appears to be about to crash right into the coffin, but at the last moment, swoops upwards to gaze at a nearby mourner, her achingly beautiful face marred with tears and mascara that has been expertly applied to appear as though it has been inexpertly applied. Her nostrils flare, her jaw clenches. We hear her thoughts as voice-over, a vicious whisper drowning out the eulogy.

"There is no other world to take her. Death is not a doorway. It is a hallway, ending in a wall that precedes nothing, and I shall defy its will." Her ruby-red lips part and she whispers, *"Death shall have no dominion."*

The image disappears, replaced by a jarringly bright white background set with black text.

Nero watched Darius slam his face into an eight-hundred-dollar ostrich feather cushion and scream. He blinked his three pairs of eyelids and lapped at his water bowl. Today was his 200th birthday, but thus far, no one had noticed. Over the course of his life, he had seen the invention of the combustion engine, penicillin, the proliferation of democracy, the First and Second World Wars, the invention of the silicon transistor, television, space travel, the internet, and the mobile phone. But this was the first time in his long life that he had ever seen a grown man scream into a cushion.

Nero cocked his head and stared at a fly buzzing against the trailer window. It slapped repeatedly at the glass, fighting to come in through the confusingly transparent yet impenetrable barrier. He licked his lips, overcome with hunger and desire. The fly gave up and disappeared into the blue sky outside.

Nero slumped into the headlamp-warmed sand and stared at the distraught man surrounded by a vastly ample supply of food and shelter, blubbering and moaning as though he would never eat again.

Humans were such odd, ephemeral creatures.

II

FIFTH BARDO

19

AIN'T NO MOUNTAIN HIGH
ENOUGH

Csaba regarded her with the expression of an executioner at a job interview. Lenore attempted to deploy her best poker face, but she'd never been good at poker. She tended to go 'all in', lose her money, and then complain that it was a stupid game for jerks who had neither the patience for chess nor the hand-eye coordination for video games. Neither of them spoke for a very long time. The bathroom tap was dripping into a bucket that had been hastily abandoned by one of the cleaning militia, its drips slightly out of sync with the ticking of the fob watch in her handbag beside her. She began counting the arrhythmic ticks and drips as a way to occupy her mind through the interminable silence between them. 1 (1) - 2 (2) - 3 (3) - 4 (4) - 5 (5) - 6 (6) - 7 (7) - 8(8) - 9 (9)…

"You know, a few years ago," she exhaled with relief as Csaba spoke at last. "I was negotiating the purchase of a property in St. Kitts and Nevis. It's a curiously named little Caribbean nation with beautiful seafront properties you can pick up for a song—a cheap song, not a real earner like *In The Air Tonight* (which I part-own, coincidentally). At the time, there was the charming bonus of included citizenship. A neat little perk, picking up a third passport. All kinds of advantages, as I'm sure you can imagine. Circling back to the point, I was negotiating with the seller. He was a man of few words. He'd stare at me with these long, intense gazes. We passed a couple of numbers back and forth. Eventually, we came to an agreement." Csaba beamed at her and sat back in the chair.

"I assume there's a point to that story somewhere?"

"Not really. Just a fun tale. And perhaps a cheeky reminder that I have the necessary resources to buy island properties and citizenships, as well as handsomely reward people who give me the things I want."

Lenore gave him her best poker face, a furious, teeth-grinding glare. She cracked her knuckles, and Csaba recoiled in distaste. "Csaba. I sincerely appreciate what you've done for me. But I have to respectfully ask you to leave." She stood up and gestured towards the door. The drips and ticks continued. *Drip(tick). Drip(tick). Drip(tick).* Csaba maintained his infuriating grin. Lenore ground her teeth and said, "Now."

"May I tell you another story?"

"*No.*"

He ignored her and continued. "When we were purchasing the property for the Amrita facility, there was a delightful couple who owned a farm that was inconveniently located right in the centre of the proposed development. We offered them a very generous package, but the land had been in the family for generations. It was their great-grandfather's legacy, etc., etc."

"*I asked you to—*"

"They were healthy, smart, and principled. You would've liked them. Eventually, we decided to let it go and find another site." He shrugged, ignored Lenore's furious glare, and blithely continued. "A couple of weeks later, something very curious happened. They started exhibiting a whole host of health problems, everything from weeping sores to fevers to memory loss. They were rushed to hospital, where they died a few days later. Apparently, the water tank on their property had been contaminated by emissions from a chemical plant a few miles away. Should've been scientifically impossible, but—"

"Just for future reference, Mr Adami, I preferred my threats to be of the 'unveiled' variety," she said through clenched teeth.

"Oh goodness *no*. My apologies, Lenore, you've misunderstood me. I feel just *awful!*" He flapped his hands in the air and insisted. "This is *exactly* why I have so many people on my PR team. I let any old thing fly out of my mouth. We're simply chatting, swapping stories! Like stories about Riley, for instance."

"If you and Elliott were so close, how exactly did you manage to miss a tiny little detail like *his teenage daughter?*"

"As I mentioned, we didn't talk for a long time. *Ri*-ley…" He was still having trouble saying her name. He sounded like an unapologetic racist being forced by company policy to use a mandated PC term. She could sense his eyes probing her, compiling data and details from her body language. It felt even more invasive than the lecherous looks from men who flicked their eyes up and down her body when she was on stage.

"If you aren't out of my house in the next ten seconds, I'm calling the police."

He shrugged. "If you feel the need. I believe the local precinct is run by Sargent Henderson. Owes me *quite* a few favours, much like the vast majority of his colleagues. I always try to help out the local constabulary as much as I can. Never know when you might need your back scratched in return!"

Lenore considered running, but didn't want to surrender the upper hand so easily. She looked directly at Csaba, irritatingly poised and relaxed. She closed the distance between them, grabbed his hand, and inspected his immaculately clean nails. He didn't resist, but merely watched her with mild amusement.

"I get it. I get the whole veiled threat as a means of getting what you want approach. But these hands? These are not the hands of a violent man. You've never had so much as dirt on them, let alone blood." She flung his hand away, and the grin slipped at long last from his face. She held up her own hands, turned them over for his inspection. "*These* dainty digits, however, have both bled and drawn blood. I'm sure you've got myriad ways of harming people via proxy, but I killed my own mother on my way into this world. I've been spilling blood since before my first breath."

His expression remained resolutely unfazed, but she noticed a solitary bead of sweat trickling down his skull. He stood up and shrugged. "I'm very sorry this little misunderstanding has gotten so out of hand, Lenore. Thank you for the tea. If you'd like the crew to come back and finish up, you have my number. Otherwise, you can consider our business concluded. Normally, I'd be quite offended by how you've spoken to me today, but you've been through a lot recently, so I can understand you putting your guard up. Rena really would have been fond of you. In another life, maybe you would've even been friends."

He turned and began walking towards the door. Lenore watched him, unmoving. He opened the door, paused, then turned to face her. "By the by, I'll pass your compliments on to my manicurist. But I'm afraid you're quite mistaken." He held up his hands and wiggled his fingers. "These feisty fingers are no strangers to bloodshed. Cheerio!" He waved goodbye and closed the door gently behind him.

Lenore buried her head in her hands, drawing deep, desperate gasps of relief as she listened to him drive off into the distance, trailing the exultant sounds of "Ain't No Mountain High Enough" behind him.

20

WHY DON'T YOU START BY TELLING ME HOW YOU DIED?

The scream catapulted Lenore into consciousness, her body convulsing so wildly, she smacked her head on the ancient mahogany bedhead. There was silence for a moment, then another scream. Now that she was awake, she could triangulate its position. It was coming from the floor. Not beneath the floor, not from downstairs, from the floor itself. A third scream pierced the early morning quiet.

"Audrey, I am going to kill you," she mumbled, picking up her phone and silencing the call. Changing Lenore's ringtone was Audrey's favourite prank, along with sending her a message saying 'Look out!' immediately before throwing a bread roll at her face when they had dinner together. The call was from Darius. She sent him a message promising to ring him once she'd properly woken up.

She'd fallen asleep in her clothes, shoes and all. She'd already dirtied the brand-new sheets Csaba's cleaning militia had provided. She stripped the bed, feeling as filthy as the sheets in her hand for accepting so many gifts from a man who was clearly some sort of criminal, if not a murderer. But then again, returning them wouldn't change anything. And she had slept the sleep of the, well, not dead, but perhaps the cryonically-preserved. She opened the duffel bag she'd borrowed from Darius. At least owning a sum

117

total of three shirts made choosing an outfit easy. She selected from the meagre offerings and stumbled into the shower. The sound of her yawn echoed across the mostly gleaming white tiles. There was a clear point of delineation where the cleaners had been kicked out; one half of the wall was significantly darkened by mould, the other ethereally bright.

Lenore made a mental note to finish cleaning the tiles, which was followed by an immediate afterthought of *'I'll never actually get around to doing that.'* She turned the tap, and the pipes shuddered ominously. She was about to wrench the valves closed again when a stream of hot water blasted from the showerhead. They ceased rumbling, apparently suffering from a little out-of-practice jitters. She sighed with relief, stripped off, and stepped into the shower.

The cleaners had fortuitously furnished her with an array of luxurious soaps and shampoos, enhanced with various elements that promised to do everything from the pleasant (*jojoba extract leaves your hair smelling FRESH!*) to the scientifically impossible (*our active ingredients harness the power of DNA to reverse the aging of proteins in your hair!*) The water pressure was blissfully strong, a welcome change from the lukewarm dribble of her old shower.

She let the hot water run over her, exhaling with relief. After threats, discovered bodies, and a variety of strangers spilling into her life in the last couple of days, the small moment of calm was a welcome reprieve. She dressed in her polyester tiger-striped t-shirt and lime-green shorts and examined herself in the mirror. She'd elected to grab the cheapest clothes available at the time—given the impending financial disaster of having to replace every last one of her possessions—but she was already regretting not shelling out an extra few bucks for clothes that would have made her look less like a glam rock groupie.

She walked back to the bedroom and texted Audrey with a request for clothes. She placed her phone down and stared at the painting of the Brindles on the back of the door before plucking it off the hook and placing it in the cupboard. She walked to the kitchen. Like the rest of the house, it was part-resplendent, part-repellent, half-immaculate, half-Dracula. She boiled the kettle, made a cup of green tea, and sat out on the balcony. There was a flock of lorikeets in the trees above, noisily devouring flowers and flitting from one branch to the next. The sun spilled through the leaves in the canopy, colouring the deck with gently shifting patches of light and shadow. She sipped quietly and stared at the shed, its open door swinging gently on its hinges. From this angle, she could barely glimpse Claire's empty dewar. She stood up and examined the pantry. Csaba's cleaning militia had gifted her a selection of tea, coffee, shortbread, and condiments but nothing in the manner of substantial sustenance. Her stomach rumbled.

Her phone buzzed with a message from Audrey:

Got a meeting with a new client this morning.

Will swing by later this afternoon.

She closed the message and checked her bank account. Between what she had in there and the handful of notes in her purse, she had enough money for an overpriced massage or an underpriced lap dance. She wondered if she could talk Audrey into bringing some groceries along with the temporary additions to her wardrobe. Lenore finished the tea, threw her cup into the sink—startling a cockroach that had already been thoroughly bamboozled by all the recent furious activity—and called Darius.

"Where the hell have you been? I've been calling you since yesterday."

"It's the opposite of a short story. Are you okay?"

"Mostly. There's the small problem of having recently discovered that the past two years of my life are basically meaningless, and this project I'm working on might actually be quite sinister, but other than that..."

"To be fair, the last twenty years of your life have been meaningless, and most of show business is sinister."

"Hilarious. How's the new house? Have you checked the taps for water pressure and/or blood?"

"Compared to what's actually happened since I got here, bleeding taps would be something of a relief."

"Seriously?"

"Seriously."

"I'm on set this morning, but I'll come over when I'm done."

"Great. Can't wait to hear all about your sinister conspiracy."

"Right back at you." She hung up and listened to the sounds of the birds outside. In the garden, a bush turkey—its red raw skull looking like the avian incarnation of death—dug away at the garden. Its mound was almost as large as the shed it sat next to. She watched it work for a while, comforted by the suburban quiet. There was a knock at the door. She let the sound hang in the air for a few moments before moving.

She walked slowly down the hall and stood in front of the unopened door. The knock came again, flooding the air with the heavy weight of possibility. Until she opened it, it represented a range of Schrödingerian potentialities. Opening the door would collapse the waveform of potential outcomes: threat-bearing debt collector, clothes-bearing Audrey, weapon-wielding Csaba, bible-clutching Jehovah's witness. She placed her hand on the doorknob and twisted it open.

Orin greeted her with a nervous grin. "Morning. I didn't know if you had any food allergies and whatnot, so I got a little bit of everything."

She pulled the door wide open. "Orin, you and I are going to be friends."

He stood staring for a moment. "Sorry, do I need to formally invite you in?"

"No, that's vampires. Which…aren't real. Obviously."

"Obviously. My mistake." She glanced at the bags brimming with pastries, fruit, and vegetables. "Not to pry, but how did you get your hands on all this?"

"Dumpster diving's rather effortless these days, what with the invisibility and all. I know you might think eating 'reclaimed' food somewhat distasteful. But, honestly, the French bakery on Kensington St. throws out so much fresh produce it's utterly criminal, and the bagel place across the road is much the same."

He opened the bag, and she pounced on an almond croissant, devouring it in three ravenous bites on her way into the kitchen. He followed her, eyes wide with stunned admiration.

"What? I wasf hun-ry," she said, mouth filled with pseudo-Parisian pastry.

"I've just never seen anyone eat a croissant that quickly."

She finished chewing and gulped it down. "Care for a cup of tea? I know how you like to watch the steam rise."

"That would be lovely."

She flicked on the kettle as he sat down. Its slow, crescendoing screech filled the air between them. When it was done, she prepared two cups, set them down on the table, and sat opposite him.

"So, where do you suppose we should begin?" asked Orin.

She leaned forward and said, "Why don't you start by telling me how you died?"

21

OCKY'S RAZOR

"Think of the last time you screamed. Was it from horror or ecstasy?"

"That's easy. Horror," Lenore answered, mumbling through the half-chewed bagel in her mouth.

"May I ask what happened?"

"The old lady in the apartment above me died in her bath while the water was still running. I woke up to find it raining inside my house. I ran out of my room moments before the roof caved in, and my apartment was filled with cadaver-laced bathwater."

Orin balked, recomposed himself, and said, "You have an interesting life, Lenore."

She laughed, tossed the bagel wrapper into the bin, and said, "It's interesting in much the same manner that a genocide museum is interesting."

Orin turned his mug around on the table, watching the steam rise. He laughed when he saw the writing on the other side: *Where there's life, there's hope.* The text sat above a small, soft-lensed photo of a sunrise. Lenore peered around to see what he was looking at. He tapped at the text and asked, "What does that mean for me then, do you think?"

"'Where there's life, there's hope. But when there's death? Nope.'"

"You have an awfully macabre sense of humour." He stared at the picture of the sunrise. "I can't say if there was a single time I screamed in the last few years of my life. I had it pretty good: roof over my head, slightly above average income, someone who I thought was the love of my life. I was the textbook definition of happiness."

"Very few people would associate textbooks with happiness."

"I suppose that's true." He waved his hands irritably. "I'm sorry. I'm making no sense. I've barely spoken to anyone in weeks. I'm out of practice. Spiders and rats aren't great conversationalists."

"Why don't we start with what you did for a living, when you were still living."

"I was a booking agent."

"For musicians?"

"No."

"Actors?"

"…not exactly."

"You might be very much deceased, Orin, but my life is ticking away while I'm patiently awaiting an explanation."

"I was a booking agent for motivational speakers."

Lenore threw her head back with laughter, slamming her hand on the table so hard that Orin's tea leapt up out of his mug, then dropped back with an audible 'plop.' She aimed a finger at his nose and said, "It looks as though I've finally met someone who has a more ridiculous job than I do."

"Why, what do—"

"Moirologist, professional mourner."

Orin laced his fingers together. "I was right. You *are* a scion of death."

"We'll get to my story. Let's finish yours first."

"Right." He cleared his throat. She tried not to laugh at the ridiculous affectation. "I would often have to go with the speakers to their engagements: conferences, universities, high schools, etc. I'd drive, check the tech was set up properly, do some admin remotely while I waited for them to take the stage. And then I'd listen. I heard hundreds of motivational speeches last year. Calls to Live My Best Life. Be True To My Authentic Self. Be The Change I Want To See In The World. Carpe Diem. YOLO. Leverage Catastrophic Collapses For Radical Investment Portfolio Adjustments."

"What was that last one?"

"You know, I got so used to it that I became rather desensitised to the sheer horror of that collection of words. I couldn't tell you how many times I've seen a group of well-dressed diners sit underneath a chandelier and zealously take notes on how to profit from catastrophe: private security, acquiring real estate at drastic discounts, chartering surge-priced private emergency transport. It's called disaster economics, utterly horrifying. But to be honest, my least favourite were the 'alternative health' gurus. Kale Cures Cancer. Vaccines Are Venom. Reiki Not Radiation. They tend to be pretty keen on alliteration as a general rule. I felt filthy, letting people preach pseudoscience, especially when it was to a vulnerable group. People dying of cancer aren't particularly risk averse. They'll try anything."

"I certainly would."

"Most people would. Anyway, I was listening to speech after speech and seeing these crowds get whipped into a frenzy over these catchy but meaningless phrases like Actualise Your Potential, Fast-track Your Success, Workshop Your Inner Peace. The road to hell is paved with nouns employed as verbs. The whole thing was slowly driving me insane, but it paid okay. And I had Wanda."

"…Wanda?" Lenore's eyebrow arched heavenward.

"She was the only thing that made it all worthwhile. We were happy."

"I'm assuming there's an 'until'?"

"Until we started to drift apart. Odd phrase, isn't it? Like lovers are just two bits of wood, eddying about at the whim of the ocean." He sighed, waved his hand back and forth through the fading steam. "I wanted to make it work, go to therapy, start doing date nights, but she seemed content to let it all drift away. One day, I came home, and there were spaces where things should have been: dirt rings in place of pot plants, depopulated bookshelves, a wardrobe devoid of dresses."

"She moved out, without even telling you?"

He nodded.

"I'm so sorry. That's awful." She put her hand on his, and they stared at it for a moment, then pulled away at the same time.

"She didn't return my calls. Emails. Facebook messages. I signed up to

Twitter just to see if she'd answer me there. She didn't."

"That's completely monstrous."

He stared at his feet. They listened to the bush turkey digging at the ground outside.

"Can I ask, is that why you…"

He shook his head. "The next day was one of my office days. No going out on the road, just sitting in the office booking clients over email. Basically, a request form would come through, and one of the ten booking agents who worked there would answer it and begin the booking process."

"What happened?"

"I didn't go in. I was too miserable to call, to do anything. I felt like every molecule in my body had been transmogrified into lead and misery. The next day I phoned to apologise. No one had even noticed I wasn't there."

"Orin. I don't know what to say."

He shrugged. "Imagine how I felt. A girlfriend who didn't even feel she had to say goodbye, colleagues who didn't notice I was gone…"

"What about your family?"

He said nothing for a while. Lenore considered escaping to the bathroom in order to give him a moment to deal with what was obviously a complicated question. She'd half lifted herself out of her chair when he said, "I grew up in a Mormon home. When I renounced the faith, they renounced me. I was excommunicated. I hadn't heard from any of them in six years."

Lenore buried her head in her hands, then looked up at him again. "You're beginning to make *Angela's Ashes* sound like a cheery summer read. If you want me to listen to this story without dissolving into a ball of tears, you're going to need to stop repeatedly smashing me with grief anvils."

He paused. Bit his nail. Stared out the window. "They came to the funeral. So that was something."

"How did you—"

"I jumped off a bridge. It was quick, felt like flying. Until it didn't."

"And when—"

"A few weeks ago." He paused again. Stood up. Sat back down. Noticed the walls for the first time. "Did I interrupt you in the middle of cleaning?"

"There were some cleaners here, but they had to leave. Quickly."

"The group that arrived in the truck yesterday?"

Lenore nodded.

"I see. I guess that's a decent segue to hear your story?"

"Depends. How much time do you have?"

"I could probably spare all of eternity, if that suits?"

"Alright then." She wrapped her hands around the cup in front of her. "What you said yesterday, about me having prophetic visions. You were right, at least in part."

He flailed his hands with wild abandon and shrieked, "I *knew* it."

She gestured for him to calm down. "*However*, it's complex. They don't just come to me when I burn incense and light a few candles."

"How do they happen then?"

"Well, not to be Freudian, but it all began with my mother—"

"I think most people could say the sam—"

"And how I killed her."

"Oh."

Lenore smiled wanly and said, "If you want the unabridged version, you'd better let me run to the bathroom first. Some of us mortal types are still beholden to the vexatious will of our bladders. Don't go anywhere."

"I've nowhere else to go."

She stood up and walked up the small flight of stairs, then down the hall to the bathroom, listening to the creaks and groans of the house.

The front door burst open. She jolted and yelled, "Audrey? You're early. Did you bring some clothes?" She opened the bathroom door. "I look like I'm auditioning for the part of 'screaming girl #2' in an 80s slasher—"

Her sentence tumbled into oblivion at the sight of Ocky strolling down her hall. His heavy boots clomped on the wooden floors. He stopped to inspect the couch, nodding in approval, then looked up at her. "Nice piece this. Danish, is it? Or possibly Norwegian? Credit where it's due; those Scandinavians know how to craft a fucken' decent piece of furniture." He flashed her a smile and gestured towards the couch in question. "A quick chat, if it's not too much trouble?"

"I assume you're aware that the basic rules of etiquette dictate that you should knock and wait for the door to be opened?"

Ocky scoffed. "Do they now? Apologies. I've never been one for the rules of etiquette. Back when I was in my twenties, this guy hired me as his bodyguard for some fancy six-course dinner, and one of his hoity-toity pals made fun of me for using the pastry fork instead of the dinner fork for the main course. They all had a right good laugh about my egregious failure to adhere to the 'rules of etiquette.' I picked it up, looked it over, and said, 'Which fork do I use to stab yer eyes out? Cause it seems like they're equally well-equipped for that particular endeavour'. I lost the protection gig, but one of the gents at the table who made his money through primarily extralegal means hired me as a 'specialist consultant,' the specialisation in question being the extraction of information from unwilling participants. Which—surprise surprise—is what I'm here to do now."

"I'm not afraid of you."

"You are. And you should be." It wasn't a threat, so much as a statement of fact. "Yer hands are shaking, yer lookin' for an escape route. That's sensible, but I'll save you the trouble of travelin' down that particular line of inquiry: you'd make it three steps, maybe four. Last time we chatted, it was all very polite and formal. You did me the courtesy of wrapping things up quickly, which was very much appreciated. So what I reckon we should—"

She glanced towards the kitchen, regretting it immediately.

He pointed in the same direction. "Someone in there?"

She shook her head.

He removed a slender wooden object from his pocket, held it up. A comb perhaps? Or possibly—he flicked the razor open, its blade flashing in the light as he walked towards the kitchen. "A lotta guys in my line of work like to use guns, or knives." He peered into the kitchen, tore open the pantry. "But you get caught with one of those, you've got some explainin' to do." Ocky walked back over to her. "But a razor? Perfectly ordinary household object." He drew close enough to reach out and touch her. He gazed up at her face, his casual threat belying his diminutive stature. "No explanation required."

"But, you have a beard?"

He nodded. "Aye, I do at present. But who says I wasn't about to get all handsome and clean-shaven?" He flicked it closed, made a show of putting it back in his pocket. "Like most folks, I operate primarily out of self-interest. Good news for you: it's in both of our interests for that razor to stay clean. If I use it?" He rolled his eyes, waved his hand in a melodramatic circle. "I gotta use this special polishing oil I have ta order in from Sweden. It's a whole lotta palaver. Let's make this clear from the outset: I don't *want* to hurt you. I know what you're thinkin', guy walks into my house, starts waving a razor around, he must be some kind of bloodthirsty sadist. But I don't like spillin' blood any more than a waiter likes clearin' glasses. It ain't *fun*, it's a job. And I like when the job goes smoothly." He gestured towards the couch again. This time, she sat.

"Csaba sent you, didn't he?"

"It's yer first time doing this, so I'll explain. *I* have the razor, so *I* ask the questions. Think of it like a talking stick. Only, you know, more stabby. Boss wants Riley for some elaborate chanty shindig he's got planned. Bunch of mumbo jumbo if you ask me. But hey, as long as his money's good, it's all gravy. Ergo: Tell me where she is, I get paid. You get to live. Win-win."

"What kind of 'chanty shindig'?"

He patted the pocket where he'd placed his razor, waggled his finger at her, and said, "Me: Questions. You: Answers. Care to try again?"

Lenore scanned for something within snatching distance she could use as a weapon. Ocky glowered at her. "You're not the first one to think about tryin' what yer thinkin' about tryin'. Word to the wise; you wouldn't be the first to die in the attempt." He took his razor out. Flipped it into the air. Caught it. Flipped it again.

"Why don't you carry a gun like a reasonable person?"

He grinned. "Razor sends a message, doesn't it? I wished to cut you, then I cut you, now you are dead because you've been cut. It's a clean story. Short. Succinct. Hemingwayesque."

"Hemingway shot himself."

Ocky considered this. "Did he now? Huh. Righto, Alice Munro then. To continue, I like clean, reasonable explanations that avoid assumption and—"

"That how you got the nickname? Is 'Ocky' short for Occam, as in 'Occam's Razor'?"

He grinned. "Indeed it is."

"Did you get the razor before the nickname, or was it the other way around? Because if it was the former, then it kind of seems like you were forcing the nickname? But if it was the latter, that would make it a rather pretentious affectation."

He put the razor away again, stroked his beard. "At this particular juncture, I've got you pegged as a…" He paused, craned his neck towards her, snapped his fingers. "Type three."

"What's a type three?"

"Someone who's neither a type one nor a type two."

"That's not very helpful."

"Not here to be helpful." He pointed to himself. "Man with a razor. Asking questions." A quiet buzzing came from his pocket. He rolled his eyes and said, "Sit tight; this won't take a mo." He stood up and pressed his finger against his ear. "Hello? No, you have to defrost it first. In the microwave. What do you mean 'what setting?' The defrost setting!"

Lenore slipped her hand carefully into her pocket. "Five minutes or so, I should think? No, you *cannot* order pizza again. Do you want to get gout? Yes, some people *do* still get gout, mostly spoiled kids who don't listen to their parents."

Lenore slid the phone carefully out, keeping it cupped in her sleeve. She unlocked the screen—the razor slid through the air as smoothly as if it were on rails, slicing through the sleeve of her shirt and nicking her skin so narrowly that she barely even felt it. She dropped the phone and grabbed at the rivulet of blood running down her hand.

Ocky kicked the phone away and kept the razor hovering an inch from her nose as he continued. "Should be done here in about ten, then I have to take yer brother to the dentist. Can you survive til I'm done, or am I going to come home to an emaciated body on the floor, withered with hunger? Alright. Love you too, pumpkin." He hung up and shook his head. "My eldest. She's studying physics, of which I can't understand a lick nor jot, but she can't bloody fix a meal to save her life. Anyway, here's what I was saying about type three." He removed a handkerchief from his pocket, wiped the blood from his blade. "You've heard of fight, flight, freeze, or fuck?" She nodded. "Right, well, personally I think that's a little off the mark. In my experience, there's type one, who either run or fight; type two, who bloody well do what they're told (my clear favourite, fer obvious reasons); and there's you folk; type three. Might try something, might not, depends on the circumstance. You tried something, I didn't kill you. Be grateful for that. But I will *quite happily* run my hand-crafted, German-made blade right across that pretty throat of yours if. You. Don't. Start. *Talking!*"

A shadow appeared in the hallway. Lenore willed herself not to glance at it and prayed that Orin had managed to lay his hands on a decent weapon. "She's hiding in 1770."

He raised an eyebrow. The shadow inched closer. "Yer saying you think she's travelled through time?"

"1770, the place, not the time. It's a little tourist town, borders the Great Barrier Reef."

"That a real thing? I ain't never heard of it."

"You not having heard of something doesn't nullify the possibility of its existence. I've never heard of your mum, but I assume by you standing in front of me that she exists." Lenore kept her eyes fixed on Ocky as the shadow drew within striking distance.

"Alright, so if I send one of my boys on a plane to this oddly named locale and he doesn't find her, you feel like taking a stab at what happens?"

"Nothing good?"

"Nothing good and then some."

The faint glimmer of reflected light danced ethereally over the hall. Lenore prayed it was from some great medieval broadsword Orin had found in one of the cupboards.

"Righto then." Ocky clapped his hands together. "Obviously, you'll be stayin' put until such a time as yer story checks out. I'll call one of my boys over to play houseguest 'til then. I can have 'im grab some food on the way if you like. What's yer preference? Indian, Jamaican, Thai, Italian? It's all courtesy of Mr Adami, so no need to cheap out, might as well get the good stuff." He started scrolling through numbers. "I'll make sure to get enough for yer friend behind me, too." Lenore's heart launched into her throat as a beaten-up pipe swung high over Ocky's head. He grabbed it with terrifying ease, dropped his phone, and flicked his razor open with his free hand. He moved with dizzying, preternatural speed. The blade flashed through the air, and it was only when Ocky's attacker jumped back to avoid it that Lenore realised it wasn't Orin at all. A black hoodie and a mass of long, matted hair covered the intruder's face.

Ocky turned to Lenore, ignoring the intruder, and commanded, "Stay right where you bloody well are." The stranger charged forward and threw his arms around Ocky's neck. He grabbed them with two hands and pulled the intruder in a judo throw over his shoulder. Ocky picked his razor up and held it against his opponent's throat as he scrambled back to his feet.

Lenore could only see the back of her would-be saviour's head, but he was lying uncommonly still for someone facing the near and immediate threat of decapitation.

"Some might admire your courage. I don't. I find it annoying. I need to take my son to the dentist. It's a non-refundable appointment. You know how much bloody dentists charge in this country? I pull people's teeth outta their heads all the damn time, don't make half as much cash doin' it. Point being: you'd best tell me all about yer good self, and if you know where Riley is, or else I'll introduce my blade here to your innermost regions."

"No problem." The voice was high-pitched, raspy, eerily chipper. It was the vocal equivalent of a clown with a machete.

"Finally, some straight talkin'. Alright then, where is she?"

"Right in front of you." She dropped the hood back, exposing a mass of matted auburn hair. Lenore couldn't see her face, only Ocky's reaction to it.

His pupils became rapidly diminishing black holes set between circular blue constellations. "Lie down on the floor," he ordered.

"No." She spoke as though she were refusing a cup of tea.

"If you don't lie down. I will kill you."

"Everyone says they're going to kill me. No one ever does. They all end up bleeding or dead. Can't see why you'd be any different."

The fear in his face looked out of place, like a child's scrawled depiction of the bogeyman amongst a gallery of impressionist paintings. It was clearly not an emotion he was used to; it didn't sit well on him. He snarled, regained his composure, and swung the razor at her neck. She didn't move. Not a flinch, not a flicker. The razor sat mere millimetres from her neck, hovering impotently in the air. For a moment, Lenore wondered if she had some sort of supernatural power over Ocky, but she dispelled this thought as Riley said,

"See? I knew you wouldn't kill me. People are looking for me. They want me alive."

"That's no lie. But a bit of bruisin' won't be a problem." Ocky dropped the razor and jumped at her, tackling her to the ground.

Riley grappled with him, bringing a knee up to his groin as he unleashed a guttural scream. There was something primal in the way that she fought; she was ungainly and wild and yet carried a surreal confidence. "Get the razor," she said to Lenore.

Lenore ran over to where Ocky had left it, snatched it up, and looked back at them just as he landed a punch to Riley's jaw. She grunted, spat blood into his face. He clawed at his eyes as Riley looked over his shoulder at Lenore and said,

"Kill him." Lenore stared at her in disbelief. "C'mon lady, off with his head!" Lenore stood frozen. Riley rolled her eyes. "Fine. Gimme the frickin' raz—"

Ocky threw his head forward, bringing it into a cranial collision with Riley's. Lenore slashed the razor, painting a red stripe on his arm. He screamed, and Riley used the opportunity to bring her fists clanging against his ears. The pitch of his wail leapt up an octave. She rolled off him, snatched the razor from Lenore's hand, and pulled it across his abdomen. The blue river of blood that gushed through the tributaries and estuaries of his veins was unleashed through the newly created geyser, blooming rusty red as it oxidised and spilled onto the newly cleaned floor.

Riley grabbed Lenore by the hand and dragged her towards the door. Lenore felt as though she had to consciously command her body to properly absorb the oxygen from the air. "Did you see a pale, skinny guy when you came in?"

"Nope."

"We need to look for him, he might—"

"If I didn't see him, he's either long gone or hiding. Either way, it wouldn't be real smart to stick around and look for him. You got somewhere safe we can go?"

"My apartment was destroyed by a dead lady in a bathtub."

Riley raised an eyebrow and said, "Okaaaay, I guess we can go to mine. You got car keys with you?"

Lenore patted her pockets and then yelped with joy when she discovered them. She held them up triumphantly.

"You want me to drive?"

"Are you old enough?"

Riley shrugged. "Depends."

"On what?"

"On whether you're asking 'are you old enough to have obtained the necessary skills to operate a vehicle' or 'are you old enough to have the state certify that I've obtained the yadda yadda yadda.'"

"Please just take my keys and don't kill us."

"Sweet. Let's roll." Lenore tossed Riley the keys. She unlocked the car and climbed in, adjusted the seat and mirrors, and gunned the engine. It groaned and grunted like a cantankerous mechanical geriatric. "Your car's a real piece of shit, huh?"

"Very much so."

"That's cool. My mum's got a '70s Volkswagen. It's even shittier than this." She slammed the accelerator, and they pulled out onto the road, tyres screeching. For a while, the only sound between them was the clunking of the engine and the angry shudder of the changing gears. "You all right?" Riley asked at last. "I know those kinds of situations can be difficult for people like you."

"What do you mean, 'people like me'?"

"People who're afraid of death."

"You're not afraid of death?"

Riley turned and grinned at her, twin rows of white tombstone teeth enshrouded by sandpaper skin. "Nah, I'm not afraid of anything." She looked back at the road, her scratchy, high-pitched voice ringing in Lenore's ears.

22

PAINFULLY QUOTIDIAN

Lenore stared at the cup of peppermint tea in front of her, eyes vacant, bones stinging with fatigue.

"Mum's at work at the homeless shelter. She won't be back 'til late. She's a real bleeding heart, y'know? Got a soft spot for freaks and outcasts. Like yours truly, for instance." Riley sat on the couch, legs crossed, slurping a cup of hot Milo.

Lenore drank in her surroundings: the mother-daughter photos on the mantelpiece, the stack of unwashed dishes in the sink, the shopping list on the fridge, the mail piled on the kitchen bench.

"You all right?"

"It's…not what I was expecting. I've been looking for you, seeing you in those paintings, dreaming about you—"

Riley balked and said, "Sorry to burst your bubble, but you're *super* old."

"I didn't mean it like that. And I'm not that old. It's just you've been the epicentre of this Byzantine mystery, and yet here you are, a teenage girl with a mum who works too much and drives a lousy car. It's all so—"

"Pathetic?"

"I was going to say 'painfully quotidian.'"

"Huh?"

"Ordinary. Normal."

Riley laughed. It was a curious thing, her laugh; abrasive, high-pitched, warm. "Lady, you are the first person to ever call me normal, for *real*."

"Well, I didn't mean it as any kind of insult. But honestly, I thought I'd find you in, I don't know, a cave in the mountains or a dilapidated castle somewhere. Not in an apartment overlooking a Woolworths and a creepy 24-hour massage parlour. I'm feeling a little discombobulated."

"Am I gonna need a dictionary to continue this conversation? Because I pulled a D+ in English last semester. But mostly because we had to write an essay on *On The Road,* and I misread the title and also skipped mosta those classes and then read *The Road* by Cormac McCarthy, which turns out to be a very different book." Riley threw her hands up in exaggerated dismay. "I gotta ask, why try so hard to find me? Why even get mixed up in this at all?"

"Aside from my conscience wanting to prevent harm befalling a stranger and the fact that I had very little choice in the matter?"

"Yeah. Besides that."

"I lost someone recently. Very recently." The words caught in her throat. She paused and steadied herself before continuing. "So perhaps it's an anomalistic combination of grief-induced irrationality and the ardent desire to spare your loved ones the same agony that I'm currently enduring."

Riley shrugged and said, "Fair dibs, works for me, even if I don't understand half the fucking words that come outta your mouth. Should we get down to brass tacks and beeswax?"

Lenore sipped her tea and placed it on the frangipani-adorned coaster. Painfully prosaic. "Yes, I think we should."

"Because I got a lotta questions for you."

"Not half as many as I have for you."

"Alrighty then, let's start with the basics. What's your name?"

"Lenore Lyn."

Riley snorted and said, "Are you fucking *kidding* me?"

"What's wrong with my name?"

"With a name like that, you really oughta be, like, an eighty-year-old librarian with a doily obsession."

"Fuck you! You sound like you swallow sandpaper and helium for breakfast." Lenore slapped her hand to her mouth.

Riley glared at her for a moment, then threw her head back with laughter and said, "*There* it is! Best to get it out of the way, I reckon. I can't stand it when people try and act all, 'Oh, I didn't even *notice* that you look like the lovechild of Godzilla and an elderly junkie!' Fuck that noise. I'm a freak. No use pretending otherwise. It's their hang-up if they're bothered by it, not mine."

"That is surprisingly insightful for a fifteen-year-old."

Riley grinned proudly and said, "Well, cheers. But it took me quite a few broken bones and noses to arrive at that little revelation." She clocked the concerned look on Lenore's face and said, "Oh, theirs, not mine."

"I'm not sure that's better?"

"Whatevs. I never met a fight I couldn't win. And that ain't braggin', cos it's true. It's like that boxer Malcolm X said, It ain't braggin' if you can back it up."

"That was Muhammad Ali. Malcolm X was a political activist."

"Really? Shit. Well, I'm not doing so good in history either. Didn't really even know much about my own history until a couple of days ago." Riley sunk back into the couch and exhaled. "Mind if I smoke?"

"Actually, my throat really itches when—"

"Shit lady, I was only asking to be polite. It's my fuckin' house." She took out a tobacco pouch and paper, then rolled both her eyes and her cigarette as she said,

"Mum never hid the fact that I was adopted. She drives me nuts, but she's straight with me. Gotta give her that. Some kids at my school were raised all, 'Grandpa's sleeping,' and 'babies are delivered by storks,' and that kinda shit. Not in this house. From day one, it's been 'Grandma's dead, kids come from mummies and daddies squishing their procreational organs together' and the whole bit. I respect her for that. And she encouraged me to take self-defence classes, which was cool. Plus, you know, it can't be easy, having a daughter with a face like desiccated coconut and a voice like helium and nails." Riley tapped the ashes into a handmade bowl with her name written in a childish scrawl on the bottom. It was crumpled and distorted, its skin was as crinkled and uneven as her own. "So...the story I get told is: my mum—my biological mum—had me real young. She adopted me out and then died in a car crash."

"They told you Claire was dead?"

Riley shot a stream of smoke from the corner of her mouth, waved the cigarette in her fingers back and forth, and said, "Claire was my mum? She told me my real mum's name was Mona. Doesn't matter. She never existed anyway. But for years, I'd regularly go and visit 'Aunt Claire and Uncle Elliott.' They were really sweet, you know? They had this crazy house filled with weird little dolls and figurines of all types of mythological creatures, centaurs and faeries and basilisks and junk like that."

Lenore fished the basilisk figurine out of her pocket and handed it to Riley. "Like this one?"

She grabbed it and turned it over in her hand as though it were a precious, living thing. "Damn. This takes me way back. It cool if I keep this?" Lenore nodded. "Sweet, thanks. Anyway, where was I? Oh yeah. They'd buy me ice cream, take me wherever I wanted, theme parks, movies, whatever. But they were always looking around, like they were scared. We always sat with our backs to the wall, facing all possible exits. They used to wear disguises, too. Sunglasses, big hats, even wigs sometimes. They called it 'playing dress-ups.' They never really explained it, but I didn't give a shit.

"Whenever they dropped me home, they'd squeeze me so tight I thought I'd burst. They looked so sad every time. Mum would never come with us, which struck me as odd, you know? Like, why didn't we all hang out as one big family? I'd see them once, maybe twice a year. I used to ask to see them more often, and Mum would just look all sad and say, 'that's not possible. It's too dangerous.' But she'd never tell me why. Like I said, she was always straight up with me, so that seemed real weird. To be honest, I think that being shut in was making 'em a little nuts. They were obsessed with getting portraits done every couple of years for some goddamn reason. And the whole house was this crazy mess, except for what they called 'my room.' I never slept there, but it had a bunch of toys and books and art supplies that I loved, and they always kept it clean and pristine."

Riley bit her lip and gazed out the window, scratched her wrist. "The last time I saw them was my tenth birthday. I remember cos I had to stand against the wall so they could mark my height and then pose for *another* fucking portrait. You got any idea how boring it is to stand still for an hour when you're ten? Anyways, afterwards they gave me a new Xbox, so that was pretty sweet. Then we went out for lunch at this fancy joint, by the river —waiters in bow ties, lobsters in tanks and alla that shit. We'd finished our meals and the waiter comes in with this massive fuckin' cake, sparklers blazing, the whole bit. They're halfway through 'Happy Birthday' when Auntie Claire sees someone outside, pulls me right outta my seat, looks at Elliott, and says: 'Tuatara.'

"I looked it up. It's this reptile from New Zealand, looks like a lizard but isn't. They've got three eyes, but the third eye is 'parietal', which means it mostly works as a light-sensor. It's visible when they're babies but gets covered with scales later on. Anyway, she hisses that word 'tuatara' like she's freaking out but trying to stay calm? Uncle El throws some cash on the table, and we stand up and walk quickly out of the restaurant, cake still sitting on the table, sparklers still sparkling.

"Claire whispers to me: 'Stay quiet. Stay still. Keep your head close to my chest.' They both don sunglasses, and we walk straight out of the restaurant, brisk but not running. What stuck with me was that they were *freaked*, but they also seemed prepared. Like they'd been practicing for it. We walked out of the building, left their car in the carpark, and hailed a cab. They didn't say a word the whole way back. When they dropped me home, Mum told me to go play in my room, and she put on this Bob Marley record real loud. I heard them talking to each other in frightened whispers, but I couldn't make out what they were saying." She shrugged. Sipped her Milo. Dragged on her cigarette.

"That was the last time I ever saw them. Mum told me they moved overseas. Obviously, I didn't believe her, but she wouldn't answer my questions. Why didn't they write, why didn't they call?" Riley stubbed out her cigarette and leaned in close, "Then, a couple of days ago, Mum came home from work early. She was bawling her eyes out. She handed me this letter and then ran to her room." Riley walked over to the bookshelf, pulled out a copy of

Watership Down.

"You read this? It's about rabbits and shit. It's cool, though. Heaps violent."

Lenore smiled and said, "I have, many times."

"Thought it would be a fun place to hide the letter. Like I'm a spy or sumthin', y'know?" She took the letter out of the envelope and handed it to Lenore.

23

URBACH-WIETHE

Our dearest Riley,

There is so much I have to say to you; apologies, confessions, gratitude—but I want first and foremost for you to know that this is a letter of love. I want you to know how proud I am of you, of the young woman you have become.

Claire and I lied to you for many years. Like most evil deeds in this world, our actions were motivated by fear. We were part of a company called Amrita. You're no doubt familiar with the publicly facing portion of our organisation—a legitimate corporation with a broad portfolio encompassing air-conditioning, construction, real estate, medical research and, most importantly, cryonics and life-extension.

The inner circle of our organisation—the Sixth Sun—is something else altogether. I'm going to refrain from revealing intimate details in order to protect you. But I will inform you that we had a few 'irregular' practices, the first of which was that all of our members swore an oath to remain childless. Claire and I employed a multiplicity of contraceptive devices. However, as your dear mother has no doubt informed you (repeatedly, I hope!) no method of contraception is 100% effective. Claire fell pregnant. I won't lie; we thought of getting an abortion. We'd grown attached to the wealth and power and influence we commanded as part of the inner circle, but as her belly gently swelled, we couldn't bear the thought of bringing an end to the life growing inside her. We concocted a fabrication about Claire being ill, claimed that she had bowel cancer and we had to go to Switzerland for several months for treatment. We did indeed go to Switzerland, but the treatment we sought was in your care and delivery.

Understand that there was no way out for us. Violating any of the sacred tenets is a cardinal offense. If anyone were to discover that we'd had a child, we would all be found and killed. We decided that the safest thing for you would be to keep you hidden nearby and carry on with our deceit. It worked well enough, for a while. But that final day we saw you, on your tenth birthday, we were very nearly caught. We made the painful decision to cut ties with you, and then searched desperately for a way to extract ourselves from the inner circle. Tragically, one fell in our lap. Claire developed the very disease we'd pretended she'd been enduring all those years (made for a tragically believable lie, a somewhat bitter silver lining, I suppose). I placed Claire into stasis here at home, and spent the next few years caring for her.

But now I've grown old, and I am utterly, unfathomably alone. I've known pleasure and luxury and love and loss. I've drunk as deep as possible from the well of life, forever fearing my own end, and now all I want to do is run towards it. Although the vast majority of our assets— including the house—have to be given away so that there's no clear trail to you, I have provided for you and Claire. Lindsay will continue to receive a stipend for your care until your eighteenth birthday when your trust fund will be turned over to your control. Amrita will learn about Claire once the deed for our home passes into the hands of the caretaker I've arranged via necessarily elaborate means. I wish I could have left it to you, but it's simply too risky. And, to be honest, I'm quite embarrassed by how much I've let it decay over the last few years. The walls and rooms have come to mirror the degradation and dilapidation in my own mind. I'm sending you a variety of communiques ranging from the routine to the abstruse, I am assuming that they will reach you over the next few days. I've sent you the letter you're now reading (direct), a tape via third-party channels (indirect), and an as-yet unassigned emissary who may be anything from trustworthy to unscrupulous (randomised). Please do not listen to the tape unless you are in the direst circumstances. It contains information that would endanger you, but under certain hideous circumstances may provide you with some leverage.

By the time you receive this letter, my consciousness will be long departed. I fear death, but I fear the thought of continuing life far more. I no longer want to wake up in the future my colleagues and I envisioned, I no longer want to wake up at all. Know that I have loved you. Know that Claire loved you. Know that Lindsay loves you. Please stay away from the house, from Amrita industries, from anyone connected to them.

I could write volumes more, but I fear my strength (physical, mental, emotional) has all but faded.

Love always,

Elliot

Lenore handed the letter back to Riley.

She folded it back into the envelope as she said, "Turns out I'm Swiss. Ain't that some shit? I'll have to take Swiss classes."

"Swiss isn't a language. They speak Italian, German, French, and Romansh."

"Fuck, I don't have time to learn four new languages. If I ever visit, I'll just yell a lot and wave my hands around. So, what kind of 'emissary' are you then; trustworthy or unscrupulous?"

"I'd like to think I have an above-average scruple quotient."

Riley's pupils darted to the corner of her eyes as she attempted to parse this.

"Lindsay's your mother, I assume?"

"Yeah."

"My friend Audrey might be able to help connect us to the Sixth Sun. What about the other messages he mentions, any sign of those?"

"What, you mean besides the one sitting in front of me? You want to give me the rundown on how you got mixed up in all this?"

"Amrita hired me to go to Elliott's funeral. I found this in his mouth." Lenore took the fob watch out and handed it to Riley.

She clicked it open and shut a few times. "So I guess you could say he died with a big fat clock in his mouth." Lenore refused to acknowledge this. Riley turned the watch over in her hands. "I shouldn't speak ill of the dead, huh? I've never even had a gift that was engraved, let alone delivered *in* a grave."

"Technically, he was in a coffin, not a grave—"

"Don't be a pun killer, LL. Fob watch is a weird choice. Never really saw the point of these stupid things. Like, get a wristwatch for fuck's sake." She tossed it onto the coffee table. "What're you, a funeral director or something?"

"Moirologist, professional mourner."

Riley laughed her raspy laugh, throwing her hands high into the air. "So you're like, a grief hooker?"

"That's not the way I explain it to my elderly relatives, but yes, that's about the gist of it."

"Okay, so you showed up at the funeral and what? They just gave you the keys to the place and said, 'have fun with the snap-frozen corpse in the backyard'?"

"Actually, Ocky was the one who gave me the keys. But he was a lot more businesslike about it at the time. I don't think Elliott thought it all through too thoroughly; it sounds like he was in quite a state by the end there. I think he ultimately meant for Claire to end up in their facility, but there's a lot I still don't understand. You didn't go back to the house earlier?"

"I mean, it's not like I totally believed they'd moved overseas, but I was a kid just getting delivered to the house each time, and I couldn't remember the name of the street. Once Mum told me he'd passed away, I decided to look more seriously. I remembered it was somewhere near the river, not too far from a cemetery. Did a bunch of recon runs on my bike until I found it. It was even bigger than I remembered." She smirked, shifted in her seat. "Hey, between you and me, I'm low-key worried about becoming a trust fund kid. They're all such entitled assholes. I gotta make sure to stay grounded, get a job or go to college or some shit so I don't end up listening to true crime podcasts and smoking weed on the couch wearing Gorman shirt-dresses every fucking day."

"You *may* have just described my ideal life."

Riley snorted a laugh. "Yeah, well. Different strokes for different folks, right?" She tossed the envelope to Lenore. "I checked the date it was postmarked; it was a Friday. Same day he died. Looks like he poured his heart and soul out onto the page, strolled down to the post office, then came home and drank a bottle of Brandy with a chaser of several dozen sleeping pills. The letter showed up on Tuesday."

"You think he wanted to delay its delivery on purpose?"

"Yeah, I reckon." She took the letter back, ran her hand over the paper. "It's a weird thing, you know? Thinking about how after he was dead, his words were still traveling around the city? Like this piece of his consciousness was still active?"

Lenore oscillated between the desire to overshare her own multitudinous experiences with mortality and stay focused on digging away at the mystery in front of her. "We leave all kinds of traces without even trying. If you stepped outside right now and looked at the sky, then five hundred years in the future, some alien species five hundred light years away could peer through their telescopes and watch that exact moment unfold in real-time, centuries after you're dead and buried."

"Fuuuuuuuuuck, that's crazy." Riley stood up, walked to the window, stuck her head out, and waved. "Hey, aliens. Make a statue of me."

Lenore laughed and said, "It doesn't work with sound."

Riley sat back down. "How come?"

"Light travels at an altogether different speed, and sound doesn't carry through space because there's no airwaves for it to travel on."

Riley considered this and said, "You some kinda scientist or something?"

"I majored in biological science for a couple of semesters. I grew up around death, so I thought it might be nice to immerse myself in its opposite, but of course, I came to realise that they aren't opposites at all."

"Two sides of the same coin?"

"More like siblings of the same family. Turned out death wasn't something I could walk away from."

"Yeah, well, you and alla humanity got that in common," said Riley as she rolled another cigarette.

"You sure you want to—"

"Lady, you really want to avoid telling me how to live my life, believe." Outside, the wail of an ambulance tore through the air. They stopped and listened to it pass.

"Can I ask you something?" said Lenore.

"Shoot."

"What did you mean when you said you're 'not afraid of anything'? I saw how you were with Ocky. It was like you weren't bothered by him at all."

Riley grinned, tapped her skull, and said, "Urbach-Wiethe."

"Is that a person?"

"Genetic condition. It's why I have the bumpy lizard skin and weird voice and can't feel fear. You know how psychopaths can't feel empathy? Their brains don't produce the right neurofens?"

"Neurochemicals."

"That's what I said. Same kinda deal. I got a calcified amygdala. Ain't afraid of *nothin*."

"You can't feel fear, at all?"

She shook her head, jumped up from the couch. "It's like that landline in my brain has been disconnected. That's how I could take out that guy back at the house. The lack of fear really unsettles an attacker. Messes with their predatorian instincts."

"It's 'predatory' instincts, not 'predatorian.'"

Riley raised an eyebrow, crossed her arms. "Remember what I said about not feeling fear? And how before that, I said the constant correcting is starting to piss me off? And before that, how I cut a guy's stomach open with a razor? You probably want to swirl alla that info around inside that book-smart brain of yours and come to some sort of conclusion, or we're gonna have issues. As I was saying. This one time, I'm tagging under this bridge, right? My graff tag is Lizard Grrrl. You've probably seen my work." Lenore shrugged. Riley scoffed and continued, "It's around. People in the know, know my shit. Anyway I'm tagging this bridge, and this guy comes up to me and says,

"'Hey cutie, you feel like having' fun?' I said, 'I am having fun; you're interrupting me.' He pulls a knife and holds it up to my face. It was real dark, and I had my hood up, so he hadn't realised I was rocking the whole reptilian look. I turn to face him, pull the hood back, and he does that weird thing you normal peeps do when you're scared— deep breath, eyes go wide. And then he gets, like, angry. That happens a lot. People act like my fuckin' face is their business, like the fact that I'm weird is their problem somehow. He grabs me and shoves the knife to my throat and says,

"'I'm going to gut you like a fish, you freak.' Punks like that are always soooo heavy on the cliché. So I look at him, roll my eyes and say, 'Either kill me or leave me the fuck alone. I gotta get this done and get home before my mum finishes work.' He just stares for a minute. I look at him like, 'Well, what's it gonna be?' and then he drops the knife and runs like a little bitch."

She laughed and shook her head. "I mean, I could've taken him anyway. He obviously didn't even know how to handle the knife. I probably would've beaten the crap outta him." She held up a fist in demonstration and said, "The trick is to keep your thumb on the *outside*. A lotta first-timers get that wrong. Hard to win a fight when you break your thumb right at the get-go. Also? Maybe, like, nine times outta ten, they're gonna come at you with a right hook, so if you can—"

"Does that mean you aren't scared of death?"

Riley cocked her head and smiled. "That one's been rattling around in that pretty head of yours for a while, huh, Lenny?"

Lenore nodded.

"Listen. I don't *want* to die. As much as I complain about this shitty existence, so far as I know it's the only one I'll ever get; I want the ride to last as long as possible. But as for being scared? When it happens, it happens, and I won't be around to feel anything at all about it. Everybody's gotta die.

That's the way of things. You want more tea?"

Lenore nodded and studied the dirty carpet beneath them as she poured. Traces of dirt were weaving into the fibres so tightly that even steam cleaning would not remove them. The dirt was becoming not something on top of the carpet, but an added component of the carpet's physical composition. "When I think about death, it's like a vacuum opens up inside me. I feel like I'm being pulled into myself. Buildings and trees seem to loom over me. There's this vast reverberating emptiness that roars in my ears. I get dizzy and nauseous, and I look at everyone around me and think, how are they doing this? How are they walking around like everything's fine? How are they not constantly crushed beneath the weight of their mortality?" Lenore winced and looked down at her finger. She'd been unconsciously rubbing at the diamond on her ring with such force that it had torn an opening in her skin. A tiny sliver of crimson emerged on her finger, a single red drop falling down to the carpet at her feet. She glanced guiltily at Riley, realising with equal parts relief and irritation that she'd been playing with her phone during her entire admission. "Riley?"

She glanced up from tapping at her keys. "Yeah?"

"I'm sorry, I think I—"

A Hitchcockian scream pierced the air. Lenore jumped an inch out of her seat, Riley leaned back and sipped her tea. It took a couple of seconds before she realised that Audrey's ringtone prank had fooled her twice, shame on her. She chastised herself for not changing it earlier, then grabbed her phone out of the bag and yelped again when she saw Darius's name. She answered.

"Darius. I'm so sorry, I completely forgot to tell you about what happened. We had to get out of there really fast, and I finally found Riley, and she was telling me her whole story, and I didn't even stop to think that I'd told you to come over and—"

"You want to stop and take a breath?"

"Okay. Yes."

"Great. Now, if you can spare your dear brother a couple of minutes, I would love to know why I'm staring at a pool of blood on the floor of your creepy and, I can only assume, haunted house."

24

I DO THIS IN SERVICE OF YOU

Darius hung up and stared at the sticky pool of red on the floor. It was soaked in the centre of what appeared to be a demilitarised zone in a war between filth and cleanliness. For a moment, he could do nothing but stare. The only sound was the sporadic tickling of tree branches on the roof. His phone bleeped with a message from Lenore informing him of Riley's address. He tapped it into his route guidance and was halfway out the door when he looked up to see Audrey stepping out of her car. "Guess she didn't tell you either, huh?"

"Tell me what?" she replied.

"That you shouldn't come over because some corporate henchman paid her a very threatening visit."

"Is she okay?"

"I think so. She's at Riley's house."

"Who the hell is Riley?"

"I'll explain on the way."

Audrey grabbed him by the shoulders and demanded, "Slow down a minute; you can't just throw info like that at me and then drive off towards the horizon. I want to see what the hell happened in there." She pushed past him and opened the front door.

"You really shouldn't."

"Don't tell me what to do!" she yelled back at him. He listened to her stilettos tap across the floor, stop, then return in double time. "You could've warned me, Darius!"

"I tried to—"

"No time to apologise! We need to get someone over here to clean that mess up. Lenore's already had a septuagenarian kamikaze into her bedroom, and a surprise ice princess appear in her newly acquired backyard. She shouldn't have to deal with whatever the hell happened here as well." She whipped out her phone and began scrolling.

"Have you got someone on speed dial who'll happily drop everything to race over here and clean up blood without reporting it to the police?"

"I've probably got a dozen guys who fit that bill. But there's one in particular who I think would be absolutely perfect." She flashed him a mischievous grin and listened as the phone rang. A timorous voice emerged from the speaker.

"H-hello?"

"Hello, pig, I have a job for you." She barked instructions and a list of cleaning products at him and then hung up. "He'll be here in about twenty minutes. We'll leave the door unlocked for him. I'm hungry. Can we stop and pick up bagels on the way?"

"I don't know if that's a good idea."

"Come on, you're so skinny. My treat." She poked him affectionately in the ribs.

"But my contract says—" His well-worn defence of being contractually obliged to stay cadaverously thin leapt to the front of his brain. It was almost a muscle memory on his tongue; he could probably recite it whilst simultaneously solving a crossword. This time, however, he brought it to a stammering halt after these first few words. After what he'd recently learned, playing dead really didn't seem like much of a life. "I'll take whichever one has the most bacon. Actually, make that two. And chips. And a thick shake."

She slapped him on the back and said, "Don't overdo it, I'm a single mum for fuck's sake. Let's take my car."

They climbed in and drove off, leaving the house still and silent. The wind gently shook the trees. A teenager bunking off school gleefully whirred down the road on a stolen bicycle. After about fifteen minutes, there was a faint stirring in the front bushes. A pale hand broke free of the leaves. Orin shielded his fingers against the glaring rays of the sun and dusted himself off. He was dizzy, nauseous, and for a moment, had no memory whatsoever of how he'd ended up in the hedge's arboreal embrace. He drew himself up, and a bolt of pain stung his jaw. "That's weird…" he said, the very utterance of these words causing nerves to telegraph furious dispatches to his brain, screaming *'That hurts. Shut up!'*

He groaned again, and the flashes of pain jolted memories back into his consciousness. He'd heard someone at the front door and gone to investigate and found himself greeted by a diminutive stranger with an enormous beard. Strangest of all, the intruder had looked directly at him. His invisibility had become thoroughly unreliable; being dead certainly wasn't all it was cracked up to be. He wished he had the intangibility of a ghost, or the telekinetic powers of a poltergeist, or a zombie's inability to feel pain. Whatever type of dead thing he was, he hadn't seemed to have picked up much in the way of superpowers. How was he supposed to protect Lenore when he couldn't even—

He yelped— causing pain to shoot through his jaw—at the realisation she might still be in danger. He shoved the door open and ran inside, then froze when he saw the pool of smeared blood on the floor. Orin fell to his knees and hung his head in his hands, whimpering. He'd failed again. He'd failed at keeping Wanda in love with him. He'd failed at living a noteworthy life. Even his attempt to escape the mortal realm had been a failure. And now here he was, failing at being an effectively intimidating post-lifeform. Lenore was missing, most likely dead. Her flesh sliced apart by cold steel, her blood spilled like wine at a pagan wedding, her skin—

A car pulled up outside the house. Orin heard the engine cutting off and the driver's door opening and closing. Only yesterday, he would have confidently strolled out the front to investigate, but now his belief in his invisibility had faltered. He didn't want to run the risk of ending up unconscious in a bush again. He ran towards the nearest cupboard and opened it to find it filled to bursting with chairs, lamps, and a collection of the most profoundly, perfectly useless souvenir in all of human creation: the snow globe. He shoved as much as he could out onto the floor, clambered inside, and pulled the doors closed. This was the second time he'd found himself hiding nervously in the closet. He really hadn't expected death to be so much like high school.

Orin peered out through the narrow slats, listening to the sound of the approaching stranger. He heard bustling and tinkling and rustling as the visitor entered, dropped something heavy to the ground, and sighed. He was dressed in a manner so bizarre Orin had to slap his hand to his mouth to prevent himself from bursting out laughing. Sadly, this slap to the mouth made his jaw erupt in pain. He clenched into a ball of agony as he stared at the doughy middle-aged man dressed in tight leather shorts, fishnet stockings, and a black and red latex singlet.

The man gasped as he saw the blood, nervously bit his nails, and then turned and walked back to the door. Orin listened as he murmured frantically to himself. He appeared to be psyching himself up for the job. He banged his fist on the wall, steadied himself, and took out his phone. "Uh, yes, hi, hello, my queen! My dark angel! She who causes, stars to…s-s-sing? Y-yes, I am a filthy grovelling worm. A thousand pardons, my queen, but I f-fear I am not up to this task. *Of course,* I want to prove my devotion! But I wondered if there wasn't something I could do that involved, ah, less, you know…blood? Well, obviously I didn't think it was human b-b-blood! I know my most glorious matriarch would never— Yes, I understand the nature of the test you've set for me. But I don't think—"

She said something to him that Orin couldn't make out, but judging from his ecstatic gasp, it was very much to his liking. "Truly, oh she who causes hearts to, ah, beat like…hummingbirds? What a great honour! Yes, I will do this task for you! Thank you, my Queen!" He hung up with an excited giggle, returned to the room, set a tablet and his phone up to record, then began lugging in buckets, sponges, and cleaning chemicals. He fell to his knees, pulled on elbow-length rubber gloves, sprayed the area with a thick mist of disinfectant, then turned to the camera and exultantly screamed, "I do this in service of you, my voluptuous, vice-ridden vixen!"

Orin shook his head in bemusement. It was times like this he was glad to be dead.

25

LET THE DEAD DIE

Audrey's rusty red Fiat clunked like it was losing the will to live. Every few minutes it would jolt and shudder in what Darius swore sounded like its death throes. He prayed for the engine's continued compliance as he devoured his bagel in ferocious, reptilian bites.

Audrey glanced at him with a blend of amusement and disgust. "You know, it's been so long since I've seen you eat an actual meal. I forgot what a pig you are."

"This bagel is better than heroin," he said.

"What made you drop the breatharian diet? Feel free to answer me *after* you've finished chewing."

He gulped, wiped his mouth with the back of his hand. "I found out the project I was working on wasn't exactly what I expected."

"It's a porno, isn't it?"

"Worse."

She threw her head back with a laugh that took her eyes completely off the road. "Spill. I could use the entertainment."

"Not ready to let the words leave my lips just yet. Too depressing."

"Fair enough. Why don't you try not letting food leave your lips while you're speaking, too?" She brushed a speckle of moistened crumbs from her shoulder.

"Sorry…" he mumbled. They pulled up at a red light and listened to the engine's remonstrations. Darius finished, wiped his hands with a napkin.

"I can feel you wanting to ask something," said Audrey.

He cleared his throat, threw the napkin into the paper bag. "Do 'financial advisors' always talk to clients that way?"

Audrey said nothing for a moment. The clacking of the indicator filled the air between them. "Yeah. I suppose you' re gonna find out sooner or later."

"Can you clarify what it is that I've found out?"

"…"

"Aud?"

"I'm what you might call a 'specialist' financial advisor. Financial dominatrix, specifically. I didn't want to tell you because I thought you'd be weird about it."

"I don't think it's weird," he protested, his voice pitch-shifting.

"It's a *job,* Darius. It's what I do to pay the bills and feed my kids, just until I finish my degree."

"I think I always knew, in a way, but I didn't allow the information to register. But I wish there was some way I could help so you didn't have to do…those things."

"You realise that's not *really* me, right? I'm acting, same as you. It's a role; I'm not really Mistress Fury, Mark Hamill isn't actually Luke Skywalker, Ben Affleck isn't actually Batman—"

"*Never* say 'Ben Affleck' and 'Batman' in the same sentence."

"Sorry to offend your nerdy sensibilities. But you see what I'm saying. They're just actors. They take off the wigs and makeup and go home, crack a beer, nap on the couch. Same here. Except for the napping."

"I know that intellectually—"

"But it's still weird?" He shrugged. "I understand how it might seem that way. But huge sections of our economy are based on constructing fantasy, and a good slice of that fantasy pie is R-rated content. People spend hundreds of dollars on perfume so they can pretend to be alluring, thousands of dollars on ridiculous fad diets in the hope that they'll get magically fit without having to exercise, millions of dollars on famous paintings so they can appear sophisticated. I'm simply filling a gap in the market. I'm not doing anything illegal, or immoral. As for weird? Hard to think of a more relative term. Plenty of people think it's 'weird' to play in a band. Look at what you and Lenore do for a living! Or, perhaps I should say 'do for a dying.'"

"Not funny."

"Fine. Not funny, but also not inaccurate. Granted, I'm no saint. But I'm also not working for a company that exploits workers, pollutes waterways, or avoids paying tax like half of my friends in corporate work. None of whom feel much in the way of guilt, by the way."

"I don't disagree with any of what you're saying. But it still seems…"

"Weird?"

"Sorry."

She sighed, drummed her fingers on the steering wheel. "I get it. My mum still thinks I work as a financial advisor for this exact reason. I just get frustrated by the fact that it's always the sex workers who're judged, rather than the clients."

Darius stared out the window, looked back at Audrey. "Part of what I find so unsettling about your job is that it reminds me that even the rich and powerful are so broken, so fragile."

"From what I've seen? More so."

"Right. Take Kyle, for instance; he's rich, famous, successful. But that fear of death still hums like never-ending feedback at the depths of his psyche. So many of our systems—biological, economic, social—are geared in one way or another towards sex; partly for procreation, partly for raw satisfaction of lust, partly—for those lucky bastards who can manage it—as an expression of genuine love towards one another. We get to enjoy that for a little while, and then we die, no matter how glorious or altruistic or brilliant we are.

"So those that can afford to do so bury themselves—pun intended—in money and sex and luxury homes, and it perpetuates this lie that if you can stockpile enough wealth, you can build a mountain of money and use it to crawl your way up to heaven. But we're all going into the ground, even if some of us will have fancier coffins. Today, seeing that blood on the floor, hearing you talk to that guy…it reminded me about how everything is ultimately about sex and death, or the avoidance of it. I mean, hey, look at this, case in point." He poked his finger at a massive billboard advertising a Michael Jackson hologram tour. "People shelling out to see holograms perform 'live.' Elvis, Roy Orbison, Tupac, Ol' Dirty Bastard. They're throwing money at digital ghosts."

Audrey stared at the billboard, looked at Darius. "Some people just can't let the dead die."

26

EDGAR ALLAN POPE

The three of them watched Riley devour her bagel with moans of primal pleasure. "It's like watching a serial killer at work," Darius stage-whispered to Lenore.

"Hey! I canmph hear you, ash-ole!" Riley protested, flecks of bacon spitting onto the floor. "I'll forgimphe you, but only cosh you brought me 'ood." She slurped her lemonade and smacked her lips in satisfaction. "I always get fis hungry afta a fight." She gulped down the last of it, popped the cap off her lemonade, and poured the ice into her mouth, crunching it as she cast her eyes over the three visitors on her faded green couch. "So," she finished chewing, waving the straw at them. "You guys are in a band?"

"Yes. The Molotov Cocktail Waitresses," said Darius, trying to look directly at her eyes and not her sandpapery skin.

"That's cool. Me and my friend Alicia are starting a band called the Reptilian Agenda. We've got the costumes and posters and logo and website and Instagram all sorted. Almost ready to roll, just gotta sort one last thing."

"What's that?" asked Lenore.

"Gotta figure out how to play instruments. I have a crappy acoustic guitar I don't really know how to use, but I'm thinking I'm probably a drummer type. She's maybe lead guitar, or something weird like baritone sax or the sitar. We wanna stand out from all those shitty samey rock three-pieces out there. Whaddya you guys play?"

"We're a shitty samey rock three-piece," replied Lenore.

Riley laughed. Audrey and Darius both tensed at the eerie sound. Lenore felt guilty for reacting the same way mere hours earlier. "Oh. Cool. Well, no offense. There's plenty of good rock three-pieces out there. Sleater-Kinney, Camp Cope, Cable Ties. Anyways, you guys aren't here to talk music. What're we going to do about this guy Soda?"

"Csaba," corrected Lenore.

Riley rolled her eyes, looked at Darius, and said, "Does she do this thing where she corrects you guys all the time too?"

"Endlessly," said Darius. Lenore punched him in the arm.

"Well, whatevs. You say 'Csaba,' I say 'let's-break-his-arm-a.' How's it gonna go down? Wanna break out the butcher's paper and Nikko pens?"

"I really think you should leave this up to us. No offense, but you're just a kid." The words had barely made their way out of Darius's mouth before Riley reached into her jacket pocket, pulled out a switchblade, flicked it open, and pressed it to his throat.

"Whatthefuckdidyoucallme?"

He held his hands up and said, "I'm sorry, I'm sorry!" as the others yelled at her to calm down. She stared directly into his eyes, her teeth bared. She dropped the knife and planted a loud kiss on his forehead, then ruffled his hair. "Just fuckin' with you, slim. Makin' a point. You know how when I held that knife to your throat, your pulse started to race? You probably almost pissed yourself?"

"I did *not*—"

"Whatevs. You got scared, right?"

"Obviously. You had a *knife* to my throat; who wouldn't be scared?"

Riley grinned and said, "L-boogie, you wanna fill 'em in?"

"Please don't call me that. Riley has a calcified amygdala. She can't experience fear; it's like a neurological dead letter."

"Makes me kind of a team asset, yeah? Plus, I probably have more fights under my belt than alla you combined. No offense."

"I'm a lover, not a fighter, sweetheart," said Audrey, scrolling through her phone and then holding out the screen. "And I have a plan that involves a distinct lack of stabbing."

Riley looked at the image on the screen and said, "Look, your kinks are your business, but how does looking at porn on your phone get us any kind of leverage on Simba?"

"Csaba," corrected Lenore again.

"You're worse than my mum."

"That's one of my clients, one of the men who pays me to yell at him and command him to perform menial tasks, like cleaning up your bloody mess, for instance."

Riley zoomed in on the image. "Oh shit, that's my place."

Lenore coughed and said, "Actually, it's *my* place."

"*Pfft.* Maybe. We can set a court date once we've roughed up Samba. But how does fishnets here help us get anything done besides cleaning and polishing?"

"A lot of my clients are well-connected, wealthy, and will do anything for me. I'm sure I could ask around, land one of these Sixth Sun guys on my client list, and hopefully convince him to give me a personal tour."

"I heard someone on set talking about the Sixth Sun, but they were very insistent that I keep quiet about it," said Darius.

"Right, so it sounds like at least a portion of the 1% are in the know. Just need to get one on my roster. The only problem is that 'personal tour' means meeting him in person."

"Yeah, and?" said Riley.

"I do my business over the internet. Some girls in my trade like the physical touch, but I try to avoid it. It can be dangerous. A lot of these guys are into some weird shit. I've only done a physical encounter once. I had to replace the steering column in my car, didn't have anywhere near enough cash to do it. So I hooked up a date, I had him tied up; a little tongue lashing, a little whip lashing, the usual."

"Your 'usual' is what most people would call 'real fucking weird,'" said Riley.

"Yes, I've been told that. Anyway. I thought we were all finished. I was packing up. I picked up the envelope with my payment and slipped it into my bag. When I turned around, he was standing there looking at me with that creepy look guys get when they decide that they are entitled to something and are simply waiting for their moment to take it." She stopped and stared at the floor for a minute, then continued in a murmur. "He didn't get what he wanted. I had to rip out a clump of his hair and almost scratch his eyes out. I got out, went home, cried for an hour. Showered. Called the cops, spun some bullshit about it being a Tinder date gone wrong because if you tell a cop you're a sex worker, then it's like you've just handed them a written statement saying, 'please don't value me as a person or make any attempt to protect and serve me.' They rolled over to the house, but it was an Airbnb he'd rented under a fake name. They never found him."

"So, TLDR, you need someone to back you up?" asked Riley.

"TLDR?

"Too Long Didn't Read. Like, 'gimme the short version.'"

"Right. I think I can get him to give me a private tour of this cryonics facility. But I don't want to be left alone with him."

Riley rubbed her hands together and said, "No sweat. We'll watch your six, Aubrey."

"Audrey."

"We need codenames! You can be Jezebel—"

"Gee, thanks."

"—I'll be Lizard Grrrl, obvs, Darius you can beeeee….Slenderman because, I mean, come on, have you even *heard* of food? For Lenore, I'm thinking Raven, like the Edgar Allan Pope poem."

"It's 'Edgar Allan *Poe.*'"

"Seriously, Lenore, if you keep correcting me, I am going to need to correct your face. With my fists."

"You're very rude, considering we're sitting here trying to figure out how to save your life."

"Yeaaaah, but I'm *pretty* sure I'm not the only one in this room who's up shit creek with a paddle deficiency. You scratch my back. I'll make sure no one stabs yours." She glanced at the clock. "Although we may need to postpone this meeting until tomorrow cos Mum's gonna be home soon, and

I *really* don't feel like she needs to know about any of this."

27

MASKS

Audrey cast her eye across her wardrobe with the careful consideration of a contract killer selecting weaponry, murmuring approvals and condemnations as she swiped through coat hangers. The trick was to partition your personality into masks appropriate to various occasions. She had her maternal mask, her rockstar mask, her work mask, her family and friends mask. Somewhere beneath the collection of finely tuned constructed personalities was what her psych textbooks would call her 'authentic self'—a genuine, unrestrained balance of id and ego.

Audrey applied lipstick, mascara, lash extensions. She sat in front of the computer, ran over her mantras, and listened to the sound of traffic outside. The first meeting was the most difficult and the most important. You had to convince the client that you were infallible, impenetrable, unfathomable. The clock in the corner of her screen ticked over to 10:01 a.m. He was late for their first meeting. Perfect.

The cheerful chirp of the incoming video call rang through her speakers. She let it ring once. Twice. Three times, imagining the caller's mounting anxiety. *'Did I get the date wrong?'* Four times. Five. Six. *'Maybe I shouldn't be doing this?'* Seven. Eight. Nine. *'Pulse pounding, palms sweating.'* Ten. Eleven. Audrey pressed 'accept.'

She scanned the man on her screen, performing a finely practiced aesthetic analysis of clothing, body language, mannerisms. Clay touched his face, cleared his throat. He was dressed in thoroughly unexceptional office drone attire (grey suit, light blue shirt) with the dissonant addition of a bright red pocket square. This suggested perhaps it had been bought for him by someone else—perhaps a daughter or wife—with the intent of detracting from his jejune sartorial choices. He was mildly attractive in the sense of lacking flaws: thick hair, no moles, scars, or excessive wrinkling. Not toned but not flabby either, but this lack of feature only added to his overwhelming ordinariness.

She shifted her assessment to the living room behind him. It was arranged in a carefully constructed minimalist design, suggesting it had been done by someone else, probably a contractor. A large flatscreen TV hung on the wall next to framed Chinese calligraphy (she would bet four figures he didn't know the meaning of the characters). Photos of family and friends were noticeably absent. The bare hooks scattered along the wall suggested he'd removed them before the call; impressive forethought. She wondered if he'd remember to replace them once their meeting was over. Clay cleared his throat and looked at her, desperate for her to speak first. Her mask was stern and vexed, but inside, she was beaming. This was going to be easy. "Um…hello! It's lovely to—"

"Did I *ask* you to speak?" His mouth snapped shut, eyes darting desperately around the room. She let him stew for a minute before continuing. "You're *late*."

"I know! I'm sorry, I had a c-c-conference call with a client in Beijing—"

"You think I *care* about your excuses? Do you know how much my time is worth, how many people I have waiting to see me?"

"Of course, I'm sorry. It won't happen again."

"It certainly won't. You've incurred your first penalty, you disgusting, dull degenerate. I don't do warnings. You will purchase one silver item from the list on your screen, express shipping. I want it at my door by the end of the week."

"Of course. Anything. Um, you're very b-b-beautiful."

She rolled her eyes and spat, "I have a mirror to tell me that, pig. I've only been talking to you for three minutes, and already you make me sick." His face fell, and she felt a twang of guilt. She glanced up at the photo of her girls she kept next to her computer, her head whirring with thoughts of textbooks and school shoes and field trips and doctor's appointments. The guilt continued humming at the back of her brain, its volume temporarily reduced. She snapped her eyes back to the screen.

"This is what's going to happen: you will tell me about yourself. Every weakness. Every dirty secret. Every secret shame and repulsive fantasy. Then, you will outline your income and assets in explicit detail—every dime, penny, and farthing. If you lie, if you leave anything out, I will know, and I will *punish* you. When you've told me everything, I will decide on your weekly offering and explain to you exactly how you will worship me. Do all of this *precisely* as I say, and you might just earn my favour. Is that clear, pig?"

"Yes," he gulped.

"Yes, *what?*"

"Yes, my…ahhhhhh…?"

"Do I have to teach you basic manners? You ignorant, impotent idiot! You may refer to me as queen, goddess, princess. I shall refer to you as whatever the fuck I feel like. Understood?" He nodded fervently. "Very well, begin. Leave out nothing." She waved her hand and sat back.

"I'm in real estate. High-end. Mansions and commercial developments. I work with, ah, Jordan. He recommended your, ah, you. I know real estate is very, um, b-b-boring—"

"A dull job for dull men."

He nodded apologetically and stammered, "Yes! But, you're the first person I've told this to. I've recently joined a very exclusive operation. A secret organisation, actually. Its members are powerful, elite."

"Do you know how many freemasons I have on my client list thinking they're the fucking illuminati simply because they engage in a little nepotism and candlelight circle-jerking?"

"No, not freemasons. We're the real deal. We're going to—ah, we have a client confidentiality agreement right, like with a doctor or lawyer?"

"How *dare* you insult me. You think I don't know how to do my job? I *know* my business. Tell me yours." The truth was that no such confidentiality agreement existed in her trade. It wasn't so much a grey area as a red area. Some of her colleagues kept extensive files of their clients' sensitive secrets to use as a blackmail database, threatening to release them if they ever mentioned the idea of ending their relationship. Audrey had never done anything like this; she had her moral code—even if it was as flexible as a circus contortionist.

"Amrita is the public-facing portion of the company; the inner circle is called the Sixth s-s-Sun. We're film producers and politicians and property developers and, well, there's one guy who's somehow rich from YouTube videos, which I don't understand, but anyway, we're not just wealthy and powerful, our inner circle—I won't get to meet them until after I've done my initiation—holds the secret to *eternal life.*" Audrey felt her stomach tighten, but kept her face impassive. "They run a cryonic centre. They're going to usher in a glorious new age. I'm helping them acquire real estate assets for their investment portfolio, which, I have to tell you, is *staggering.* I mean, I've worked with some big operations before, but nothing like this."

She leaned back, painting her face with a barely perceptible trace of intrigue. She watched his eyes widen with delight. "You have piqued my interest, pig. Perhaps you are *marginally* less pathetic than I thought."

He jolted upright like a child at the promise of ice -cream and continued, "R-really? Oh wow. You are…I adore you."

"The word you are looking for is 'worship.'"

"Yes, I worship you."

She smiled and waved her hand. "Let's get to the fun part. Take off your clothes and get on your hands and knees."

28

VOMITING ON THE ASTRAL PLANE

"Passion. Loyalty. Ambition. These are the qualities that defined Nicholas." Lenore watched the sea of product-laden, side-swept hair nod in agreement. "He was generous in spirit, a gifted musician, a true friend. I can think of no better way to honour his memory than to listen to one of his greatest creations, a song that truly speaks to who he was as an artist and human." The speaker paused, a mischievous grin transmogrifying the landscape of his face. He nodded to someone off-stage. Lenore glanced to see a grinning brogrammer flash a thumbs up. She groaned and buried her head in her hands. This did not bode well.

"Ladies and gentlemen, I give you Young Bedlam's hit jam *Dat Ass Won't Quit (And Neither Will I)*!" The speaker grabbed his air horn from the lectern and blasted it triumphantly into the air. Lenore slapped her hands over her ears as the speakers began blasting an aneurysm-inducing party track that she'd heard in an asinine beer commercial. A cadre of women clad in revealing black dresses emerged carrying shot trays. The bass made the church walls reverberate as the recently departed extolled his manifesto.

I wake up and then I party!
Do I ev-er stop? Hardly!
Ipartytilthedawn and then I party on
you moth-er-fuck-ers cannot stop me!
Lenore's stomach churned with disgust. She'd been to a few of these

FUNerals before, and they inevitably ranged from tacky to appalling. *If humans can't even find the time to be sad at a goddamn funeral anymore, we might as well surgically alter our faces into permanent jokeresque smiles, our thumbs perennially pointed heavenward in praise of get-up-n-go.* She rubbed the ash-diamond on her hand, trying to conceal her irritation. One of the hostesses handed her a shot glass. She was wearing a stripper's smile; superficially, it promised pleasure, leisure, licentiousness, but beneath the surface lurked an ocean of fatigue and irritation. Lenore begrudgingly took the shot glass, then looked at her and asked, "Just out of curiosity, you do a lot of these gigs?"

The hostess leaned in and whispered, "Honestly? I'm getting more of these 'party funeral' gigs every month. Pays as good as pole dancing, and no one grabs my ass. Usually."

The plastic smile returned to her face, and she turned to the man across the aisle from Lenore. Adorned with gaudy gold cufflinks, a numberless watch the size of a beer coaster, and a condescending half-smile, he was the human embodiment of the concept of smarminess. She leaned in and purred, "Hey sweetheart. Shot of vodka? This round's on Nick!"

"Baby doll, I'll take anything you want to give me."

Lenore performed an action she liked to describe as 'vomiting on the astral plane'— the essence of her being expelling a potent expression of revulsion whilst her physical self maintained its composure. She stared at the shot of vodka in her hand. It had been served in appallingly poor taste, given that the recently departed had met his end in a drunk driving accident.

She took out her phone and typed:

> *I'm about to do a vodka shot at 1 p.m. on a Wednesday.*
> *At a funeral.*
> *For money. Guess that's got to be a new low, right?'*

She hit 'send' and tipped the vodka down her throat.

It tasted like liquid misery.

* * *

Darius sat in the make-up chair, eyes closed, and listened to the sound of the other actors flirting with the make-up artists. He tried to push down the image of the blood smeared on the living room floor, but it kept rising back to the surface. It was like trying to force a cork to stay at the bottom of a swimming pool. Ordinarily, this was his favourite part of the day, this transition from who he was to who he might be. He liked to imagine that he was not being made up to appear like a putrefying cadaver but rather a glamorous, masculine lead. He was about to star alongside Natalie Portman, Chris Hemsworth, Samuel L. Jackson. He was about to engage in meaningful artistic dialogues with Martin Scorsese, Darren Aronofsky, Sofia Coppola. He was about to feature on a panel discussing story-telling as a mechanism for revolutionary ideas, or his involvement with a charity sponsoring the creative careers of underprivileged inner-city youth. In these transitional moments he was his former self, his potential self, his aspirational self, his father's projection of himself, his professional self.

He felt the staccato tapping of a manicured talon on his shoulder.

"Darius? Helloooooooo?" his eyes snapped open to be greeted with Ruby's raised eyebrow and coffee-stained teeth. "Oh hey there. What were you dreaming about? Or should I say who?" she giggled.

"Technically you should say whom."

As her face crumpled with irritation he realised he'd aimed for 'playful bantering' but landed on 'condescending grammar prescriptivist.' "Ah, sorry, that was rude. I didn't mean—"

"Whatever dude, ex-*cuse* me for not studying, like, advanced punctuation." She whipped the cloak off his chest and stormed off. Darius examined his reflection. His potential selves had resolved into the same one as always; a failed actor pretending to be the one thing that he would certainly, inevitably, ineluctably become—

a corpse.

29

BONE MUSIC

The clock ticked thunderously on the kitchen wall as Audrey stared out her window, watching the flurry of ordinary people making their home commute. People who worked in jobs with predictable paycheques, retirement funds, staff Christmas parties. Audrey leapt out of her seat and popped the battery out of the clock. The silence was a thick winter blanket. She sighed with relief and leaned her head back against the wall, only to feel it shudder with the calamitous force of her neighbours' hot water system.

Audrey roared with frustration and opened a beer. Footsteps echoed in the stairwell, closely followed by Lenore's signature knock: *tap-tap-tappa-tap-tap*. She opened the door and hugged her. "Hey. How was the funeral?"

"Like a frat party in black." Lenore walked to the fridge and took out a beer.

Audrey handed her the bottle opener and said, "Len, are we going to be putting ourselves in the line of fire here? Because you know I'd take a bullet for you, but only if I can make it home from the hospital in time to make dinner for the girls." There was another knock at the door. Audrey ignored it, staring at Lenore expectantly.

"Aren't you going to answer that? It's probably Darius and Riley."

"Not until you answer my question."

"I'm not going to answer your question until you answer the door."

Audrey groaned, stomped over to the door, and pulled it open. "Hey Riley, hey Darius, how was your day? Get the fuck inside. Your annoying sister is annoying me by being annoying."

Riley ran over to Audrey's record collection and whistled in appreciation. "Niiiiiice collection. I can't believe you own actual, real records. Are you, like, a thousand years old?"

"Lovely to see you too, Riley. You make me positively thrilled about my future as a mother of twin teenage girls."

"Yeah, get ready for that. Imagine the drugs they'll have in ten years' time. Good luck keeping them away from affordable magic euphoria pills with zero side effects." Riley selected a shabbily packaged record from the shelf, pulled it out of its sleeve and grunted with confusion as she inspected two spectral, skeletal hands.

"Be careful with that. It's a collector's item."

"Why do you have X-rays in your record collection?"

Audrey snatched it from Riley and slid it carefully back into its sleeve. "That's a Bill Haley & His Comets album printed on an X-ray. It's called bone music. Rock'n'roll was banned during the 50s in the Soviet Union, so people had to find ways of secretly distributing it. Vinyl was hard to find, but some weird genius figured out you could press directly onto X-rays. This group of people called the *stilyagi* raided hospital bins for discarded X-rays, then printed the songs on and burned cigarette holes in the middle so they could be played on a turntable. It's a testimony to the enduring power of art in the face of oppression."

"Get the fuck out. They took illegal music and printed it on stolen material, and then set up underground distribution? That's badass."

"I'm glad you appreciate it. I picked it up at a record fair a few ye—Hey. Don't smoke in my house."

"Fine. Whatever. I didn't realise this conspiracy meeting would have so many *rules*." She glanced at the bottle in Audrey's hand. "Can I—"

"Absolutely not."

"You are the lamest criminals *ever*." Riley kicked the recliner right back and began tapping at her phone.

Lenore leaned forward and said, "Let's start with what we know. We know what Csaba wants: Riley—"

"But we don't really understand why. I mean, she's pretty annoying."

Riley raised her middle finger at Audrey without looking up from her phone.

"Not helpful, Aud. He wants Riley, he wants to keep Claire's body, he wants money, power, influence. We only have one of those things, and we don't want to give it— her— to him."

"Fuckin-a."

"'Fuckin-a' indeed. So that means we need to find a way of getting leverage."

"I could try and get Kyle to help us?" suggested Darius.

"Look at this guy, name-dropping like an LA socialite."

"I'm not 'dropping' his name. I'm just using it. He could be helpful."

Lenore frowned. "I don't think so. The paparazzi tail him everywhere he goes."

"You catch those pics of him skinny dipping in Costa Rica? Boys got abs for days."

"Riley, do I really need to remind you to stay focused on a meeting whose sole agenda is 'figure out how to stop you from getting kidnapped and/or killed'?"

Riley threw her hands up defensively and gestured for Lenore to continue.

"Our best bet at doing that is by finding out incriminating information and arranging a deal."

"Sooooo…blackmail?" said Darius.

"Investment opportunity," corrected Lenore. "We are giving him the opportunity to invest in a future where he doesn't go to prison. He not so subtly alluded to a range of shady activities in the short time we spoke. His closet must be bursting with skeletons."

"You're assuming he's stupid enough to keep incriminating files just lying around," said Darius.

Audrey grunted and said, "Guys that rich and narcissistic are always stupid enough 'to keep that stuff just lying around.' Nixon. Trump. Madoff."

"So we're gambling on the fact that 1) we can get into his office, or file storage or whatever, 2) that he'll have something incriminating in there 3) that he'll be willing to broker a deal that doesn't end up with all of us wearing cement sneakers 4) we don't get caught in the act—"

"5) Shut up, Riley. Here's what's going to happen: Audrey has set a date for tomorrow night with a Sixth Sun devotee; she's already recorded compromising footage of him—"

"Oh, *sweet!* Get that shit on-screen!" Riley picked up the remote. Audrey snatched it off her.

"To continue: We're going to make him do the legwork, organise a discreet visit when security is on skeleton crew. She'll spike her client's drink, and we'll sneak in, find what we need, and then stop him from talking with the threat of releasing the—could you please stop *texting*? You really aren't doing much for the stereotyping of your generation you know? Keeping you focused is a Sisyphean task."

Riley groaned and rolled her eyes with near audible force, "Did you say something about syphilis? Don't sweat it girl. I think they have a cream for that these days. Happens to the best of us."

Lenore shot Darius a look of desperation. "Don't look at me. You're the one who brought off-meds Lindsay Lohan to the meeting."

Riley flicked open her switchblade and pointed it at his nose. "Call me Lindsay Lohan one more time, see what happens."

"Hey! I am instituting a firm 'stop pointing knives at Darius' policy!" barked Audrey in her well-practiced, angry mother voice.

Riley flicked the knife closed and said, "Fine. But only because I have a general policy of listening to angry statuesque boss bitches."

"Well, fuck you for being rude. But also, thank you for the compliment."

"Just telling it like it is, Gigantra. So, are we gonna get our hands on some military hardware? Tech-9s, IUDs, that kinda shit?"

"IUDs are contraceptive devices. IEDs are explosive devices. *Seriously,* not something you want to mix up."

Lenore slammed her hand on the table and yelled, "ENOUGH! We are about to do something very dangerous and highly illegal. If you could stop arguing like a pack of irascible teenagers—no offense, Riley—that would be great."

"I'm not irascible, you're irascible!" she murmured irascibly.

They stared at the carpet in silence for a moment. Lenore took a deep breath and said, "Okay. I'm…sorry for yelling. It's been a very surreal few days. Let's try this again."

* * *

Audrey slipped on her gloves as her computer began bleeping, the incoming call alert flashing on her screen. "Shitshitshitshit…" She checked the camera was positioned properly, tied her hair back, rolled her neck, and accepted the call.

"Hello, my queen!" Clay yelped excitedly.

She treated him to a sultry smile and blew him a kiss. He made an odd, ecstatic giggling sound. "You have *pleased* me, slave. If you continue to please me, I may number you amongst my favourites. Would you like that, you pathetic piece of excessively effusive effluvium?"

"Yes, my queen! Very much! Ah, I don't mean to be rude, but…"

"Spit it out, scum!"

"You have s-s-something on your cheek. Toothpaste, I think?"

She swore internally, turned away from the camera, snatched a tissue, and wiped her face in one fluid motion. She turned back to the camera, lit with anger. "You disgusting pig! How dare you lie to me. I am perfect, infallible, faultless!"

"Of course. I, ah, I was mistaken. Must have been some d-d-dust on my screen. A thousand apologies, oh, um, most divine and delicious one. She who makes my heart sing and my loins as warm as summer sand—"

"I suggest you shut your weird little mouth-hole, slave. As I was saying. You have pleased me. And I promised that if you completed your little task to my satisfaction, I would reward you. The reward is this: I would like to meet you, in person." The colour drained from his face, and a squeal of delight escaped his throat. "This is a rare and priceless honour, do you understand that?"

"Y-y-yes, my mistress."

"Very good. Now, if you wish for me to bestow this precious gift upon you, you will need to prove that you are worthy. Prove that you can show me something all my other pathetic little grovellers cannot. Take me somewhere that they cannot give me access to. Do you think you can do that?"

"Y-you mean like one of my properties? There is a spectacular beachfront mansion I've just agreed to handle. Or if you prefer a penthouse, I know one with a rooftop—"

"I don't want to set foot inside your gauche, opulent McMansions. I want somewhere as unusual and magnificent as I am. Somewhere secret, somewhere special—"

"Oh, you mean? Ah, I'm s-s-sorry, but I don't think that I can..."

She fixed him with a furious glare, pushed down the guilt that welled up when she saw the disappointment in his face. "I thought as much. This session is now over. I may choose to—"

"No, wait. I can...I think I can do it. Ah...you promise that we can, that I can see you in person?"

She leaned in close to the camera so that her lips filled the screen and said slowly. "You. Can. Touch. Me."

He gulped, nodded, sweat pouring down his reddening face. "Let me make some calls."

30

FAMOUS LAST WORDS

The Amrita cryonics centre sat large and imposing against the horizon, a sentinel of glass and steel squatting beneath the black blanket of the sky. Darius drummed his fingers on the dashboard, murmuring to himself. Lenore glanced at his fingers, checked her phone. Riley flicked her knife open and shut. Lenore's hand darted out and stilled Darius's hand. He rolled his eyes and said, "Calm down. Audrey knows how to look after herself."

"We don't know who's in there. What if that dwarf with the razor—"

"Would you call him a dwarf? I mean, he has a beard, and he's fairly small, but I'm not sure if he'd qualify as a dwarf. Also, isn't that considered an offensive term these days?"

"You guys always this boring when you argue?" asked Riley, spinning the closed knife around in her fingers. "You really oughta have weapons, you know. I mean, shit, at least get a baseball bat or something."

"I'm a pacifist," said Darius.

Riley snorted a laugh, "Famous last words."

"No one will be doing any stabbing or bashing or slashing." barked Lenore. "We are going to be like ninjas. In regards to the silence, at least. Not so much the 'highly skilled warrior' part."

"Speak for yourself. I'm about ready for some action."

"You can't solve all your problems with violence, Riley."

176

"Oh yeah? Tell that to all my dead problems." Even after all this time with her, Riley's sandpaper and helium voice was still unfathomably eerie, especially when she said things like that. "You been back to the house today?"

"I swung by to check no one had burned it down. Honestly, though, I couldn't even bring myself to make it through the front door. It creeps me—" Lenore's phone buzzed.

Two guards on a circular patrol. Seen them twice in twenty minutes.

I'm in the bathroom. I'll send this guy to sleep and come and hit the door release in about ten minutes.

"We good to go?" asked Riley.

"Ten minutes."

"Arggggggh! That is nine minutes too long. Let's play a game or something. Two lies, one truth? Or what about Chinese whispers?" Darius and Lenore groaned. "What. Did I—oh, I guess that one's kind of a shitty name, huh?"

"Pretty much. Riley, what does your mum think you're doing tonight?" asked Darius.

"Studying for a chemistry exam. Which, you know, we're at a cryo lab. So that's... sciencey."

"You probably want to avoid the word 'sciencey' in that exam tomorrow."

Riley shrugged. "Okay, two lies, one truth it is. I'll go first. I once found a syringe in the local swimming pool, I once made out with a guy who had a peanut allergy, and I'd been eating a peanut butter sandwich earlier that day, and I gave him anaphylactic shock, and my real dad was apparently involved in some kind of weird cryonic undeath cult."

* * *

Audrey's two-inch heels echoed cavernously across the cement floor as she strolled past the allegedly hibernating bodies, row after row of serene, frozen faces. Their eyes were all beatifically closed, condensation collecting on their lips and eyelashes. Audrey's heart clenched as she saw two twin girls lying side by side in eternal slumber. She tried not to let her mask slip, but she noticed Clay staring at her. She snapped back into character and glared at him, "Don't stare at me like some pathetic, pandering puppy!" He mumbled an obsequious apology. She snapped her riding crop against the back of his knees. "Stand up straight! Are you a man or a mouse?"

"S-s-sorry, oh she who makes dark roses blossom in winter moonlight."

Audrey fought back the urge to laugh by biting her lip and snapping the crop against the side of her thigh and then swept it in a wide arc around the room as she said, "Worm, you have impressed me." The words hit him as though he'd been struck by linguistic bullets. His body convulsed, and a garbled yelp of glee escaped his lips. She smiled, nodded at the bag carrying the wine and glasses he'd brought, as per her instructions. She leaned in close and whispered, "Take me somewhere private." She pitied him a little, as she watched him melt and tremble over the slightest hint of physical contact. Perhaps one day he'd find a nice girl and worship her on a non-mercantile basis. Maybe he'd be a good father, raise sons who would treat women with respect and adoration. Then again, maybe he was just another weird, spineless pervert.

They walked past the cryonic chambers—he'd told her the technical term was 'dewars'—and towards the elevator. "There's a meeting room. I, uh, had to grease a few palms to get the access pass, but I think you'll be impressed."

"I had *better* be."

The elevator doors pinged open to reveal two hirsute men of wildly varying stature. Audrey had glimpsed them earlier from the entry mezzanine. The shorter of the two was dressed in a tight-fitting black suit, his companion clad in standard security guard attire. Clay nodded at them both, shook their hands in turn.

"You Clay? I'm Ocky." Audrey's pulse increased to dubstep speed. "Welcome to the club, squire. You got your entry fee?" He nodded and handed him an envelope. Ocky opened it, flipped through the notes inside. "Righto, we're good here. We'll make sure there's a 'glitch' in the video footage. But if you break anything, take anything, or—" he stopped and examined Audrey with a long, lascivious leer, "—leave any kind of fucken mess, there will be consequences of a highly corporeal nature. Carry on, young lovers." He slapped Clay on the back so hard he almost fell over.

They exited the elevator as Audrey and Clay entered. She heaved a sigh of relief as the doors closed, wondering how Ocky would feel if he knew that Clay had recently cleaned up his blood whilst dressed in tight leather hot pants. She examined the elevator buttons. They'd entered on the ground level and were currently leaving B1, but beneath this was listed 'B2', alongside which was a magnetic security card reader.

Clay shrugged. "Ah, a thousand humble apologies, oh she who—"

"Spit it out." She froze. The events of the last few days had left her shaken. This was one of the few times she'd broken character since her very first weeks on the job. Confusion swam in Clay's eyes; she brought herself up to her full imposing height and placed her gloved hand against his cheek, the lace and leather returned to her voice. "It would make me very, very happy if you would tell me." She held his eyes with her hypnotic glare.

The doors pinged open as he gulped and said, "Ah, yes. I would, but sadly…I'm a new initiate, and so, they, ah, haven't told me. Even g-g-getting in here tonight was very difficult. I mean, if we get caught, ah…well, you heard what the security guard said."

She glared at him and seethed, "You have disappointed me, you miserable, maladroit mole!" the architecture of his face collapsed into a dejected ruin. She snatched at the wine, twisted the top open, skulled a mouthful, then said, "So why don't we go into the meeting room so you can make it up to me?"

He nodded, the grin on his face so wide it threatened to engulf his ears.

* * *

Lenore's phone buzzed. She checked the message and said. "Okay. He's passed out. She's coming to meet us. Small problem though; Ocky's there."

Darius gasped. Riley grinned and said, "So what's the problem?"

"Come on, Riley, I know you've undergone 'fear castration'—" said Darius.

"That is fuckin' offensive. Although, to be fair, it's also kinda funny."

"—but the rest of us losers have to deal with the rather encumbering fear of death. Besides, you must still be worried about pain and dismemberment on a logical level, right?"

"Yes, I am *logically* aware that getting sliced up by a bearded dwarf is not exactly an ideal scenario. But 100% of the times I've met this dude, I left him bleeding. How's *that* for logic?"

"Terrible," said Lenore. "A sample size of one is vastly inadequate for any kind of accurate data collection—"

"Can you save that for tomorrow morning when I need you to help me cram for this chem test? Anyways, back to my plan. I'm gonna run up in there and in the immortal words of Beyoncé, 'I'mma fuck me up a bitch' while you guys go and get all Nancy Drew."

"That's not the plan!" protested Lenore.

Riley grinned maniacally, opened both the door and her switchblade, and said, "Wait for my signal."

"What's your signal?" called Darius, and she ran out the door.

"I'll come running out of the building with a couple of security guards trying to kill me." She tore off down the road towards the facility at dizzying speed, her sneakers flashing in the moonlight. Darius and Lenore shared a fleeting, confused glance and then followed her.

In the distance, a delivery truck approached, its driver's brain illuminated like a pinball machine as the amphetamines he'd snorted stimulated his synapses into high gear. The cryonics centre always caught his eye when he passed this way. He noted a rust-red Toyota parked a little way up the road. He stared at it, wondering if someone had broken down, then watched in bemusement as a skinny figure emerged from the boot. Even from a distance, he could see his clothes were ragged, and his skin was eerily pale. The driver's drug-addled brain sparkled and spun with theories and fantasies until he was snapped back into focus by the blaring horn of an oncoming car into whose lane he'd drifted. He yanked at the wheel and watched the strange pale figure disappear into the distance of his rearview mirror.

31

BLOOD

Ocky's not-so-dearly-departed father would've described recent events as 'a buffet of shit and shenanigans.' He'd been inhaling military-grade painkillers ever since the episode at the Brindle house. The drugs were inducing a heady mix of nausea, dizziness, and nostalgia. After both his pride and his lower side had been severely injured by the very girl he'd been searching for, he'd had to invent an elaborate deception to tell Csaba. Failing to capture Riley via mere incompetence would've most likely resulted in his death (he knew this with some authority, given that he'd often played the role of executioner in many a similar scenario).

Csaba had listened calmly to his story about some routine debt collecting gone awry and thus postponing his pursuit of the girl who was not supposed to exist, but Ocky was not convinced that he'd been utterly convincing. Ocky scratched at the stress hives on his wrist as he ran some mental calculations, numbers jumping and whirring in his head as he paced down the hallway. The bribe he'd managed to pick up from allowing the new initiate to give his escort a private tour of the facility would let him pay off the car repairs and the electricity bill, but he still had his family health insurance to pay off and—due to his extensive list of occupational hazards—his premiums were heinously expensive. On top of all this, he'd had to hire a tutor to help his son with his math homework, some snot-nosed undergrad who fancied himself worth thirty dollars an hour. People liked to call math 'the universal language,' but it was one in which Ocky was barely conversant. He was infinitely more fluent in the language of pain, which he argued was far more widely understood. He rolled his neck and shoulders; a series of cracks shuddered through his body. He couldn't keep doing this kind of work forever, and his retirement fund was a far cry from ready. Most of all, the thought of his kids ending up in the criminal arts was not something he wanted to entertain.

"Hey, what do you think of my new tattoo?" asked Haberschmidt, with the chirpy excitement of a first grader during show-and-tell. He pulled back his sleeve to reveal the word 'Becky' written in lurid graff font.

"To fuckin start with, I think the same thing about your tattoo as I do about all tattoos for guys in our line of work: Not a good idea. We're working for a sub-legal inner circle of a corporation with all kinds of skeletons in its closet: big ones, skinny ones, ridiculously tall ones that don't have the courtesy to fit neatly inside a standard-size body bag, making disposal exceedingly fuckin' onerous ones. I use a nickname for a reason. You want to make yourself harder to track, not draw a bunch of dots for the pigs to connect. You know, the first thing they ask witnesses at the scene of a crime? 'Did the perpetrator have any distinguishing features such as *tattoos?*' Secondly, you've not only elected to add a distinguishing feature, you've emblazoned the name of your, what, girlfriend?"

"Fiancée."

"Mazel tov. So now they've got an identifying feature *and* a name. A nice, searchable, indexable, cross-referenceable name."

"Well, technically, her name's Rebecca, so…"

Ocky glowered at him; his mouth snapped audibly shut. "One more piece of advice: while I'm doling it out like candy, a sub-dermal emblazoning of yer beloved's name ain't the smartest thing to do until the deal's locked down. If you ain't exchanged rings, don't make with the ink."

"Hey. Becky and I are—"

"Look, I been married. Twice. And I thought the same thing both times. I get it; love's an adventure and all that. But I woulda taken a bullet dipped in bleach for Vanessa and Anoushka, during the various durations of our romantic entanglements. And you know where they are now?"

"No?"

"Me either. And that's exactly the fuckin' moral, point, and precept."

"I had no idea."

"Not the first time those words have left your mouth, I'd wager." Haberschmidt raised a tentative hand in a slow arc towards Ocky's shoulder. "Don't."

His hand dropped. He coughed and rolled his sleeve back up. They paced down the hall in silence. The banging on the glass echoed through the empty foyer.

Ocky jerked his head at the elevator and trotted towards it, Haberschmidt trailing behind him.

"Who the hell do you think that is?" Haberschmidt asked as the elevator moaned its ascent.

"Something that's about to get its fuckin' head kicked in, I presume," Ocky answered, trotting down the hall, flicked his razor open. Haberschmidt followed him, staring at the flashing blade. "Got something you wanna say?"

"No, I mean, it's just…why don't you carry a gun?"

"I do carry a gun."

"But why don't you *only* carry a gun?"

Ocky glared at him, decided the question didn't warrant a response, turned the corner, and then stopped dead in his tracks.

"Woah. What's wrong with her face?" said Haberschmidt, staring at the girl grinning and waving in the window.

"She's mine. Do you understand? Do not shoot her. Do not touch her. You back me up, follow my lead. We clear?"

Haberschmidt said nothing as he watched the lizard-skinned girl tap at the imaginary watch on her wrist, then inexplicably burst into a maladroit hip-hop dance routine.

"Stand by the door release. Wait til I tell you to open it."

"I'm waaaaaitiiiiiing!" the girl yelled. Her voice was coarse and freakishly high-pitched.

Ocky stepped to the other side of the glass and stood opposite the lizard-skinned girl, twirling the razor in his hand. She breathed fog onto the glass and drew a smiley face, flashed him a thumbs up.

"Is she on drugs or something?" asked Haberschmidt.

"No. Open the door on three."

"I mean, couldn't we just leave it locked? It's not like she's trying to break in or anything?"

"One."

"Hey, Ocky, come on, man, she's an unarmed teenage girl."

"Two."

"Listen, I don't want to overstep here—"

"So don't. Three."

The lizard-skinned girl brought her nose to the glass. Ocky lifted his blade up. Haberschmidt stared at the fat green button. He felt Ocky's eyes on him.

He looked at the girl.

At the blade.

At the button.

The doors slid open with a mechanical yawn. The girl turned and took off across the carpark, whooping gleefully. Her sneakers slapped the pavement as she laughed and taunted. Ocky ran after her. Haberschmidt tried to keep up, but Ocky pounced on her while he was still trailing. He proceeded to pin her arms behind her back as she let cry a stream of verbose vociferation. Ocky held his razor to the girl's neck.

"Ocky! Ease up; she's just a—" Haberschmidt was interrupted by the arrival of an eerily pale young man who ran towards his partner with a warbling noise that may have been either a faltering battle cry or a pre-emptive wail of defeat. He leapt at Ocky, his pallid, slender frame soaring through the air like he'd been thrown from a trebuchet. Ocky swung his razor in a wide arc, cutting his attacker in the same instant he was tackled to the ground. Riley cackled with delight as she jumped up and ran full-tilt in Haberschmidt's direction. "S-stop! Don't make me shoot you!" he yelled.

She ignored him, a freakish grin consuming the lower portion of her face.

He fired off a couple of warning shots. She didn't even flinch. He may as well have started juggling for all the good it did him. For the rest of his days, Haberschmidt would label this moment as the most terrifying of his entire life: watching a teenage girl stampeding toward him, utterly unphased by the threat of mortal injury, leaping into the air, hands outstretched as she screamed, her eyes lit with joy and bloodlust.

* * *

Lenore watched in horror as Riley bolted across the parking lot, her ragged red Converse slapping the asphalt with meth-head staccato taps, Ocky racing after her. A second security guard ran out the sliding glass doors after them both. Once they were at a safe distance, Lenore slapped at her brother and yanked him towards the entrance.

"What about Riley?"

"We'll have to trust that she can handle herself."

"What if she can't?"

"I'll try and withstand the urge to say 'I told you so' to her limp, dead corpse."

Audrey waved at them from behind the glass doors, then pushed the release button, allowing their entry. "Where's Riley?"

"Running interference."

"What? Why would you let the person we are trying to protect be bait?"

"I didn't 'let' her do anything. Find anything interesting?"

"Not yet. Meeting room's through here." She led them through a heavy oak door. Clay was laid out on the meeting room table with his legs akimbo and his consciousness in limbo.

"You sure he's out?" asked Darius.

Audrey picked up his hand and flopped it around, and said in a high-pitched cartoon voice, *"Hiiiiiiiiii, Darius! This is me proving how unconscious I am!"*

"Can we please stop ventriloquising the insensate?" chided Lenore. "We should split up and search other areas. Anywhere else you think they might

185

be hiding the juicy stuff?"

"There's a lower level that he doesn't have access to. I think if we can get in there—"

Two shots cut through the air. They froze and stared at each other. "What kind of security guard opens fire on an unarmed girl?" asked Darius.

"Might've been the girl who did the firing," said Lenore.

"We have to call an ambulance. Even if it is for the security guard. I'd rather not be responsible for some minimum-wage muscle bleeding out in a parking lot."

"The longer we stand here arguing, the closer someone gets to a grave."

Darius and Audrey looked at Lenore, waiting for a decision. She glanced down from the mezzanine's railing at the rows of silver canisters below, each of them filled with a body attempting to cheat the fundamental rules of existence with an underhanded barrage of chemicals, cryonics, and cash. She scanned the slew of faces: Old men. Young women. Dark skin. Light skin. Bodies of every colour, creed, and gender railing against the one thing that truly united them. She imagined Quan lying in peaceful repose alongside the bodies stacked like supermarket soft drink cans. She felt nauseous, the floor began undulating beneath her boots. Time trickled like treacle.

"Len! We're running out of time," Audrey snapped. Clay murmured something unintelligible, slapped his face with a clumsy, half-dead hand.

"Sorry. I thought…ah, what should we do?" They looked at each other, lit up with fear and confusion. The glass doors slid open as Riley charged into the foyer, covered in dirt and blood. "Whattup noobs. Got you a present." She tossed Lenore a security pass. "Let's go shopping!" She ran to the elevator, waving them in.

Audrey leaned into Lenore and whispered, "I know she can't feel fear, but is she also incapable of feeling empathy?"

Lenore examined Riley, casually wiping the flecks of crimson from her face with the back of her sleeve. "I'd say that is distinctly within the realm of possibility, yes. Let's try and not piss her off." They ran into the elevator.

Audrey turned to Riley and asked, "What happened to the guards?"

"A lady never brags about her conquests," Riley flipped her hair in imitation of a shampoo commercial model.

Lenore tapped the security pass against the scanner and hit B2. It beeped angrily at her, and the elevator remained obstinately still. She swiped again, another angry bleep.

"Here, let me try," said Darius, snatching it from her.

"Sure, it must be my technique. I obviously wasn't slapping a magnetic strip against a reader with the correct amount of *finesse.* Please, show us how it's done."

Darius glared at her, turned the pass over in his hands a few times and placed it gently against the reader. Lenore didn't bother to mask her satisfaction when it responded with an identically irate bleep. "I don't get it. Why would a security guard not have clearance for the place they're supposed to be securing?"

"Oh, I forgot to tell you! Your boy Orin showed up," said Riley.

"What?"

"Yeah, credit where it's due. He helped some. Ocky had me pinned at one point, and ghostface pulled him right offa me. I grabbed the blade and manage to tag him in the leg. But the other guy popped off a couple of shots before I managed to grab his gun. Orin helped gaffer tape 'em up."

"Where is he now?"

"Said he'd wait back at the car. He got roughed up pretty bad, wanted a breather—"

"Who the hell is Orin?" asked Darius.

"—he was bleeding some, but he said not to worry, something about being 'impervious to the blades of mortal men' or some shit. That boy is crazy."

"Who is Orin?" yelled Audrey and Darius simultaneously.

"The person I have to get to a hospital before he dies. Again." Lenore ducked out of the elevator and ran towards the entrance.

Riley threw her hands up in frustration and said, "He said he'd be fine. He was *barely* bleeding."

Audrey took three long strides towards Lenore, grabbed her shoulder, and said, "I hired a wildly overpriced babysitter, then drugged and blackmailed a client to get us in here tonight. I could end up in prison for this. Or a coffin. So if you're telling me we have to abandon ship and walk out of here empty-handed, I am going to need you to tell me: Who. Is. Orin?"

Lenore looked at her friend, then out at the velvet-black abyss of the night sky. "I'll tell you on the way to the hospital."

32

DEAD STARS

The halogen light buzzed with a low, unsteady whine. Much like many of the nearby patients, it flickered sporadically between on and off. Lenore glared at it, willing it into steady silence. Across from her, a young mother—hair frizzled, black bags blossoming beneath weary eyes—fidgeted with the mass of jewellery adorning her fingers as her daughter slept in her lap. The television was playing an ad for funeral insurance, which seemed unaccountably cruel given the setting. Lenore leaned back and took out her phone.

I'm waiting at the hospital to hear news about a recent acquaintance who got stabbed whilst trying to help me break into a cryonic facility.

As you do.

She hit send. The TV was now showing an interview with a politician who had some months earlier advocated the bombing of Syria and was now making countless TV appearances condemning the recent 'unanticipated' influx of Syrian refugees.

"Mrs. Lyn?" The doctor was a middle-aged man with a neatly trimmed beard and horn-rimmed glasses that consumed the bulk of his face.

She stood up, and he greeted her with a professional smile and a firm handshake. "It's 'Ms.'"

"My apologies. I'm Darren Landy. Pleased to meet you."

"I thought doctors always introduced themselves as 'Dr Suchandsuch.'"

"Only on TV. Or, occasionally, if they're pretentious young pricks. Not naming any names." He tilted his head towards a lanky junior doctor who was now pummelling the young mother with a barrage of medical jargon and flamboyant hand gestures.

"Duly noted. Is Orin going to be okay?"

Darren cleared his throat in the way that people often do when they're considering the best way to be professionally euphemistic. "Have you known him for long?"

She shook her head. "We only met recently. He told me he was dead—ah, dead keen. On the band. At the gig we were attending. We met at a gig. In a bar."

"I see. Would you have the contact details for someone in his family who might be able to—"

"His family severed ties. It's complicated. I don't think he has anyone else."

"Very well, I should mention that you'll want to file a police report in regards to his assault. Do you know who the assailant was?"

"Random drunk pub pugilist."

"Yes, well, I'm afraid that's an all too common story. If you ask at the admin desk, they'll guide you through the process of contacting the police and reporting. As for his ailments, there's a lot we're going to need to work through, but let's start with the good news. Physically, there's nothing life-threatening, although there's going to be permanent cosmetic damage. The gash was quite deep. We've stitched it up, but it's going to leave a prominent scar. He'll need physical therapy for the damage done to his legs and back, and there's a good chance there will be long-term consequences. He'll be lucky if a limp is the worst of it, and pain management is going to be an issue for at least the next few months. The cut on his hand is infected. We'll need to treat that with antibiotics. He's also severely malnourished. I don't think he's been eating much at all from the looks of things, there's also some hygiene-related skin issues, nothing chronic. I realise that's a lot of information to digest. But hopefully, Oliver will be—"

"Orin."

"Pardon?"

"His name is Orin."

Darren frowned, checked his chart, and said, "Oliver Struckel, twenty-nine years old, admitted with a cut to the face and repeated blows to the back and legs."

"Yes, but—"

"Your friend's name is Oliver. He's going to need more assessment from our psychiatric wing, but my initial diagnosis is that he's suffering from a condition called Cotard Delusion, also known as Walking Corpse Syndrome. Basically, the patient believes themselves to be deceased. It's quite rare, certainly, the first time I've come across it in my career. Might explain his decision to use a different name. It appears he had a mental breakdown after his failed suicide a few weeks ago. He was actually admitted here after that attempt, but he managed to slip out before we could properly treat him, and no one's been able to locate him since."

"You're saying he's crazy?"

"Not the term I'd use. He's experiencing a prolonged psychotic episode."

"So he's not a scion of death," she murmured to herself.

Darren laughed and said, "No signs of actual death, no."

"Can I see him?"

"He's asleep right now. We'll need to keep him for observation for a few days, at least. But you're welcome to visit him tomorrow. We'll have to organise care for him once he's released, do—"

"I'm so sorry, but I'm unbelievably tired. It's been a rough...existence thus far. Could we talk about this tomorrow?"

He nodded. She thanked him again, turned, and walked outside. The doors slid open. The thick, humid summer air slapped her skin. Outside, a woman sat with her head buried in her hands, sobbing. Lenore approached, stopped a few feet behind her. Her brain lit up with her professional arsenal: clusters of clichés, quivers of quotes, platters of platitudes. She discarded them, walked over, and placed her hand gently on the woman's shoulder. She snapped up and stared at her in surprise, tears running in twin salty streams down her cheeks.

"Hey. Fucking sucks, doesn't it?"

The woman's face shimmered from confused to offended to relieved before finally setting on amused. She laughed, tears spilling into her mouth, and gripped her hand. "Yeah. It really fucking sucks."

Lenore placed a hand on her shoulder; the woman held it for a moment. Her skin was clammy with sweat. Lenore offered a sympathetic smile. Waved goodbye. Stepped into a cab. She watched the woman wipe at her tears and gaze up at the night sky, staring at a sea of tiny points of light. So many of them were the mere memories of stars, hurtling through the cold vacuum of space at incredible speeds over incomprehensible distances, finally arriving millions of years later in the tired, weeping eyes of a woman mourning the impending death of someone she loved, unaware the stars themselves were as dead as her lover soon would be.

33

THE NEXT AND FINAL APOCALYPSE

"Gaze upon the instrument of your death, villain!"

The gunman's adversary stared at the revolver, removed his own weapon, and replied, "I have rendered death impotent! Savour this moment. It will be your las—"

The sneeze echoed through the field, implausibly loud. A hundred heads snapped to stare in its direction. From amongst the pile of putrefying bodies, a single hand rose in awkward apology.

"Sorry everyone…" Darius reeled from the force of hundreds of eyes blasting him with lasers of loathing. "I got some dust in my nose."

For the next three seconds of icy, impenetrable silence, Darius wished he were actually dead rather than failing to achieve the illusion of being so. "Well, that's as good a time as any to go get lunch. Let's try it again in an hour. Wrap it up!" Jason pulled off his headphones and walked off to his trailer. Darius felt a knee clip him in the back of the head as the pile of bodies slowly transformed into a crowd of hungry background actors. He couldn't be sure if this was intentional, but in his current mood, it made sense to assume this was the case.

He looked up to see Kyle leaning over him, hand extended. "Wanna get lunch?"

"Sure, I feel like I am a stomach with limbs and a head at this point. But you really don't have to keep slumming it with me. I'm sure the actual cast is keen to share a meal with you. I mean, Stella is always making eyes at you."

"Nah, man, I'm not slumming. Shit, you're so down on yourself. Besides, Stella's *super* gay. She wants to keep it on the DL until she gets nominated for an award and then come out of the closet so that if she doesn't win, she can claim it was because of discrimination. It was her agent's idea."

"Doesn't that kind of exploitative behaviour undermine the LGBTQI community's ongoing struggle for equality?"

"Dunno, probs. Anyway, you like Mexican? Because I had the chef cook some up." He pushed his trailer door open. The smell of salsa and tacos struck Darius's nose like an olfactory sledgehammer.

"Oh god. I think I just had a foodgasm."

Kyle laughed and slapped him on the back. "See? This is why I like hanging with you. You're so fuckin' *weird*. Oh, man, check it. He made the special guacamole. This stuff is better than cocaine."

Darius sat down and began piling up a plate, trying to ignore Nero's creepy reptilian stare boring into him from behind the glass of his two-foot tank. "You look kinda tired. Everything okay?"

"Huh? Yeah. I was up late last night. At a gig."

"Who'd you see?"

"Ah, this band called the…Failed Escapades. They weren't great. Had a lot of technical issues. I left early."

"I can't remember the last time I went to a gig that wasn't at my agent's bidding. He's always telling me to go network at some concert for a lame DJ with Dragon Ball hair or a tween actress releasing a pop single to 'expand her personal brand.' I should come with you some time, check out some real musicians."

"Wouldn't you get mobbed with people bugging you for autographs and photographs and locks of hair?"

Kyle sucked salsa from his fingers and said, "Nah. I've got a get-up: fake beard, wig, baseball cap, big glasses. I'm good to go."

Darius glanced over at Nero, the allegedly three-eyed lizard was indolently masticating on a grasshopper. "Hey, listen, I gotta get your opinion on something. I talked to my agent, but sometimes I feel like I can't trust him.

I mean, he talked me into doing *Death Glove 5*, not to mention that yum-e-snax commercial with the dancing centipedes, soooooo embarrassing. Although I did use 90% of the cash from that commercial to pay for funding vaccine research…or maybe it was awareness of the dangers of vaccines? Something to do with vaccines anyway."

"You should probably check which—"

"But no one ever talks about that, do they? So, I'd really appreciate a normo's opinion. Someone who's not involved in the industry."

"I am involved in the industry?"

"Well, yeah, but not like, 'guest list to Daniel Day-Lewis's secret sex parties' involved."

"Daniel Day-Lewis's secret what?"

Kyle ignored his query and sighed dramatically, hurled a paper napkin into the bin. "Sometimes I feel like this acting business is all so *pretend* you know?"

Darius laughed and then immediately transferred this outburst into a fit of coughing when Kyle regarded him with a confused expression. He loaded up another taco and said, "Sorry, I was thinking about…" his eyes darted around the room, landed on Nero. "What Nero would say if he could talk."

"Man, that'd be funny as hell. He'd be all like, 'oh, look at me! I'm two hundred years old and look like a lizard, but I'm not a lizard.'" Nero eyed them both with ancient reptilian contempt before scuttling into his plastic cave. Kyle propped his tablet open and said, "Anyways, watch the whole thing before you make a judgment, okay?"

The clip showed a room illuminated by the flickering light of dozens of gigantic black candles. A low droning began, slow and ominous. At first, it appeared to be coming from some hidden speaker, but when the hooded figures entered, it became clear that it was a ritual chant. The camera shifted to focus on a large stone table with a man in his late fifties clad in bright white robes. At first, he appeared to be dead, but tiny twitches revealed he had not yet left this mortal coil. The hooded figures gathered around him, and their dirge changed pitch. One of them held out an elaborate chalice, and the man in white sat up. He took the chalice and looked at the hooded figures. They raised their hands and chanted,

"Tu-a-ta-ra! Tu-a-ta-ra!" he examined the contents of the chalice, looked up at them, then became suddenly stricken with panic. He tried to pass the chalice back, swung his legs over the side of the table. One of the figures grabbed him, whispered something in his ear. He nodded, and his body slumped with resignation. He sat back on the table and murmured, "Death shall have no dominion."

The others chanted back, "Death shall have no dom-in-i-on! Death shall have no dom-in-i-on!" The man in white drained the chalice, raised his hands in supplication, and yelled

"I sleep, but shall awaken!"

"He shall a-wake-n!" The hooded figures chanted, exultant. The cup was taken from his hands, and he slumped into unconsciousness. He disappeared from view for a moment as the hooded figures swarmed over him like ants on a corpse. When they pulled back, he was loaded onto a trolley bed. The camera followed him as he was wheeled towards a silver cylinder and lifted inside. The door closed neatly shut.

The chants of 'He shall a-wake-n!' repeated and repeated, gaining in both volume and intensity, transforming into canonical patterns, swirling and eddying around each other, the syllables consuming and birthing one another in ceaseless cycles, ourobouric chains of sound and supplication.

The screen went black. Darius looked at Kyle, unsure of what to say. "So, like, it's kind of weird, huh?" he offered.

"It's 'kind of weird' in the same sense the Marquis de Sade was 'kind of kinky'. Where exactly did you get this from?"

"You know that whole thing I told you about how I was going to live forever?" He mentioned this as though he was recalling a discussion about a new diet or favourite vacation spot. Darius nodded, and he continued, "Well, okay, so I thought it was going to be a science thing, you know? Like, once upon a time, people thought diseases were because of an imbalance in your fluids, right? So, 'oh, no, you're sick, better get some of that pesky blood out of you.' Then we figured out it was all about germs, viruses, etc. So, hello penicillin, goodbye influenza. And *that's* what I thought I was signing on to.

Not this weird cloak and hammer stuff."

"It's 'cloak and dagger.'"

"Yeah, that. Anyway, everyone's talking about the Sixth Sun."

"Really? I only heard of them recently."

"Oh, ah, I meant everyone who's a, you know…"

"Richo?"

"Yeah. When they told me about this cryonics thing, I thought I was signing up for the equivalent of penicillin for death. But it turns out they're more into the rituals and chanting. The name 'Sixth Sun' comes from the Maya. I looked it up, apparently, they believed every age—each with a new sun—had its own apocalypse; fire, floods. There was one with jaguars, apparently? The Sixth Sun supposedly begins after the next and final apocalypse. Everyone who signs up gets reborn and runs around in paradise after the great unwashed are all wiped out."

"The great unwashed being the 'normos.'"

"I guess they weren't too specific about that bit. I'm getting cold feet about the whole thing, but I've already agreed to waive my fee for this project and paid a huge deposit, I had to sell my house! Well, one of my houses. The one in Oakland. Can't remember if it was the place in Oakland, California, or Oakland, Florida. Somewhere sunny, anyway. I think Csaba and these Sixth Sun people want me to be the Tom Cruise to their Scientology. They want me to officiate some big important ceremony they've got coming up, but I hate giving speeches! I don't know if you heard about it, but I announced last year's Oscar for 'Best Lighting and Sound' as 'best *lightning* and sound.'"

"No, I didn't hear about that," Darius lied. *Everyone* heard about it. #bestlightning had been a trending hashtag for days.

"I don't know what to do. Csaba keeps telling me how great I'll be, says if I do it, they'll waive a bunch of fees for me and my family, promises he'll set up some meetings for a few films I want. He reckons if I do it, he can get me in Scorsese's next picture. I'd *kill* to be in one of his movies." He mournfully placed a handful of cheese on his tongue and said, "Oh, hey, just FYI, Csaba said if I showed this to anyone, he'd kill me and whoever saw it, so you know, keep it on the DL."

"He said *what?*"

"Relax, big shots always talk like that. 'You leak this script, and I'll throw you off a bridge; you talk to TMZ, and I'll have you beheaded; you sleep with my wife again, and I'll feed your nuts to my pitbull.' It's just industry slang. Csaba's totally chill."

Darius pictured the pool of blood on the floor at his sister's house and said, "Sure. He's a real puppy dog." He pointed at the screen and said, "Could you send this file to me?"

"No probs, what's your email?"

Kyle merrily tapped at the keys on the screen as Darius spelled it out for him.

Nero watched the two of them with silent reptilian rancour. He was growing weary of his transparent cage. He longed for the feel of wild new stone beneath his feet, the thrill of the hunt, the blazing heat of the sun instead of the effete embrace of the heat lamp. He blinked his three eyelids and stared at them, dreaming of blood and freedom.

34

TUN STATE

Lenore watched the elderly woman throwing bread to the murder of crows dancing coven-like at her feet. Her wrinkled, papery skin was peeled back into a euphoric smile. Her granddaughter clapped her hands as the feathery symbols of death feasted on the lumps of wheat and sugar. "They like it, Granny, they like it!" Her grandmother nodded sagely and said,

"Bread is very good for birds."

The girl waved at Lenore and announced, "We're helping the birds grow big and strong!" She considered whether she should covertly whisper into her ear, 'Actually, you're feeding them more sugar than their body can handle and hastening them towards a joyful but unquestionably early death,' but she thought better of it and simply flashed her a thumbs up as she continued up the gravel path. The glass doors slid open, and she was greeted with the familiar aroma of the retirement village—cheap aftershave, mothballs, and the heavy scent of death lurking by the bingo table.

Ray was wheeling a purple-haired octogenarian down the hall as she recounted tales of her granddaughter, a successful singer of a jazz quartet. In actual fact, the granddaughter in question had been a full-time heroin addict for some years now, but this little detail had conveniently slipped from the ragged suitcase of her memory. Ray flashed Lenore a smile, parked the purple-haired woman at her preferred card table, and strolled over.

"Nice of you to drop by. I assume your phone suffered a toilet-related death, seeing as how you haven't returned any of my messages?"

"Sorry. Things have been rather strange lately."

"Stranger than your ceiling collapsing and finding a watch in the mouth of a corpse?"

"Yes."

He reached for her hand, but she pulled away. "Not feeling overly amorous at the minute. I'm going to pop in and say hi to Dad."

"Fair enough. Well, my shift finishes in about half an hour if you want to…"

She stared at him. The floor. The window. "Maybe a cup of tea and a chat would be nice. I could use a friend right now."

"Great, I've gotta keep going with my rounds. Mrs. Battersby has been complaining that her 'gentleman caller' has been making eyes at the other ladies. Unfortunately, he's just a very persistent hallucination, so I'm not sure what I can do about it. But if I don't at least talk to her, she'll set the curtains on fire again. Catch you out front in thirty."

He waved goodbye and walked off. Lenore continued on to her father's room and found him seated at his computer, compulsively clicking a pen and muttering to himself. This in itself was entirely typical, but his surroundings had undergone a drastic transformation, as though a reality show focused on extreme makeovers of the living quarters of elderly widowers had recently paid him a visit. Books rested neatly on shelves, couches were oddly bereft of half-eaten sandwiches, and his desk looked like it was from a display home. "Dad?"

He whipped around, beamed, and said, "Two visits in a single week, praise the good and assuredly fictional Lord and Saviour! Either my daughter has finally decided to reward me for the tiny favour of making her into the woman she is today, or you're here to borrow money."

"Actually, I was looking for some advice." She sat down on the faded blue couch. It was strange to sit without having to first move mountains of books and papers.

"You've come to the right curmudgeon. Let's see; the term 'superfood' is bullshit, our societal obsession with staring at screens will eventually result in a slew of physical and mental ailments, timeshare properties—"

"Dad, could you listen, please?"

He noted the quiet sincerity in his daughter's voice and mimed zipping and locking his mouth.

"After Mum died, how did you keep going?"

He moved from his office chair to sit beside her on the couch, and wrapped her hands in his as she continued.

"Since Quan died, everything seems grey and hollow. I feel like I can't carry the weight of my own body. I'm happy sometimes, but there's always this constant, quiet feedback of misery." She pulled her hands away from his and stared at them. "I find myself staring at my hands for minutes at a time. I look at this tenuous alliance of atoms, temporarily tolerating its existence as fingers, nails, palms, skin, and think about how easily that alliance can be broken."

"Sweetheart, it's only been what, a month? You can't expect to—"

"Everything feels meaningless and profound at the same time. There's a part of me that wants to believe that death is just a doorway. But honestly? I think it's just a hallway ending in a blank and infinite wall of nothingness. And nothing I do or say or promise or pray is ever going to bring him back."

Richard put his arm around her and said, "When Christine died, I felt like there was a hole in the universe in her shape. I felt furious at the joyful, perfect families I saw in parks. It made me lose all faith in any kind of justice in the universe. If I hadn't had you and your brother to deal with, I probably would've buried myself in booze, maybe something stronger. Luckily, you little brats, with your endless nappy changes and spilt food didn't really leave me too much time to wallow in my grief. You were literal and metaphorical pieces of her that I could still cling to. I'd stare at the two of you some days and think about how portions of Christine's DNA were swimming around inside the source code for your software." He stood up and passed her a photo of the two of them, aged perhaps two and three, half-naked and covered in spaghetti, beaming proudly at the camera.

Lenore examined the photo and smiled, then handed it back to him. "It's supposed to get better, I should know. I tell people the same thing every day. The same clichés. The same bullshit. 'One step at a time. Time heals all wounds.' But I still feel like I'm having my heart ripped out of my chest every morning."

"I know, I know. But that wound is still new. It won't ever heal completely, but I promise it'll get better with time. And yeah, I know that's a cliché. But the thing about clichés is sometimes they're simply truths occurring at a high rate of frequency." They sat in silence for a while. Outside in the hall, a cleaning cart squeaked by.

"Dad, are you afraid of death?"

He exhaled and leaned back into the couch. "If I can answer your question with a complaint—which is going to happen more and more as I get older, by the way—when I hear someone decades younger than me complaining about 'getting old' and worrying about death, all I can think is 'gimme a freaking break, enjoy your knees while they still work.' But look, I'm a rationalist, not a robot. Of course, I'm scared. It's part of that fear that motivates us to do something with these tiny little lives we have, right? To create a legacy."

"Some days, it's all I can think about. I look around at people driving, shopping, getting married, walking their dogs, busking, applying for home loans, and I want to scream, 'what's the point? Don't you know you're all going to end up in the ground no matter what you do'?"

"I wouldn't suggest it, might be frowned upon."

"I know. I just feel like there's a vacuum inside me, trying to make me collapse with the fear of what's coming." She rubbed at the diamond on her finger and stared out the window.

"Sweetheart, you ever think it might be time to look for a different job? I understand that dealing with Quan's death isn't easy—and it shouldn't be—but going to two funerals a week wouldn't be a great idea, even for someone who wasn't dealing with the recent death of a loved one."

She shrugged and said, "What else am I going to do: telemarketing, erotic massage?"

"I know you're joking, but please don't give me a heart attack. No daughter of mine is going to end up working in telemarketing." He handed her a box of tissues, and she dabbed at the tears in her eyes, then gestured around the room.

"Did you get yourself a house elf? I feel like I haven't seen the floor in here since you cleaned up for Christmas."

He grinned proudly. "Well, I wanted to tell you and your brother together, buuuuuuut…." He glanced in the direction of the door, leaned in close. "I've finished my research."

Lenore made a guttural sound of confusion, the hybrid bastard child of a sneeze, a snort, and a choke. "You…what?"

"I'm done with the research phase. Time to stitch it all together, get it ready for publication." She would've been less surprised if he'd announced that he was giving up sleep. "You've 'finished' your research? The research you've been obsessing over incessantly since before I was born?"

"Has it been that long?"

"You said you couldn't come to my graduation because you had to monitor 'potentially apocalyptic anomalies in the Nasdaq.'"

He shook his head, "Really? I was sure I went to your—oh, no, wait, that was your brother. Well, look, I'm sorry. I know I've been spending a lot of time on this. But this is my life's work, my legacy. I'm telling you when people read this," he gestured at his computer as though it were a black monolith recently descended from space, "things are going to get wild. It'll take me a few months to put all the pieces together, but that's good. It'll give me time to buy a new suit."

"Why do you need a new suit?"

"For all the TV interviews. This is going to be the next *Tipping Point*. This is going to make Machiavelli's *The Prince* look like the unauthorised biography of the artist formerly and then once again known as 'Prince.'"

"*The Death Dollar: A Study Of The Interconnectivity Of The Economics of Mortality, Late Stage Capitalism, Entropic Systems, and the Alteration and Augmentation Of Human Life* is going to have a global impact on par with *The Tipping Point*?"

"You sound skeptical."

"I'm sorry, I meant to sound utterly incredulous. I mean, I know it's been nice for you to have this work, as a hobby—"

"You did *not* just call my magnum opus a hobby!"

"Well, come on, Dad, your expertise is in high-school math, and you've written this conspiratorial mash-up of economics and biology and entropy and—"

"Tell that to Chomsky. His degree is in linguistics, but he's considered one of the world's foremost political experts!"

"Well, sure, but—"

"And I do not take kindly to being called a *hobbyist* by someone who hasn't ever held down a full-time job."

"That is not fair. I've been playing in the band for six years. Touring, recording, invoicing, booking gigs. There's a difference between level of income and level of dedication."

He grunted and turned away from her. It'd been a while since she'd seen him this querulous. She'd almost forgotten what these tantrums looked like, all the petulance of a cookie-denied kindergartener transplanted onto the wrinkled visage of a geriatric. "Dad, I didn't mean to upset you, but can we be realistic here? You haven't got a publisher, you haven't got a relevant degree or expertise, you haven't even had an opinion article published in over a decade—"

"I've published plenty since then."

"On your blog—"

"Old media paradigms are dead. Newspapers are basically worthless. The modern transmission of information should be—"

"'Fluid, frictionless, and fathomless.' I know you don't want to hear this, but—"

He wrenched his desk drawer open, rummaging like an addict in search of his lost stash. "Dad! Could you calm down?"

"I am calm!" he barked, removing the drawer entirely, then upending its contents onto the floor. "Here somewhere, wherethefuckdidI—ah! Here's what I wanted to show you!" He shoved the photo triumphantly in her face. It was a doughy, eight-limbed creature that looked like a vacuum cleaner bag made flesh. "Tardigrade!" he yelped. "Remember I was talking about this when, when you and Darius were here, remember?"

She pushed the photo aside and said, "Yes, Dad, I remember. You don't need to yell."

"I'm not yelling! Just listen. Okay, so we think of tough animals, we think of bears, sharks, lions, whatever, right? Apex predators, right?" He waved his hands erratically. Lenore pulled back slightly, wondering how long his manic episode would take to run its course this time. "But that's so wrong! You want tough? You want *tough*? Look at these freaky little eight-legged bastards! They are mi-cro-scop-ic; they live all over the earth, from the Himalayas to backyard ponds, there's probably some in the garden out there, and they're damn near indestructible. They can survive radiation levels 1000 times greater than most animals. 1000 times! Extreme temperature, extreme pressure, shrug it off like it's *nothing! Nothing!*"

"Yes, I know, we talked about this last—"

"Dehydration? These little buggers take it in their stride! You or I can't go more than a couple of days without water; they can go ten years! Ten years!"

"Is there a point here, Dad?"

"Hold your horses. Okay, but the most amazing thing, they took some of these things into space, the cold, hard unforgiving vacuum of space. No air, no nutrients, nothing! Brought 'em back to earth, gave them a little water, and pow! They sprung back to life like they'd been taking a nap!"

"Hold on, you're saying they hibernated—"

"Not just hibernated! They shut themselves down completely; they were essentially dead! It's called a cryptobiotic state, or 'tun' state."

"And they revived?"

"Yes! Ah, well. Some of them. Others died. But still! In-cred-i-ble! And and and my point is, I'm like this tardigrade! Weird lookin', small, but you can't keep me down! The research they're doing on these things, I mean, there's implications for space travel, life extension—"

"Cryonics?"

"Of course!"

Lenore examined the bizarre micro-organism, imagining it entering a death-like sleep and then reanimating with a drop of water. Richard gulped at a can of Red Bull. The fact that she'd taken an interest had calmed him a little, but he was still trembling, eyes darting around the room. "Say, when are you going to get this thing finished up?" he jabbed a finger at her tattoo.

"I thought you hated tattoos?"

"I do! But it looks ridiculous half-finished."

"I'm not sure. When I have a spare day free of escaping kamikaze bathtubs and haunted houses, I suppose." She placed the photo back on the table, helped her dad return the contents of his drawer to its rightful state, then paused. Lenore took her phone out of her purse and wrote:

I can't believe I'm saying this, but do you think what they're saying might be true? What if we really can cheat death?

She hit send and listened to the sounds of the crows cawing in the courtyard.

35

I LOVE THOSE EARRINGS! I'LL MAKE SURE YOU'RE BURIED IN THEM.

Audrey stared at the teetering pile of porcelain that rose from her kitchen sink, adorned with a smeared collection of reds, greens, and browns that would have been entirely at home in a Georgia O'Keefe painting. She stared at the message from Clay on her work phone for the hundredth time.

Can't talk now. Call you at 11.

It was brusque and utterly bereft of grovelling or apology, which was not encouraging. On the other hand, it also didn't contain the threat of legal action, so there was that to be thankful for. She removed her favoured diamond earrings from her jewellery box. They were a gift from a client, by far the most expensive thing she'd ever owned. Those two shiny rocks that served no function besides dangling either side of her skull for aesthetic effect were more valuable than her car, her computer, and all her guitars combined. She would've sold them long ago if not for the fact that the client in question requested on seeing her wear them. She only ever wore them whilst working. They were a perfect totem for the ridiculousness of not only her economic situation, but the concept of desire-based economics in its entirety.

She sat in front of the computer and watched the digital clock in the corner tick over to 1:57.

Do I plead with him, break character? Maybe I could tell him I'm in love, I've never felt this way before?

1:58

What if I get arrested? What would happen to the girls?

1:59

I wouldn't last ten seconds in prison. Some butch she-nazi would make me her bitch in minutes.

The call came in, and she hit 'accept' before the first ring had completed. "Hello darling!" she purred, leaning into the camera, her shoulders pushed together to emphasise her cleavage.

"Hello," his voice was curt and clipped.

"Ohhhhh…is someone a bit grumpy today? Maybe because he was up all night like a very, very naughty boy?"

He scowled and said, "What you did, was…I-I woke up with my pants around my ankles on the boardroom table, cops shining a flashlight in my face and barking orders at me!" The cops had found him, not security. That was good.

Maybe.

"I bet you liked that, didn't you? We both know how much you like being ordered around you saucy, sexy stallion!"

"Not like that, I don't! I have a reputation. What if this ends up in the papers?"

"What, that you slept with a beautiful woman on the boardroom table of a prestigious scientific facility? I should think that would do wonders for your reputation."

His eyes darted up and to the left as he scratched at the locked doors of his memory. "D-did we…?"

"You don't remember? I have to say, I am a little offended!"

"We…ah, that is to say, you and I did…um?"

"For hours and spades in dozens of ways! I don't know about you, but I am ex-*hausted*! You really know how to give a girl a workout! I had to cancel all my other clients today so I could stay focused on my number one favourite."

His finger shot involuntarily towards himself, joyous disbelief surging over his skin. "M-m-me?!?"

"One. Hundred. Per. Cent." She let this sink in, tried not to pity him as he tittered and very nearly looked like he was going to actually clap his hands in glee.

"But, I mean, if my company knew that I'd hired a…um, working girl…"

"Sweetheart, I won't tell if you don't."

He considered this and then grinned, nodding fervently. "Huh. Okay! I think…I guess, I guess that's fine! I really shouldn't drink so much…"

"I have to take a little heat for that. I talked you into taking a little something extra, I wanted our time together to be really special. I did explain that one of the effects was memory loss, but, you know, the ironic thing about explaining memory loss is that people often forget that they've been told about the memory loss."

He laughed and said, "Yes! I imagine so. It's been a while since I've done any kind of drugs. I smoked a bit of weed way back in my twenties, the odd bump of coke now and then, but I'm not very adventurous these days!"

"I've got an aching back that very much says otherwise, Clay." She used his actual name. In fairy tales, knowing someone's name gives you power over them. In her line of work, knowing the name and refusing to use it was a mark of this power; its official use rather than a denigrating epithet denoted an admission of that power balance dramatically shifting. His face lit up with joy. "I want to see you again soon. Would you like that?" He nodded so fast he looked like a bobblehead in an earth tremor. "Wonderful! I have a few urgent things to take care of over the next couple of days, but you keep your pretty mouth closed about us, and I promise that by the end of next week, I will make it very worth your while, understand?"

She wasn't sure what her next move was. She couldn't keep drugging him and claiming they'd slept together, but as a delay tactic, a woman saying 'I promise I'll sleep with you if you do X' was a method that had been tried and tested throughout history.

"Sure! No problem! I can't wait!"

The knots within her slipped apart, and relief flooded through her, but she took care to maintain her perfect grammar school posture.

"Right back at you, handsome," she ran her finger suggestively down her jaw towards her plunging neckline as she pondered how to best wrap up the call. An array of scripts hovered in her consciousness, awaiting selection like a fighter selecting between a range of finishing moves.

Clay opened his lips, about to say something, but was interrupted by a bright flash that tore across the screen and set him screaming. He held up his hand and stared at the red, pulsing mass in horror, his fingers hideously misaligned, delirious fleshy worms struggling to escape his palm. Audrey screamed as the hammer flashed across the screen again, this time colliding with his skull. A fleck of blood caught the camera lens, partially obscuring Clay as his eyes rolled back into his head. He slumped forward and struck the table with a dull thud.

A hand pushed him onto the floor, took his seat, and dabbed at the lens. A finely groomed older gentleman looked at her as though he was appraising an antique vase. "Would you prefer I address you as 'Mistress Fury' or 'Audrey'?"

"How do you know my—"

He held his hand up, shook his head. "Not the most important question to be asking right now. Oh! I just *love* your earrings! I'll make sure you're buried in them." He smiled at her as though he'd offered to help her with her groceries. Her hand reached to snatch the screen closed but froze when he held a photo of her daughters up to the camera. "Don't go! We've got so much to talk about."

36

RED. VERY RED. EXTREMELY RED.

Ray stared at the kettle as its angry scream began to crescendo. Lenore rotated the salt and pepper shakers as he made tea and hummed quietly to himself. "You know that humming is quite annoying."

He raised an eyebrow at her and placed the mugs down on the table, then plucked the salt and pepper shakers out of her hand and put them on the bench. "Must be nice, being the only person in the world without any annoying habits, free to pass judgment on us lesser mortals."

"Sorry, I didn't mean to—"

"I'll let it slide, given your whole mourning situation. But just a heads up; you have three weeks' worth of leeway left, and then I'm going to start treating you like any other annoying person."

"That's fair."

"Lenore, I was kidding! Grief makes us all crazy. When my brother died I was a reckless, self-indulgent maniac for at least a year."

"You never told me you had a brother?"

"Yeah, well. You never asked too much about my family. Or anything else."

She sipped her tea. Said nothing.

"I didn't mean for that to sound like an admonishment."

"Uh-huh. Guess I'm not the only one passing judgment. But you're right.

I know I always bail up in here wanting to unload and…"

"Have sex?"

"I was going to say unwind. Would it redeem me at all if I told you I just wanted some company today? It's been a rough week."

"You don't have to redeem yourself. You're flawed and annoying. You've got that in common with the rest of the human species."

"Thanks."

Outside, the roar of a lawn mower ruptured the afternoon quiet. Ray dropped a sugar cube into his tea; watched its angular forms dissolve into the murky liquid.

"How did he die?" asked Lenore.

"Suicide." The word left his mouth like a body jumping from a bridge. He gazed at the table and continued, "His wife Patricia found him when she came home from work, sprawled on the floor next to a note and an empty pill bottle."

"God, Ray, that's…"

"Yeah. I know. The hardest part was the guilt. Both Patricia and I kept asking ourselves if there was something we could have done, signs we could have looked for. We knew he had depression, obviously. But he seemed like he was doing so well. We became obsessed with going over photos, diaries, Facebook posts, trying to look for the signpost of where things went wrong. As if knowing would be of any help anyway." He paused, looked up at her. "One night, both of us bleary-eyed after too much wine and scrolling obsessively through his photos. We, you know…"

"Ah."

"Yeah. It was wrong on a number of levels. We chalked it up to grief and inebriation, that's a potent combo, but I've barely spoken to her since. What I'm trying to say is…I get why this is happening." He waved his index finger back and forth between them. "And why it's not a long-term thing. Even if I'd like it to be."

Lenore nodded. Probed her mind for something to say, but found only a yawning conversational abyss.

"How did Quan die?"

"You just pointed out my solipsistic tendencies, then you go and ask me to open a vault of grief that you know is an endless source of lamentation and self-pity?"

"Yes. The difference is you're not telling. I'm asking."

"Right."

"Also? Although you've talked endlessly about how hard it is to cope, about your grief, about your fear of death, I don't actually know anything about Quan. I don't even know how he lived, let alone how he died."

"Forgive me for thinking it'd be weird to talk about my recently deceased boyfriend with my—"

"Your what?"

"Friend. Very good friend. Very good friend with very good benefits."

Ray laughed and said, "Yeah. Okay. I'll take that." He motioned for her to continue.

"Quan was a tattoo artist. When we met he thought it was astounding I didn't have any ink. Eventually, after years of trying to talk me into getting some work done, I acquiesced. I decided on the raven because I'm trying to confront my fear of death by hurtling towards it, despite the fact that this strategy has thus far been thoroughly unsuccessful. He told me that if we waited for a slow day at the studio I could drop by and he'd do it for me, but if he had any paying clients drop in he'd obviously have to attend to them. He was a little over halfway done when a customer showed up.

"He looked after them, then another showed up straight after, and then it was time to close up shop. We decided to leave it for another time. I went away on a little East Coast tour for a couple of weeks. When we came back, his schedule was booked solid for a few days. After that, we kept putting it off, it was something we'd argue about now and then. I'd yell at him to finish it with a home kit, but he insisted he wanted nothing less than his best equipment and his best work for me. It dragged on and on. Then, we finally scheduled a day when he had another slump in bookings. I was actually looking forward to it. I felt like I'd had a half-finished laundry list on my arm for weeks. I woke up, excited like a kid on Christmas morning to get into the studio. And he was gone."

"He left?"

"He left this world. Brain aneurysm. Happened in his sleep. No prior symptoms."

"That's awful."

"I don't disagree." Neither of them said anything for a while. "I still text him. I'm sure the phone company will cut off his service after a couple more months of unpaid bills, but for the moment, it still works. His phone's sitting in a box at the top of our closet, along with all his stuff I can't bring myself to throw away, all of it now drenched in cadaver-laced water. I send him little messages, pretending he might respond. Pretending he's still alive."

"I get that. I left voicemails on Allan's phone for months after he was gone. Hearing that little prerecorded message before the beep made it feel like a piece of him was still here. Eventually, the storage filled up. I kept thinking that maybe by some miracle a message would—"

Lenore's phone buzzed and they both jumped and then burst into relieved laughter. She grabbed it out of her handbag and read the message from Riley.

Yo, my dumb school just told me that there's been a package waiting for me for four days

It was sitting @ the reception desk.

you believe that shit?

Fkn bureaucracy.

No note inside, just an unmarked cassette tape.

I got a free period @ 1, can you meet me at my place with a tape player?

Yr old, you've got a walkman or some shit right?

I'm not old, I'm technically a millennial! My car, however, is ancient, and just so happens to have a cassette deck. I'll swing by this afternoon.

"Please tell me that wasn't a message from beyond the grave," said Ray.

"No, just a friend of mine. I'm sorry. I'll turn my phone off."

"You don't have to do that."

"Battery's about to go anyway." She turned it off and tossed it in her handbag.

Ray took her hand, raised her ring up to the light. "I've been meaning to ask you, is this an engagement ring? Were you two planning to get hitched?”

“No, this is my mum.”

“Your mum had excellent taste.”

“I didn't say it *belonged* to my mum. I said it *is* my mum. It's an ash diamond. They compressed her remains into this shiny little stone, and now I always have her with me.”

He released her hand, leaned back in his chair. “You carry a lot of death around with you.”

She shrugged. “Part of being alive.”

Ray nodded. “Do you mind if I take a shower real quick? I know it might seem odd, but if you knew the specifics of my job, well, let's just say I deal with a prolific collection of bodily fluids. You can hang out here. We'll chat more when I'm finished.”

“I should probably go. I'm exhausted anyway.”

“No, don't rush off. Honestly, I'll be fifteen minutes. Take a nap if you want.”

“That does sound euphorically appealing...”

“Great. I'll be back in a few.”

Lenore rose from her chair, staggered over to the bedroom, took off her jeans and studded belt, and slipped under the covers.

* * *

The sound of cheerful whistling roused her from half-sleep. She fluttered her eyes open, attempting to refocus the world out of its blurry, soft-lensed state. The first thing she saw was a mass of red. A jolt of fear brought her suddenly upright. Ray was standing in his towel, wreathed in steam, in front of a large canvas coloured in an abstract wash of crimson. Lenore's hand shot to her mouth, and she shook her head violently as the familiar image washed over her.

He laughed and said, “Didn't notice this when you came in, huh? I didn't think it was your kind of thing. I know it's red. Very red. Extremely red. It was a gift from my mum. I can take it down if you hate it that—”

"*Get out!*" she screamed and clambered out of the bed.

"What the hell are you talking about?"

She glared at him and said, "You need to get the fuck out of here. It's going to happen. Now!"

"I don't understand, what's going to—" His sentence was obliterated by the fear blossoming in Lenore's eyes. "Now? Right now?"

"Yes! Run, just fucking run!"

The front door creaked open, followed by feet stomping up the stairs. "Who the hell is that?"

"I don't know, but you have to—"

The door flung open, and gloved hands gripped Ray's shoulders, hairy arms pulling him tight against the body of the intruder. Lenore felt time slur and stumble as the blade was drawn across Ray's throat, mirroring the vision she'd seen dozens of times before. Ocky let the body drop to the floor, flicked the blood off his razor, and said,

"Tell you what, when I first started out in the criminal arts, tracking people down was a seriously onerous endeavour. Now I just pay off a few guys at the major telephone companies, get live satellite tracking data for any number I want. Technology eh? Now, I should emphasise the fact that, although I have, by virtue of professional dedication to eradication of witnesses iced this fucking numpty, I'm not contractually obliged to kill you, just bring you to see the boss. My *personal* preference is to carry you outta here in a neat polymer body bag, but I *might* be inclined towards leniency if you can come along quiet-like."

Lenore stared at the lump of blood and bone that had moments ago been her friend and began to cry in great, heaving sobs.

"Come on love, ain't no need to make with the waterworks. Csaba's been known on occasion to be entirely genteel and reasonable. He's a businessman first and foremostly. If you agree to whatever he asks, you'll be all good and gravy."

She pulled on her jeans and began fastening her belt, then stopped and stared at it. She glanced at Ocky and watched the flicker of recognition in his eyes as he studied her stance and expression. He seemed to send a probe into the inner workings of her mind, watching intently as her impulse turned to action, anticipating her movement before she was even aware that she was moving at all. He ducked as she whipped the belt out from its loops and flicked it wildly in his direction. It missed him entirely, the buckle slapping lamely against the wall.

She struck again as he charged towards her. This time, the belt landed heavily across the side of his head. Blood spat out from his cheek; his left hand grasped at the wound as he grunted, then snatched the belt with his right hand. He yanked it before Lenore had a chance to release her grip, dragging her towards him. She pulled her fist back as she was drawn violently towards him, using the force of her own body being yanked forward to carry her fist like a comet. Riley's words of wisdom about keeping her thumb on the outside surfaced amongst the surge of panic and adrenaline. Ocky snapped his head back, then pulled himself back into position and stared at her.

For a moment, she thought she'd only caught him with a glancing blow, then he dropped the bloody razor, grasping at his throat, his breath coming in sickly, desperate gasps. Lenore looked down at her hand. Her ring was missing its ash diamond, golden claws clutching at newly empty air.

Ocky coughed and spluttered, blood gushing from his face. Lenore reclaimed her belt and jumped behind him, wrapping it tight around his throat. Ocky's fingers scrambled in vain to get underneath the belt and pry it free. His struggling became weaker, then ceased entirely. She unfastened the belt, and he fell to the floor.

Lenore stared at the two blood-splattered corpses lying still and silent at her feet. She'd seen many bodies these last few years, but this was the first time she'd witnessed death actually crossing the threshold rather than merely being privy to the results of its visitation. Her head screeched with an infernal choir of fears and strategies. She ran to the bathroom and scrubbed the belt clean, watching the water run red, then sickly pink, and finally clear, as it was continually swallowed by the yawning abyss of the plughole.

37

I'M IN THE DEATH BUSINESS

Lenore climbed out of the taxi, unlocked her car, and clambered in. She started the ignition and plugged her phone into the charger, resting her head on the steering wheel for a moment as her phone buzzed back to life. She screamed at the space between her feet, relieved to finally be able to unleash her despair after maintaining a forcefully neutral expression in the cab ride over. The cab driver had talked to her about the weather, his kids, camping. What macabre banality, to discuss camping stoves and hiking boots moments after watching Ray's throat sliced by—

Her phone bleeped a series of message alerts. There was a sharp tap on her window. She glanced up to see a bespectacled man miming at her to wind her window down. She obliged irritably and barked, "What?!"

"Are you leaving? I need the space."

"In a couple of minutes. I have to make some calls."

"Well, could you do it later? I've been looking for a park for ten minutes."

"I will make my calls and then leave. If you say another word to me, I will ram your car on the way out. Thank you, and have a nice day." She wound the window back up and ignored his furious complaints as she glanced at Audrey's message.

CALL ME NOW!!!

Audrey picked up before the first ring had completed.

"Are you okay?"

"I…did something wrong." She was sobbing violently. The twins were arguing in the background.

"Tell me what happened."

"…"

"Audrey?"

"I told Csaba."

"Told. Him. WHAT?"

"…where Riley lives."

Lenore screamed and slammed the dashboard, then took a deep breath and said, "How *could* you?"

"He threatened my girls! He had photos of them in their school uniforms. I just picked them up; we're going to stay at Dad's place for a few days." Lenore listened to the cars honking and twin girls yelling through her phone speaker. "Len? Are you still there?"

"When?"

"When what?"

"When did you tell him?"

"Maybe…ten minutes ago?"

Another car was sitting behind her, indicator blinking. Its owner made eye contact and beeped the horn, flailing arms frantically. Lenore flipped him off, wishing her car had something superior to hazard lights to indicate her level of urgency, a police siren perhaps, or retractable spikes. "Have you called the police?"

"Csaba said he has a bunch of cops on his payroll; if I call them, he'll know about it. Do you think he's telling the truth?"

"There's no way to know for sure, but it's more than likely. I'm going to Riley's place now. Hopefully, I can beat him there."

"But…what are you going to do, beat him up?"

Lenore's head stung with visions of blood-red, bulging eyes. "If I have to. Call me when you're safe."

She hung up and messaged Darius, then punched Riley's address into her GPS, perched her phone in its cradle, and reversed out sharply, clipping the car behind her. There was an explosion of showering glass, then a brief interlude of blissful silence before the furious honking of the driver's horn began. She turned around, met his enraged eyes, and mimed an apology before shifting into drive and screeching out of the parking lot.

* * *

She surveyed the apartment. It didn't look like a crime scene. Door (unlocked), plates (unwashed), mail (unread), bills (unpaid). It was—as upon her last visit—painfully quotidian. For a few euphoric moments, she allowed herself to believe that she had arrived in time. That Riley was somewhere within the apartment, cyberbullying someone or online shopping for hunting knives or whatever she did for fun, but when she called out, she was met with only sinister silence.

She ran through the apartment, checking each of the tiny rooms, found nothing. The room began to tilt and spin. She wished, not for the first time, that she had Riley's ability to be completely fearless, to examine the rooms with cold, clear logic, unencumbered by thoughts of razors drawn across throats, guns placed against temples, pliers clenched around teeth—

Her phone rang, and she snatched it out of her pocket, answering it without glancing at the screen.

"Hello, Ms. Lyn! My name is Samantha. I'm from Amrita Industries. Have I reached you at a convenient time?" her voice was clinically effervescent. Lenore took a moment to compose herself, restraining the urge to scream violent threats at a lackey of unknown importance who was doubtlessly calling from a recorded line.

"Sure. Talk."

"I hope you're having a lovely day! I have some wonderful news on behalf of Mr. Adami. He's let me know that negotiations on your contract have concluded, and you will now be paid in full. There's nothing else he needs from you."

"What negotiations?"

"My apologies, but I'm not privy to the particulars of your arrangement. Mr Adami assured me that you were in possession of all the details. He has, however, requested me to inform you that the final settlement amount is fifty thousand dollars."

"Fifty thousand?"

"Yes. His note says here, 'fifty thousand dollars payable subject to conclusion of negotiations.'"

"So, translation: if I stay out of it, he'll pay me."

"That would be the gist of it, yes! And, um, you'll have to excuse me if this next part sounds a tad aggressive, but in order to make sure the message is accurately conveyed, I want to avoid using any sort of mitigating language on the grounds that—"

"Spit it out."

"As you wish! Mr. Adami has noted, 'should Ms. Lyn wish to continue negotiations, please advise her that I will consider pursuing aggressive action.' Now I want to clarify that is, of course, a legal term meaning—"

"I'm well aware of what he means."

"Okie-dokie! Well, Ms. Lyn, I'm not sure what your line of business is, but I would suggest that celebrations are in order!"

Lenore let the chirpy sing-song of Samantha's voice rattle around in her brain for a few seconds and then replied, "I'm in the death business. And you can tell your boss to keep his blood money."

Lenore hung up and sat down on the couch, staring at the filthy carpet. There, half-hidden behind a table leg, a cigarette stained the carpet with ash. She picked it up. It had landed right next to the drop of blood she'd spilled there a few days earlier. She stared at the blood and ash, realising Riley must've been sitting in the exact same spot when they took her. She wondered if she'd gone in a flurry of wildly imaginative adolescent profanity or if she'd been drugged and taken out quietly. She picked up her phone and saw that Darius had sent her a video message. She ignored it and tried to call him, but was greeted by his voicemail. She typed a message and lay back, staring at the ceiling.

She savoured a few divine seconds of serenity, then decided to search Riley's room for the tape. It was predictably chaotic: an adolescent apocalypse of clothes strewn across the floor, books haphazardly stacked around the room, make-up and aerosol paint cans scattered across the dressing room table. Her backpack was gone, they'd most likely taken it with them. There was no way of knowing whether Riley had had time to stash the tape before they'd arrived. Lenore dug into the annals of her memory, trying to think about her favoured hiding places for illicit substances as a teenager. She found nothing under the mattress. An inspection of various shoe boxes in the closet revealed only a couple of baggies of weed. She sat on the bed, tried to see the room through Riley's eyes. She scanned Riley's 'floordrobe' at her feet, the spray-paint cans lined up like cylindrical soldiers on the windowsill, the chaotic collection of bracelets and bric-a-brac. Her gaze fell upon the beaten-up acoustic guitar leaning against the wall in the corner, its thick coat of dust broken by a couple of smeared handprints. She picked it up and shook it. Something heavy clunked inside.

38

THE TAPE

C LACK.

"—rry Csaba, I don't understand, we're already offering *immortality*. It's the perfect product; universally appealing, future-proof, elastic pricing schedule. Why package it with all this chicanery?"

"I'm not talking about chicanery. I'm talking about the utopian society that will usher in a new age."

"So it's a cult. Listen, Csaba, we all know that you've been having a hard time since Rena died—"

"If you utter her name again I will instruct my new security guard here to tear your eyeballs from their sockets and feed them to you." *Hisss. Click. Hisss. Click.* "I'm *kidding*! I'm not a monster!" *Nervous, awkward laughter.* "This is Ocky, my new PA. Ocky, could you get us all a round of coffees? I had our preferences printed out for you. Jeffrey here has a sweet tooth, he takes three sugars, but don't tell his wife, he's supposed to be on a diet, isn't that right?" *Laughter, footsteps. Click. Hiss. Click. Hiss.* "Allow me to explain my thinking before we get into the questions. As you've so eloquently stated, we have the perfect product, and to a great degree, it will sell itself. I mean, the first time I explained it to all you greedy bastards you were handing me a cheque before I'd even finished the elevator pitch!" *Laughter. Click. Hiss.* "Over the next few months we will be forming an elite sub-organisation within Amrita Industries called the Sixth Sun. Think of it as

223

the members lounge, the VIP room. The Sixth Sun takes its name from the Aztec eschatological system."

"Eschka-whatsit?"

"Eschatological. The stories and mythologies surrounding Armageddon. The Norse have Ragnarok, Judeo-Christians have Revelation, Capitalists have Communism—" *Laughter. Click. Hiss.* "We all have our stories surrounding the final end. In Aztec mythology, humans are believed to have lived through several distinct eras, each represented by a new sun. There was an era destroyed by flood, a popular apocalyptic motif across many religions, one by fire, one by jaguars—"

Laughter. "No, I'm serious! This is *important*. Jaguars are of particular significance to Aztec culture, and symbols are key. You all have logos for your various companies, am I wrong? John, yours is a real work of art, kudos; Karen, you have the lion and the bull, classic archetypal symbols of strength and power; and Leon you have that weird squiggle that looks like it was drawn by a toddler on meth."

Laughter. Click. Hiss.

"I'm *kidding*, I'm *kidding*! I'm sure it tested very well in the focus groups. Symbols are important. We'll circle back to that. So, the Sixth Sun will borrow somewhat from the Aztec culture in terms of myth, but we're going to make a pastiche of a number of traditions; Judeo-Christian, masonic, Hindu, Buddhist, Gnostic, etc. A good artist borrows, a great artist steals, am I right? Think of it as a sort of mythological Esperanto. We want to appeal to everybody."

"But you can't just invent a cul—ah, philosophy, overnight."

"Really? Tell that to Joseph Smith. How many Mormons are there these days? I recently inked the deal on the air-conditioning units for the new Mormon headquarters in Utah and let me tell you they are not short on cash nor members. Although they are a little lacking in common sense, drop the middle 'm', and you've got a pretty good descriptor of their members, but you didn't hear that from me. And let's not forget L. Ron Hubbard. The man started his career as a pulp sci-fi author, for crying out loud, now look how many people he has under his wing? And signing up Tom Cruise as an ambassador? Stroke of genius. We're going to look to do something similar.

"The cornerstone of our philosophy is the three 'M's: Myth, marketing, and mystery." *Murmur. Hiss. Click. Hiss.* "Much like the Aztecs, our myth requires a symbol. Something beautiful, mystical, and, above all, enduring." *Shuffling. Click. Hiss. Gasp.* "Take a good long look! You can touch it if you like. It's perfectly harmless. It's called a tuatara. Not actually a lizard, despite appearances. This living fossil has a lifespan of up to 200 years. Imagine that? 200 years ago our ancestors didn't have electricity, plumbing, penicillin, the steam engine, automobiles, aviation, television!

"In Māori culture—another one of the traditions we want to stir into our pan-cultural jambalaya—they're thought of as guardian spirits of knowledge. When they're born they have three eyes, the third is initially visible but as it reaches maturity becomes covered by scales and is used as a light sensor. Three-eyed bicentennial reptile? I mean, the marketing copy writes itself! Alright, this little guy's going back in his tank for now. Oh, coffee's here! Ocky, you're a gem. Thanking you!

"On to part two: marketing. This is an organisation unlike any other, so we can't just be running magazine ads, television commercials, 'dial the number on your screen NOW' etc. Wouldn't work. Ridiculous. We're going to try something a little more specialised. First of all, distribution. We're going to leave physical, tangible paraphernalia in planned locations; cassettes, VHS, letters will be placed in Presidential suites, conference halls, first-class flights, VIP lounges. Amrita is the public-facing front, open slather for the hoi polloi. The Sixth Sun is strictly invite only. We want to make the Bildeberg Group look like the YMCA. Now, I know what you're thinking, won't those barriers make it harder to achieve market capture? And let me assure you, the answer is *no*. Making our clients part of something secret and elite assures their secrecy, their allegiance, and most importantly, gives us leverage.

"For example. Each of you in this room has—in addition to your highly profitable legitimate operations—been involved in some, shall we say, 'sub-legal' entrepreneurial efforts."

Remonstrations. Protests. Click. Hiss.

"Come on, come on! We all know each other! Let's not beat around the shrubbery! Look, I'll start. Ocky isn't actually my PA. He's a hired thug who assaults and, on occasion, kills people for me. *Wow, does* it feel good to get that off my chest! You should try it, really! Paul, how about you?"

"Csaba, I'm sure I speak for all of us when I say that I had a very strange and temporary ringing in my ears for the last five seconds that prevented me from hearing whatever it was that you just said, so that's all fine. And we don't need to talk about it anymore. But I assure you my investment portfolio is entirely above—"

Gasp. Click. Hiss.

"Ah, that's, I mean, I can explain!"

"Can you? Go on then."

"Ah, I mean, I was—"

"That *is* a picture of you, isn't it, Paul?"

"Well, yes...?"

"And the gentleman you're shaking hands with is the notorious dictator Idi Amin?"

"Yes, but there's context!"

"Oh, there's always 'context'! I'm sure your shareholders would completely understand if you explained it in terms of 'context.' And before the rest of you start throwing stones, just let me flip through these next few slides...oh-ho! That's a juicy one of you there, Carlos! A little blurry, admittedly, but I'm sure a human rights tribunal would get the gist of it. Annnnd...Felicia, you little minx, is that Senator Ewing? There's one of Leonard and Muhammed with something that looks awfully similar to weapons-grade plutonium. Here's Patrick with—gosh, she's only a spring chicken, isn't she? Exactly how many Springs has she seen, would you say, fourteen, fifteen?"

"Enough! You've got dirt on us; we get it!"

"That's not the point I'm making at all. We all have dirt on *each other*. We are dirty, but we shall never be buried beneath the dirt. Ha! Maybe we should make that into an inspirational poster, put it up in the boardroom? Anyway, we are bound, all of us, by blood and by money, but most importantly, by belief. The belief in a better world."

Silence. Click. Hiss.

"To continue! Our marketing campaign will be extravagant, esoteric, and far-reaching. We will hire famous actors, not just to be in our promotional materials, but to be ambassadors. To use their influence to bring people into our fold. Say what you will about Scientology, they've made some real leaps and bounds in terms of outreach. We'll definitely be borrowing a few moves from their playbook, with some notable improvements. We have a publicity project in the early stages right now that will be a world-first in terms of scale and reach. A whole new level, big names, big budget, huge outcome. And that brings us to the final, and most important principle: mystery. Like any esoteric philosophy, we will have rituals, ceremonies. These will be the glue that binds our practice together. We want to create a rich melting pot of cultural influences, blend in a little pomp and poetry. I've been reading a lot of Dylan Thomas lately. He's certainly got some stuff we can use, 'Death shall have no dominion' and all that. We're going to be workshopping ceremonies over the coming weeks—"

"*Workshopping* ceremonies? You can't just make up a spiritual practice like you're designing an ad campaign!"

"Why not?" *Silence. Click. Hiss.* "I'm serious. Give me a solid, logical reason why we shouldn't design a new utopian philosophy using the same tools we employ in the business world in which we're so thoroughly distinguished?"

"It's just not what's done!"

"Not a logical reason. And, if I may be so bold, the kind of thinking that will see your business dead in the water in the next decade if you hold onto it. Some of these rituals will be more...elaborate than others. We can't splash around in the kiddie pool if we want to really create something transformative here. It's got to be more than secret handshakes and codewords. One day, not too far from now, I will be lying in one of these dewars, waiting to be reborn in a new and glorious age. I expect all of you to do the same, not merely out of fear of death, but out of hope for a bright new future. And I really don't think that a quick high-five and farewell is going to cut it for such an occasion. After all, none of us is ever going to have a funeral, so we might as well have a substitute ceremony of equivalent grandeur!" *Laughter. Click. Hiss.* "There's much to discuss, and we can spitball plenty of ideas in the coming weeks and months. I want you all as partners on this. But for now, I'm going to pass you over to my colleague and dear friend Elliott, who is going to run us through the sacred tenets."

Murmur. Click. Hiss.

"Hold on, hold on—"

"Please save your questions for the end, Enrico."

"Come on, seriously? The 'sacred tenets?' I am here for a business opportunity. I'm an atheist! I can't worship some god who—"

"I'll take it from here, thank you, Csaba. Enrico, no one has said anything about God. The Sixth Sun considers the concept of God (or Allah or any other prime deity you care to name) to be part of humanity's past ages, a sort of juvenile philosophical phase. We recognise that the collective energies, accomplishments, and discoveries will make the idea of God obsolete. We have no god, but we have our devil, and her name is death. If each of you can abide by the tenets we've devised here, you shall never see her face.

"A quick reminder: we are sparing you from death. All the tummy-tucks and nose jobs (and face creams and superfoods, I could go on) in the world aren't going to keep you from the grave. The only thing that will keep your feet firmly and permanently planted on this mortal coil is our work here at the Sixth Sun. When we are awakened in the new age, all of us brought together by a unified set of principles, there will be no more sickness, no more death, no more conflict. A utopia for the chosen few.

"On top of all that? Make no mistake, this is a business opportunity. This is *the* business opportunity. Do you know how much the Catholic Church is worth? And they have something that none of us in this room have: tax exemption, the capitalist holy grail! Businesses could learn a lot from religion. We want not just customer loyalty, but customer *allegiance*. Belief, devotion, these are the things that will make us not just a business, but a bold new civilisation."

Murmur. Click. Hiss.

"So, the nine sacred tenets. Nine because it is the largest single digit number, a trinity of trinities, and (while ten is traditionally the popular figure for commandments like this) well, to be honest, 'ten tenets' didn't test well with the focus groups. Sounded a bit too much like 'ten tenors'." *Laughter. Click. Hiss.* "If I can draw your attention to the screen: behold. The first sacred tenet." *Uproar, yelling.*

"Listen! Each of you here has been chosen via a select set of criteria. I'm sure you've all deduced that these included extraordinary wealth, substantial influence, and criminal dealings. However, the fourth thing that unites all of us in this room? None of us have children. Whether by choice or fate, we are without heirs. Some of you may be embarrassed about that, but at the Sixth Sun we aim to achieve stability. Equilibrium. One select group of people living forever. A stabilised population with no fluctuation in numbers. No deaths. No births. No. Children. Ever. Anyone who violates any of the sacred tenets, now or in the age of the Sixth Sun, will be instantly expelled."

"A perfectly stabilised population? Come on, Elliott, that's impossible."

"Do you really think so? In 1895, the renowned physicist Lord Kelvin declared that 'heavier-than-air-flying machines will never exist.' He was proven wrong a mere eight years later, and he was infinitely more intelligent than any of us. Impossible, as we are so fond of telling our clients, is a relative term. We shall have a select, stable, controlled society. You know what upsets a stable society? Children. Youth. It's never the elderly leading the marches and protests and sit-ins, is it? New blood brings new ideas. Thus, if we want a perfect, warless, peaceful utopia, we must all commit to never having children. Ever."

"But what if the population is depleted, if someone dies in an accident or something?"

"We already have rudimentary technologies allowing us to clone, grow new organs, map genetic structures. By the time we awaken in the new age, we can extrapolate that those technologies will have advanced enough to reconstruct and regrow any of us and transplant our consciousnesses into new vessels, identical save for whatever improvements are available."

Murmuring. Click. Hiss.

"I can see the disbelief in your eyes. Think about this, Henry: you have a pacemaker in your chest, don't you? Twenty years ago, that would have been unimaginable. Melissa just underwent stem cell regeneration. David over here has a liver taken from another human being, and we are only on the very bleeding edge of these sciences. After one or two hundred years? We will feel like gods."

"What about the location?"

"Elliott, darling, do you mind if I step in here?" *Shuffling. Microphone rustling.* "Trust the real estate mogul to ask that question, hey Terry? My husband and I have arranged for a number of veritably Edenesque locales to be purchased and maintained on a variety of continents once our funds have been pooled. When the time comes, we will simply have our caretakers choose the most appropriate location, reward them with entry into our new society, and close the gates to the rest of the world. And Csaba, I hope you don't mind me saying this, but many of you here were fortunate enough to know his beloved Rena and were as devastated as we all are by her loss. I want you to call up the memory of that grief or the grief of losing any of your loved ones. Let it simmer for a moment. Let it marinate. Then tell me if you're really sure you ever want to suffer like that again."

Silence. Click. Hiss.

"I'm sorry, Claire, Elliott, Csaba. I can't be part of this. Lily and I have been trying for a child, and, to be perfectly candid, it all sounds a bit mad. I mean, I was on board for immortality; who wouldn't be? But all this utopian society malarkey, Sixth Sun, nine sacred tenets? Come *on*! I just want to wake up when the science is advanced enough to restore me to youth, not spend my days chanting in togas and whatnot."

"That's highly regrettable, Yannis."

Scraping chair. Silence. Click. Hiss.

"No, Csaba, please don't look at me like that. I mean, I saw the photo you have of me! These lips are sealed! No one will ever know I was here! But I have to politely decline—"

Screaming, gasping. Thud.

"Ocky, be so good as to lift him into the demonstration dewar over there, would you? Thanking you! Well, ladies and gentlemen, as you can see, Yannis has had to enter hibernation a little earlier than planned. Silver lining? This is a *perfect* opportunity to workshop the departure ritual! Now, I've got a few different chants I want to try out, but if you could all start by putting on these lovely robes. Pure Italian silk, courtesy of our good man Salvatorio here. Any objections?" *Silence. Click. Hiss.* "Splendid! Alright, I'll just light these candles…mmm, white gardenia-scented! These were Rena's favourite." *Click. Hiss. Click. Hiss.* "Sorry, I had something in my eye. Let's all gather in a circle, shall we?"

39

VISUAL RATSAC

The corpses lay three feet deep, baking in the heat of each other's bodies. They had become a singular, unified mass, a many-limbed, multi-headed monstrosity that reeked of death and decay. There was no sound but the howling of the desert wind—interrupted by a cheerful rising ringtone. "Who the *fuck* forgot to turn their fucking phone off?" screamed Jason, dropping his headphones.

Darius wiggled his face out from the mass of groaning bodies and was about to offer a grovelling apology when he was interrupted by Jason's continued tirade. He was somewhat notorious for his tirades, which had in the past included N-words, T-words, and C-bombs and had resulted in an extensive variety of slaps (literal, legal, physical, and fiscal).

"Hey, I recognise you! Darren, right?"

"It's Darius, actually."

"Well, Darius actually, do you know how many people would fucking *murder their own saggy-tittied grandmothers* to work on this set?"

The offending phone bleeped in Darius's hand. He found his eyes scanning the screen before he was even conscious of the action. As Jason stormed across the set to reach him, the message surged through Darius's brain like a firefight in a munitions warehouse.

Jason's eyes were bulging out of his head as he seethed, "Put the phone away. Now."

"My sister's in trouble. It's urgent."

"Who are you, Liam Neeson? You gotta go fucking rescue somebody from the mafia? Get the fuck back to work! How does someone suck so hard at playing dead?"

Darius looked up at the scowling face, the latest in a lengthy series of arrogant, talentless, overpaid directors. Somewhere inside him, a long-sealed pressure valve eased open, gently at first, but then with full-fathom force. He felt rage and indignation surging through every fibre of his being before bursting out of his mouth as he yelled: "Do you not understand the meaning of the word 'urgent'? My sister is in trouble and, this may be news to you, but some of us have more important things in our lives than this Kafkaesque pile of *elephant shit.*"

"Get the fuck off my set."

"Fine. I can't wait to leave." Darius attempted to move, but was somewhat encumbered by several hundred kilos of emaciated extras on top of him.

Jason flailed like a car dealership inflatable and screamed, *"Get off him get off him get off him!"* The faux cadavers awkwardly scrambled back to life and Darius managed to finally stand upright.

"Your films are *terrible.* They are visual ratsac. They are cinematic crimes against humanity. I would be embarrassed to have your name on my résumé, and that's coming from someone whose résumé includes *Deathbike 2: the Spokes of Pain* and *Frogger: The Movie.*"

"You're never fucking working in this town again. You're *done!*" The words flew from Jason's mouth, a swarm of furious semantic wasps that wrenched mouths apoplectically open and caused faces to burn a bright, communist red.

Darius let the aura of shock hover and hum for a few seconds before he broke out into a grin. "Even your dismissals are weak and clichéd." He turned to the crew. "It's been a pleasure working with all of you. Most of you. Some of you. Just so you know, this isn't a feature film. It's a series of elaborate commercials for a cryonic centre run by a secret society of deluded robber barons who think they're going to live forever. Break a leg!"

Darius marched off set, surprised by the feeling of righteous calm that had descended over him. He slammed the studio door behind him and headed out to the parking lot.

Kyle leaned out of his trailer, Nero cradled in his hands and said, "Yo! D-money! I thought you weren't going to be done til lunchtime?"

"I just quit. Or got fired. Whatever. I don't work here anymore."

"Oh, man! That sucks. Who am I going to hang out with?"

"I'm in a hurry Kyle. My sister's in trouble."

"Is it serious?"

"Very."

"Can I help?"

Darius glanced at the minuscule reptile in his grasp that had outlived kings and empires. Nero's eerily independent eyes scanned their surroundings, each of them pursuing divergent retinal feeds. He took a few steps closer and said,

"Is it true that most big-shot actors have a 'fixer'?"

"A mixer? Sure, all the time! There's an actor's guild party this weekend at—"

"Not 'mixer,' '*fixer*.' Like, someone who takes care of…complex problems."

"Ohhhhh, right! Like to cover up sex scandals and stuff?"

"Would you mind whispering?"

"Sorry! Is this better?" He said at an entirely undiminished volume. "Yeah, I have someone. Got me out of a bind at Chris Hemsworth's place once. We'd all taken waaaay too many mushrooms, and this llama fell in the pool, or maybe it was an alpaca, which one do they eat in Bolivia? Doesn't matter. What size problem: sedan or minivan?"

"Sorry?"

"How big is the problem? Or problems. They gonna need a sedan or a minivan to get it all cleared up?"

"I think it's a sedan-sized problem. SUV at worst."

"Got it. Here, hold Nero."

Kyle handed the ancient reptile over and pulled out his phone. Nero studied Darius's sweaty, anxious face and wondered what a gigantic primate so comfortably at the top of the food chain could possibly have to worry about.

40

A SURPRISE CELEBRITY GUEST

It was strange to think that she'd first walked through this door just a few days ago. At least it was clean now, resplendent even. She would have to pass on her thanks to Audrey's paypig. He certainly knew his way around a bottle of bleach. Lenore slumped onto the couch. The house creaked and groaned like a retiree murmuring complaints about the economy. She stood up and walked around the kitchen, then sat down at the table and pulled up Darius's video message. Her thumb hovered above the play icon, then swept the message away and pulled up a new conversation.

Hi. It's me again. I'm going to do something dangerous. I might get hurt. Maybe even get killed.

I know we're all afraid of death, but I feel like, for most people, that fear exists as a quiet murmur, whereas mine is an unceasing, stentorian Gregorian chant.

I've been trying to look in the face of death and laugh, but all I've been able to do is demurely bow my head and whimper, waiting for its final embrace, which looks like it might come sooner than I anticipated. If I don't write to you again. This is why.

I love you, Quan.

She sent the message and watched it slide onto the screen, where it joined the stream of hundreds of unanswered messages she'd sent over the last few weeks. She wiped the tears stinging her eyes, navigated back to the video, and hit play.

*　*　*

Darius pushed the door open and said, "Hey Len, I brought a surprise celebrity guest."

She stared, eyes and mouth wide open, a series of guttural noises sporadically leaping from her mouth.

"Great to meet you. I'm Kyle," he held out his hand in greeting.

"I know who you are. *Everyone* knows who you are." His gigantic, muscular arm hung in the air for a moment before she could bring herself to touch it. It didn't seem real that such a perfectly sculpted limb should exist outside of a cinema screen. The very act of shaking hands with him should have been as far-fetched as the existence of unicorns or the efficacy of trickle-down economics.

"You're really...you?"

Kyle took this question far too literally, chewed his lip, and said, "Wow, that's, like, sort of a philosophical question, I guess? Like, are any of us really *us*? How many types of self are there? I suppose right now...I am the self that is pleased to meet you."

"Yes. Me also as well. To meet you." She marvelled at the sight of her hand wrapped in his.

Darius leaned into Kyle's ear and said, "I think she's a little starstruck. She's not used to meeting famous actors."

Kyle laughed and said, "Oh, I'm nothing special. I have my servants put my pants on one leg at a time, same as everyone else." They stared at him. "That was a joke, you guys."

Lenore laughed effusively and slapped at his chest, then left her hand resting there for a while, gently stroking the bulk of muscle.

Darius lightly lifted it away and whispered, "Let's not grope the house guests, Len." He motioned for Kyle to take a seat on the couch.

"Nice place. I like the Art Deco ceilings. Ohh! Check out the light fittings! They must beeeeeee…Danish, am I right?" They looked at him, confused. "I'm dating an interior designer. She's trying to teach me this stuff. It's pretty interesting, actually. She recommended I get these new carpets made out of recycled corn husks. Isn't it crazy that they can do that? How the hell do you turn corn husks into *carpet*? What a world!"

Lenore stared at him. Darius rolled his eyes and slapped her leg with the back of his hand. "Sorry. I was rather distracted by—" she waved her finger in a slow rotation around Kyle's face "—this whole situation. So. Handsome."

Darius snatched her hand and pulled it down. "You're *embarrassing* me!"

"Right. Sorry. We should get down to it. Are we sure that your guy has taken care of the…unexpected mess?"

"You mean the dead bodies? Oh yeah, he said it was totally no problem. Just made it look like a burglary. That guy Ocky had a rap sheet a mile long, so it's all pretty plausible. He said he wished all his clean-up jobs were this easy."

"Kyle, I don't know how to thank you?"

"Nah, it's cool. Anything for Darius! Ohhhh, is this an Artemest chandelier? Niiiiiiice!"

He stood up to inspect it, took a few photos with his phone. Darius turned to Lenore and said, "I told you about how the Sixth Sun was grooming Kyle to be their new spokesperson—as of now, he's officially accepted the position. They've asked him to do a speech at the ceremony tonight."

"The same ceremony as on the video you sent me?" Lenore asked, managing to finally pummel her libido into submission for long enough to focus on the life-threatening situation at hand. Eros and Thanatos continued trading blows in her brain.

"Well, we're not *totally* sure. I'm not a full initiate into the Sixth Sun inner circle yet. So it might be a different ceremony. I hope they don't make me do anything weird. My cousin Jeremy was in a fraternity where they all had to have sex with a dead sheep to get in. He won't tell me who else was in the fraternity, but he swears that several of them are CEOs and senior politicians these days. Hopefully, it's one of those fun initiations, like where you have to do a bunch of shots and then go streaking?"

Darius watched Lenore's eyebrows jettison up her forehead at the suggestion of Kyle's nudity and snapped his fingers in front of her face. She jolted back into focus and said, "That's promising. I found a tape Elliott sent to Riley. Csaba talked all about how rites and rituals are core to their whole ethos. Their '11 secret herbs and spices,' as it were. Kyle, if you can stall whatever whacky séance-type activity they're up to, that should be able to buy us some time to sneak past security."

"No problemo! I'll go in and sign a few autographs, FaceTime their nieces or whatever. I can definitely drag an easy ten minutes of distraction out of that. Ceremony starts at midnight. If we go in sometime after close of business hours they should be on skeleton crew. That gives us a good window to get in and out."

"Assuming, of course, that both Csaba and Riley are there," said Darius.

Lenore frowned and said, "We'll have to hope that they are. I'm afraid we don't have any other options. Next question: Riley will most likely be on the locked floor, which we couldn't get into last time. How do we get access?"

Darius removed something small and shiny from his pocket.

"What is that?" asked Lenore.

Darius grinned and replied, "God mode."

41

ZOMBIES IN LOVE

Alastair Twombly was having a bad week. His IBS had been particularly brutal of late, and his girlfriend was seriously pissed at him for cancelling their date at the new Italian place to take a last-minute fill-in shift. Ocky—normally as reliable as gaffer tape—had been unavailable for some reason. To make matters worse, Twombly had been paired with Keith Haberschmidt, who asked questions like:

"You like music?"

"…who doesn't?"

"Yeah! Cool. Cool cool cooooool-i-o. I like music too, big fan. Big, big fan. I like, let's see, fugues, sonatas, dirges, psych jams, mash-ups, medleys—"

"I get it. You like musical collections of sound. Me too. Can we talk about something else?"

"Sure thing! You like TV?"

"If I say yes, are you going to list—"

"I like drama shows, comedy shows, new shows, old shows, foreign shows, old foreign shows, shows about cops, old foreign drama shows about cops—"

"Can you please stop listing things!"

"Sorry, just making conversation." He pulled out his torch, clicked it on and off, put it back again. "You like food?"

"*Everyone* likes food. It is impossible NOT to like food. Eating is a basic human urge, it is hard-wired into us that we must consume calories to survive. Have you EVER met anyone who did not enjoy the experience of eating? That is a NON-question. What else are you going to ask? You into breathing? What about sleep? Does the fundamental human requirement for sleep number amongst your daily activities?" Twombly paused, looking at the puppy-like disappointment in his partner's eyes. He sighed and said, "Look, I'm sorry. I'm having a rough week. You mind if we skip the chit-chat?"

"You'd prefer complete silence."

"Yes."

"Sure, I can do that."

Twombly grunted with relief and sat down in the thick plush office chair behind the receptionist's desk.

"I like silence. For sure. For sure, I do. I like silence in nature, silent movies, silent graphic novels, John Cage's *4:33 of silence*—" Haberschmidt was then stunned into silence (which was ironic given that this was the next kind of silence he was about to list), as Kyle Abrams strolled towards the glass entry doors. "Ohmygodohmygodohmygod!" Haberschmidt screeched, hopping from one foot to the other.

"What the fuck is your problem, man?"

"It's really him! Kyle Abrams, he's the reason why I became an actor!"

"But...you're a security guard?"

"No, I'm an actor! I only took this job as research for my role as Zombie Guard #3 in *Zombies In Love*."

"What the hell is *Zombies In Love*?"

"It's a zom-rom-com!"

"A *what*?"

"A zombie romantic comedy! Starts shooting next week. I've got a couple of sweet lines. Well, sounds anyway."

"You're playing a zombie guard?"

"Yes!"

"So, shouldn't you be researching zombies? I mean, do zombie guards act any differently from zombie Pilates instructors?"

"Of *course*! It's all about movement. You've got to have layers to your characters. Shhh, be cool, here he comes!"

The doors slid open, and Kyle strode in, flashing his Hollywood smile. Haberschmidt leapt forward and shook his hand exuberantly. "I'm so excited to meet you. I've seen everysingleoneofyourmovies except *Vampires In Space* because it was only released in Japan. I tried to download a torrent once, but it turned out to be the porn parody which wasn't totally without its own merits but obviously disappointing nonetheless. *Death-hunter* is my all-time favourite movie, followed by *Death-hunter 2* and then *Death-hunter: the director's cut* usually director's cuts are the superior version, but in this instance, I think the studio really—"

"Whoa, slow down, bud! Always good to meet a fan. Thanks so much for the compliments, you two!"

"I didn't say anything," grunted Twombly.

"Right, but you were going to. I have, like, a second sense for these things."

"Could I get a picture? My brother is not going to believe this!" Haberschmidt held out his phone.

Kyle grabbed it and extended his gigantic arms, one around Haberschmidt and the other reaching for Twombly, who stepped away and said,

"I'm good."

"Ok, wanna take the pic?"

"Sure." He held up the camera, but Kyle interrupted and said,

"You know what? The lighting's not so great in here. How about the boardroom?"

"I don't think—"

"Please? Do this one thing, and I promise I'll shut up all evening!" pleaded Haberschmidt.

Twombly considered this and said, "Not a single word?"

"Not a single *sound*. Not a sneeze, wheeze, or cough!"

"Fine, but let's make it quick." The three of them hurried into the boardroom and closed the door. Seconds later, the glass entry doors slid quietly open.

42

RENA

Darius pressed the 'stop' button, looked at Lenore, and said, "I wish Quan was here."

"He probably would've talked us into doing something reasonable like staying at home."

"Exactly. That's why I wish he was here. Instead, I find myself pondering the legal implications of misusing elevator fire keys." He took out the two keys that Kyle had gifted him, passed one to Lenore.

"And this firefighter he was sleeping with just…gave these to him?"

"You wouldn't believe some of the things fans gift him. Everything from hair and toenails to stolen museum pieces. It's wild. Still, her misdemeanour is our window of opportunity." He unlocked the service panel and inserted the key inside. "Kyle said that once we unlock God Mode, there's a good chance an alarm will sound. If that happens…"

Lenore inhaled and nodded for Darius to continue, but then grabbed his arm and pressed her finger to her lips. She pointed at the doors, cupped her ear to the cold metal surface. "I think someone's here. I can hear music."

Darius leaned in next to her, "On this floor?"

"Yes. What's going on?"

"I don't know, I can't make it out either."

"No, that's the song. Marvin Gaye's *What's Going On.* I know Csaba's a Motown fan, it might be him."

"Do you think Riley's with him?" asked Darius.

"Yes. I do." She reached for the 'open' button. Darius grabbed her hand and stared at her with imploring eyes.

Lenore pulled her hand away. "There's two of us and only one of him. Unless he's got some of his hired thugs with him. You're free to come with me or not, but I'm going in there." She hit the door release and ran towards the sound of Marvin crooning over the swelling strings.

"Len!" Darius hissed, rushing after her.

The office's blinds were drawn across the floor-to-ceiling windows, the bass causing them to tremble and shake. Lenore pressed her finger to her lips and looked back at Darius, who glared at her angrily. She grasped the handle gently and turned, but it was— unsurprisingly— locked. "What's going on? Ohhhhhhhh, what's going on!" Csaba sang exultantly from inside.

Darius grabbed a fire extinguisher from a nearby wall and mimed for Lenore to stand back. Mouthed '1,2,3' and hurled it at the glass.

Lenore covered her ears with her hands, expecting an ear-drum-shattering crash, but there was only a dull 'clang' as the extinguisher bounced off the glass and sent Darius flying back onto the carpet behind him. The door flung open, Lenore leapt back just in time to avoid being slammed in the face. The barrel of a gun poked out from where the door shielded her vision. Marvin's voice was now twice as loud, his velvety baritone pulsing through the hall.

"Well, hell-o! You look familiar." Csaba snapped his fingers. "I've seen you on set, haven't I? You usually look a lot more…corpse-y. Step into my office, if you'd be so kind. Tell you what, those reinforced windows just paid for themselves!"

Lenore watched in horror as Darius stepped into the office, she waited for a few terrifying seconds before slipping in behind them.

"If you'd be so kind as to clamber into that dewar there?" Csaba yelled over the music. "It's not powered, it's an archaic model we keep for display purposes. Locks quite nicely, though, so there's that." Darius did as he was commanded. Csaba placed the gun on the table to secure the lock.

Lenore ran to the table, snatched the gun, and yelled, "Hands up!"

Csaba turned around, surprised and irritated. "I really need to hire better security. It's like a Club Med in here." He glared at her and said, "Ocky's dead, I assume?"

She nodded.

"Unfortunate. I liked Ocky. I'll have to make arrangements for his children. Don't suppose you thought about *them*, did you?"

Lenore said nothing.

"I'm impressed by your gumption. Ocky was a tough customer. And I'll confess: 50k was a lowball offer. I can see now you're worth much more than that. Should we call it an even hundred?"

"I don't fucking care about money. Where's Riley?"

He tilted his head up, indicating the wall behind her where Riley lay sleeping beneath a crisp white sheet, her leathery skin covered in a series of arcane symbols. "You're a shrewd negotiator. I'll give you that. Let's call it…900 000? Nine is an important number in the Sixth Sun, you know, a trinity of trinities. Very auspicious."

"Stop *talking!*"

"Well, that's not how negotiations work *at all.*" Marvin Gaye was now asking *What's Happenin' Brother?* The music was so loud it filled not only her ears but her lungs, her muscles, her bones, her blood. Everything was shaking, spinning, sinking all at once.

"Turn it off!"

"The music?"

"Yes!"

"Alright. I have to reach into my pocket to turn it off with my phone. It's on Bluetooth." She glowered at him. "Happy to leave it, if you prefer. I mean, interrupting a James Jamerson bassline is a crime against humanity if you ask me."

She looked at Darius's pleading eyes, at Csaba's nonchalant grin. The air became thick and viscous. The ring on her hand—its claw newly emptied— was trembling. "Fine. Do it slowly."

"Sorry? Couldn't hear you," he said, pointing at the speakers.

"Do it slowly!" she yelled.

He nodded, made a show of slipping his hand inside his jacket and removing his phone. He pressed the screen, and the volume increased from loud to deafening. "Sorry!" he yelled, "Butterfingers! Just let me—" he dropped the phone, clambered to pick it up, and with a speed belying his fleshy frame, whipped a bizarre stone blade from his pocket and slashed her arm. She screamed, her voice joining Marvin's warbling croon. She dropped to the ground in pursuit of the gun, but Csaba planted his foot on top of it and held the blade in front of her nose, ushering her towards the nearest chair. She clenched at the gushing wound in her arm and sat down.

Marvin fell swiftly silent. Lenore's ears rang with a high-pitched squeal. She could barely make out Darius's muted yelling from inside the chamber. His fists banged frantically on the glass, dull thumps penetrating the screeching in her ears. Csaba picked up the gun, put the knife on the table, and sat down opposite her. For a while, he said nothing, then he clicked the safety back on and placed the gun on the table in front of him before folding his hands and resting his chin on his thumbs. He regarded her with a Cheshire smile and said, "To think that it was only a few days ago that the two of us were sharing a cup of tea and exchanging pleasantries. And now here we are."

"I need an ambulance."

"That's a fair assessment of the situation, yes. Take this for the time being." He reached into his pocket, pulled out a silk handkerchief with a magician's flourish, and tossed it to her.

She tied it around the wound and watched the virginal white quickly change to red.

Csaba nodded at the knife in front of them. "This is the ceremonial knife we'll be using later tonight. It's an original Aztec artifact, seven hundred years old! This blade has been drawing blood since the days of geocentrism. Odd design though, isn't it? The teeth, the bulging eye? Looks like something an 8th-grader would come up with for their D&D campaign. It's called a 'smiling knife', because they believed that the sacrifice was a joyful thing that would halt the destruction of their era— our current era—the fifth sun.

"I told you once that Rena would've liked you. I'm even more certain of that now. You're every bit as stubborn and reckless as she was." Darius's thumping continued; Csaba shot him an angry look, picked up the gun, and pointed it at Lenore, mimed firing it. Darius lapsed into silence, and Csaba turned back to her. "Your brother, I presume? The family resemblance is strong."

"..."

"If you were in my position, what would you do?"

"You mean if I was a delusional megalomaniac who'd started a death cult—"

"We're the very antithesis of a death cult."

"—as a money-making venture?"

He snorted, sat back, and said, "How did you arrive at a fanciful little conclusion like that?"

"Elliott had a tape of one of your early meetings."

Csaba nodded, impressed. "Which meeting was it, just out of curiosity?"

"The one where you blackmailed your co-conspirators and outlined the sacred tenets."

Csaba laughed. "Really? Wow. I wouldn't mind hearing that, for old times' sake. Seems like an eon ago now." He paused to look over at Riley and said nothing for a while, then said, "You interrupted one of my all-time favourite albums, *What's Going On.* An absolute start-to-finish masterpiece. Do you know how Marvin Gaye died?"

"His dad killed him."

"You know your music history! There's a little more to it than that, though." He took his phone out again, touched the screen, and the music resumed, this time at a more reasonable volume. "Back in the early eighties, Marvin wasn't doing so well; he had issues with drugs, mental health, debt. Fame and fortune hadn't been good for him, and he'd hit an artistic slump. He managed a comeback hit with *Sexual Healing* and hit the road, even though—like a surprising number of musicians—he hated touring. He became very paranoid. He actually wore a bulletproof vest for much of that tour, convinced that some stranger in the crowd was going to kill him. Can you imagine? Working your way through uplifting pop masterpieces like

Ain't No Mountain High Enough whilst scanning the crowd for some lunatic you were convinced was about to bury a bullet in your chest?

"He made it through the tour alive and ended up living back at home with his family, not exactly living the dream. He was buried in debt, despite his immense income, and losing himself to drugs. His father, Marvin Gay Sr., was—like you, like me, a complex character—a man of contradictions. He was a preacher and had a strict moral code that he enforced on his children throughout their upbringing, whilst himself indulging in heavy drinking, domestic violence, and—according to some—cross-dressing.

"The two of them never really got along. And here they were, both grown men, years of resentment boiling away underneath them, living under the same roof. The whole situation was a fuse just waiting for a match! Christmas day, 1983, Marvin the younger gets his father a very strange gift: a Smith & Wesson .38 special 'to protect himself' from intruders.' Beyond ironic. A few months later, Marvin and his dad had a fight. Marvin Sr. pulls the gun, you know the rest. Tragic sidenote: according to Marvin's brother Frankie, the prince of soul's final words were 'I got what I wanted…I couldn't do it myself, so I made him do it.'" He spun the revolver in a slow circle on the table. "Elliott told me he wanted out, more than once. I wouldn't let him go. But he got what he wanted in the end." He picked up the gun, turned it over in his hand. "See what make this is?"

"Smith & Wesson."

"That's right, .38 special. I carry it with me to remind me that it's the ones you love who can hurt you the most." He placed it back on the table. Blood leaked through Lenore's bandage, crimson tears dripping onto the aged oak. From behind where Csaba was seated, Lenore glimpsed a quick shimmer of movement. "I'm envious that you were able to attend Elliott's funeral. I still can't believe he banned me from going. He really knew how to hold a grudge, even in death. I loved that man. People like to say, 'I loved him like a brother,' but my brothers were violent sadists, so personally I don't find that to be a useful comparison." He rolled up his sleeve to reveal a series of scars and cigarette burns. "Got a whole list of reasons right here why they never got an invite into the fold." He wiped tears from his eyes, sniffed. "The thing you have to realise, Lenore, is that the tape you heard was recorded a very long time ago."

Lenore tried to keep her eyes locked on Csaba as Riley's eyes fluttered open. "It's true. Back then, I was a mere entrepreneur. I thought of it as a simple combination of self-preservation and the pursuit of profit. But after years of research and reflection, ritual and communion, my belief is as pure as that of any Buddhist monk or Hindu sadhu. The Sixth Sun is the future of the human species. I would kill for this cause. I would die for this cause, or refuse to die for this cause, as the case may be."

Riley surveyed her surroundings and attempted to lift herself off the table, but her left hand was cuffed to the bed. Lenore kept her eyes laser-focused on Csaba. "I'm not some bloodthirsty villain who enjoys killing, there's a reason why I usually pay people to do the wetwork for me. I find the very concept of death to be repulsive. And no, I'm not going to kill you, or your brother. We'll probably have to work out some sort of permanent internment. However, I'm afraid Riley's death is non-negotiable. Her sacrifice is the centrepiece of our ceremony tonight. Her very existence is an affront to our sacred tenets, so there's a beautiful symmetry to her immolation."

Riley's eyes lit up with anger, she pointed at the cuff on her hand and then looked at Lenore, held up her right hand, and began counting down with her fingers 5, 4, 3…

"You made all of this up, you lunatic!" Lenore screeched as Riley yanked at her thumb and clenched her entire body in an attempt to stop herself from screaming. Even through the fog of the fading sedative, the pain rioting from her dislocated thumb was significant. She was grateful for the sound of Marvin's soulful voice masking her movements.

"I used to think that too, but now I realise I simply discovered it. It was my own arrogance that led me to believe that I could invent something that is simply the fundamental truth of the universe. I didn't anymore 'invent' the Sixth Sun than Newton invented gravity. They were inevitable discoveries. It simply took the right men to stumble upon them. The Sixth Sun is the synthesis and advancement of all humanity's prior belief systems merged into the one true, absolute religion; godless and pure."

Riley slid off the bed and inched quietly towards him. Lenore yelped and grabbed at her arm. "It hurts! I have to get to a hospital."

Csaba leaned in to look at her arm, then snatched up both the knife and the revolver and spun around just as Riley was about to dive towards him. "Lenore, you have many talents, but acting doesn't number amongst them. Riley, stay where you are, or I'll kill you where you stand."

Riley peeled her lips back to reveal a parade of jagged teeth. "But you're going to kill me anyways, right?"

He recoiled and raised the gun higher. Lenore realised he was hearing her unnerving broken-glass-and-helium voice for the first time. "Let's talk about this calmly."

"We passed 'talk about it calmly' a while's back, Csabs." She took another step forward, closing the distance between them.

"I *will* shoot you!"

She shrugged and said, "So do it then." She grabbed his wrist and pressed the gun against her forehead, staring directly at him.

He stared into her unblinking green eyes. They were wholly, utterly, impossibly fearless. Csaba had built an empire around the fear of mortality. He'd killed and bribed and blackmailed to avoid ever facing up to the terror of his own non-existence, and here was this frail teenage girl who was staring into the face of her death, completely unafraid. A mere squeeze of the trigger and her consciousness would be forever obliterated. And yet she regarded him with all the boredom of a weary bank teller at the end of a twelve-hour shift.

This tiny neurological glitch had granted her the power that he'd been seeking ever since the day he'd set eyes upon Rena's cold, still corpse. In that instant, more than anything — more than angry, more than vengeful, more than afraid—Csaba was envious. He felt that insidious envy surge through him as Riley gripped his wrist and pulled the gun from his hand at the same moment that Lenore grabbed his left hand and shoved the ceremonial blade he was clutching between his ribs. The ancient stone pierced his flesh, violently relocating his viscera, its toothy smile jutting grotesquely from his side. He flailed as Riley extracted the knife, staring directly at him as she drove it deep into his heart.

The world melted around him like ice cream on searing summer asphalt, the walls liquefying, Marvin's voice blurring and distorting. He stared at her fearless green eyes as he fell, the journey to the floor seeming to last aeons and epochs. The memories of his life eddied around him—emancipated from their linear structure into the terrible and beautiful chaos of the infinite present; every kiss and kindness, every song and smile, every mistake and malfeasance—all rushing, swooping, diving like spirits around and through him as the life he had clung to so desperately rushed out of his body and dissipated into the void. As he crashed onto the floor and felt death swallow him, Csaba at long last felt unafraid. He could not hear the occupants of the room around him over the titanic roar of his memories filling the fading corona of his consciousness. As his last breath, last pulse, last thought shuddered through his body, Csaba whispered his final word:

"Rena…"

43

ANTIQUARIAN FUTURE

The silence had texture: thick, gnarled, nodular. The four dozen men and women in that hermetically sealed room—shielded against sound, radio signal, nuclear radiation— stood still and unspeaking. Cumulatively they controlled tens of billions of dollars in assets, hundreds of thousands of employees, entire nations' worth of property. Their payrolls included police and politicians, activists and artists, criminals and cardinals. They owned property, companies, concepts, data. They had arrived from every corner of the globe in private jets and limousines and yachts and helicopters. But in that room, utterly disconnected from the outside world, they were simply still and patient bodies, almost indistinguishable beneath their wine-red cloaks.

Another cloaked figure entered the room, slightly taller than the rest. He strode confidently onto the stage, his footsteps beating like war drums. He stood in front of them, raised his hands skyward, and chanted "Death shall have no domin-i-on!"

"Death shall have no domin-i-on!" The crowd chanted back in unison.

He lowered his hands, reached into the box on the table behind him, removed an ancient reptile, and held it aloft. Nero regarded the cloaked assembly with independently rotating eyes. What the hell were these humans doing dressed in those weird red skins? Not only were they the only species on earth to be so ashamed of their own bodies that they kept them constantly covered, now they had these odd hoods so you couldn't even see their beady mammalian eyes.

"Tu-a-tara! Tu-a-tara!" the crowd chanted. Nero gaped his mouth open and flicked his tail, displaying his disdain for the humans, but they failed to understand his incredibly unsubtle body language, the contemptible fools. He was placed back in his box, where he lay in the cool, dark space and dreamt of hunting beneath sun and open sky.

There was a pregnant pause as the figure on stage surveyed the crowd. "Children of the Sixth Sun, I bring you glorious news!" A few of the cloaked faces turned to look at each other. They had been expecting Csaba to perform the sacred ceremony. The question boiled and bubbled on their lips, the speaker answered it before it was given voice. "Csaba shall soon join us. But first, I have been bequeathed with the task of making a grand elevation!" A cough erupted in front of him, the speaker waved his hands in apology and said, "Sorry, *revelation*. A grand revelation!"

Murmurs broke out amongst the crowd, the speaker held up his hands and commanded "Silence!" with a stentorian boom, the room fell deathly silent. He raised his hands to his hood and held them there for a moment, milking the dramatic tension. With a grand sweep, he pulled the hood back, a luminous smile filling his famous face. A sea of reactions swelled and surged in the room, ranging from coquettish giggling to high-pitched yelping to awed profanity. Kyle raised his hands and said, "Brothers and sisters, it is a great honour to meet you at long last!"

"*Werewolves On Wall St* is my favourite movie!" screamed one woman with all the tittering delight of a high-school cheerleader (she owned the world's second-largest real estate company).

"You rock, dude!" yelped a tribal-tattooed investment banker, his voice breaking in nervous excitement (he owned three yachts and a Caribbean island on which he moored them).

"I love youuuu!" squealed the CFO of one of the world's largest tech companies, (she regularly hosted world leaders at her ski villa).

"Please, brothers and sisters! You honour me with your kind words, but we are all equals under the light of the Sixth Sun! We are all the chosen few, seeking an antiquarian future!" Again, a figure in the front coughed. Kyle glanced down and then said, "Ah, I mean, an equestrian future!" Silence. The figure murmured again, and Kyle said, "Sorry! I mean e-qual-it-ar-ian future." The crowd cheered and applauded in equal parts due to the stirring of their hearts, their fame-tickled egos, and their inflamed ovaries.

"Now, for the great revelation from Csaba himself." He swept his hand dramatically towards the elevator entrance. The doors slid open, and Csaba appeared, but not in the manner his brethren had been expecting. A cloaked devotee wheeled him in on a stretcher trolley, sheet drawn up above his hips, his bare chest covered in the arcane symbols he'd pilfered from a plethora of ancient esoteric traditions, including Gnostic, Coptic, Sufi, Hindu, and—he'd never admitted this to his brethren—a couple of borrowed glyphs from the fantasy card game *Magic: The Gathering*.

Covered in this pastiche of chicane iconography, he looked transcendent, regal, mystical. However, the most eye-catching part of his appearance was the gaping red chasm in his left breast. Hushed, awed whispers filled the room. "Behold! The great Founder has given his life for us! The blood sacrifice *is his own*!" Csaba was wheeled into the centre of the room as the chanting swelled, effulgent with the awe of Csaba's ultimate sacrifice.

"Tu-a-tara! Tu-a-tara!" They roared, fists pumping with Super Bowl-esque fury. Kyle pushed forward a table containing a silver tray with a small collection of eye droppers and a slender flask.

"My brethren and uh, wait, what's the female equivalent of brethren?" Kyle bit his lip and searched his memory, the crowd waiting expectantly. The figure in the front row coughed irritably, and Kyle said, "Anyway, brothers and sisters! Before he made the grand sacrifice, Csaba revealed unto me one final revealing, ah, revelation!" He studied the enraptured crowd. Kyle hadn't done any live performances in over a decade. He'd forgotten how much he missed the rush of standing in front of an enraptured audience. "The night of ascension has come sooner than was expected. There have been great new, ah... Augustines and portions?" More angry coughing. "Sorry, *auguries* and *portents*! All is in order..." The crowd stared up at him, eyes and mouths wide with wonder. He could taste their anticipation on his tongue. "Our preparations are complete. At last, we greet the age of the Sixth Sun! Now we ascend!"

He threw his hands exultantly upwards, awaiting an uproarious cheer, but was greeted with only deathly silence. Kyle suddenly remembered why he'd stopped doing theatre. Long repressed memories of lukewarm applause came rushing back. The spectre of failure ran through him, hungry and enraged. His eyes crept down, looking at the crowd who were now glancing nervously at one another. Finally, the tribal-tattooed banker broke the hideous silence and said,

"Ah, bro? Just to confirm, you're saying it's happening, like, *right now?*"

Kyle coughed nervously, recovered his composure, and roared, "Do you question the founder's blood sacrifice?!"

"No way! Ah, I was just, like, confirming? 'Cos, y'know, we're all basically good to go, as per the schedule, but Csaba said that before we jumped into cryo, we'd have a chance to run upstairs where we can get a phone signal and talk to our estate lawyers, and VPs to make final arrangements?"

"Who else among you requires counsel with your lawyers before the ascension?" A forest of fingers sprouted in front of him. His mind raced, which was a difficult change of pace for a brain that was far more accustomed to a lazy saunter. "Very well! First, drink of his blood, then go make your arrangements. *Then* shall we begin the grand ascension!"

The cheer that erupted filled the room, his ears, his heart, his soul. The hooded figures formed an orderly line (they were not used to queuing for anything, so this was in itself a miracle) as he dispensed a single drop of blood onto each of their tongues before they moved in small groups to the elevator.

At last, only three hooded figures remained in the lower chamber. They looked up at Kyle. He put the eye-dropper down and said, "Thanks for the help with my lines, D. That was my best performance since *Hamlet 2: Son of Hamlet!*" Darius, Lenore, and Riley threw their hoods back, looking at each other with profound relief.

"Don't get too fucking comfy. It ain't over 'til the chunky señora solos."

"Riley's right. We shouldn't really relax until they're all in the chambers."

"What did we use for blood anyway?"

"Csaba had some tomato juice in his fridge. It's pretty dark in here, can't really tell the difference," said Lenore.

"Yeah, okay, but how come, like, no one noticed that the tomato juice tasted like, you know, tomato juice?" said Riley.

"I guess no one wants to be the guy who says, 'Hey, this doesn't taste like real blood!'" She stared at Csaba's lifeless body. He looked like he was smiling. Even in death, he was a smarmy bastard.

"The cloak really suits you, Slenderman."

Darius groaned and said, "I *told* you not to call me that."

"Yeah, well, in the last couple of hours, I escaped a ritual sacrifice and ran a 700-year-old ceremonial knife through the heart of a cult leader, so, you know. I'm feelin' a little fancy-free."

Lenore sniffed. The three of them turned towards her. "It's after midnight, which means it's been forty-nine days. Quan is officially gone. He's passed through the final bardo. If you believe in that stuff. Which I don't." She buried her face in her hands, and Darius pulled her tight into a hug. "He's properly, finally gone."

They stood still and listened to Lenore's crying for a few seconds before Riley blurted, "Who the fuck is Quan?"

Lenore mentally fumbled with the idea of explaining everything to her, but was interrupted by the 'ding' of the elevator arriving. They swept their hoods back over their faces and stood solemnly waiting as the Sixth Sun devotees began filing back into the room. Lenore's tears slipped silently to the floor, invisible and unnoticed.

44

USUALLY THERE'S A SEX SCENE OR A CHEERING CROWD?

Mass ritual suicide turned out to be surprisingly clean and expedient. Each of the Sixth Sun devotees climbed into their custom-built chambers, said a few final words (these ranged from prayers to self-confidence mantras to requests for the universe to manifest their destinies), then pressed the activation button. One by one, the chambers flooded with liquid helium and left them frozen, static, and silent. Lenore and her companions pretended to be busying themselves with tidying up after the ritual as they waited for the last follower to enter his chamber. Their bodies tensed in simultaneous apprehension as the portly man climbed into the dewar, murmured his goodbyes, closed his eyes, reached for the activation button, then jerked upright and yelped, "Wait! I left my phone upstairs!" He was halfway out when he froze, looked at Lenore in stunned silence, then broke into uproarious laughter and said, "Gosh, how silly of me! My iPhone's going to be a *teensy* bit obsolete by the time I wake up! So embarrassing. Well, here I go, see you in the new world!" He chuckled to himself, closed the lid, activated the chamber, took slow heavy breaths as the blue liquid travelled up his feet, his lips, filled his mouth, his lungs, his chest. He closed his eyes for the last time, surrendering to eternal sleep.

257

Everyone pulled their hoods back and exhaled. "Are we mass murderers now? How many people do you have to kill for it to be a 'mass'?" asked Riley.

"They don't believe it to be death," said Darius.

"Yeah, but we do?"

"We didn't actually *do* anything to them. Let's call it passive observance of a religious ritual resulting in an alteration of states of consciousness," said Lenore.

"AKA 'mass murder'. Pffft, whatever floats your boat on your moat. Those fuckers had it coming, they were going to ritually sacrifice someone. Specifically me. Quick Q: What are we gonna do with him?" She pointed at Csaba's corpse, then noticed the prominent erection that had formed a pale tent in the centre of his sheet. "Holy fuck, he's not dead!" she screamed, leaping behind Kyle's gigantic chest.

Lenore patted her shoulder reassuringly and said, "Relax, it's just rigor mortis."

"Huh?"

"Rigor mortis. The body stiffens a few hours after death."

"Dead people get *boners*? Ugh. Humans are so gross."

"No argument here. Anyway, his chamber is waiting. I suppose we might as well use it."

"Of course, it's the one that's ornate and lavishly over-designed," said Darius, wheeling him to the dewar.

"Funny how the founders of these allegedly egalitarian cults always find ways to emphasise hierarchy. I once worked at a funeral where the guy was buried in a diamond-encrusted coffin. *Diamonds!* I felt like going back and digging them up, even if only to donate them to a charity or something."

"Where was this grave, just out of curiosity?" asked Riley.

Lenore shook her head and said, "Nice try. Help me lift the body."

"Okay, but if that dead man boner touches me, I am going to need therapy for, like, ten billion years."

Kyle pushed his bulging shoulder underneath Csaba's back and lifted him with a grunt, the rest of them helping to manoeuvre his limbs. They pushed and squeezed until he was inside, then attempted to shut the lid. "It won't close," he said.

"Can't we ram it shut?" asked Riley

"We're not jamming bread into a freezer!" said Darius.

"Yeah, because bread in a freezer still has a purpose. This is the dead body of a violent psycho."

"Fair point."

They pushed and groaned until at last the lid sealed with a satisfying vacuum hiss. Lenore fell to the floor and leaned with her back against the wall. She stared at the array of blue-lit cadavers, the quiet hum of the refrigeration units filling the room with a low sonic drone. "I should call Audrey and Orin, let them know that they're safe. I just need to sit for a minute. My head is spinning."

"Yeah, I oughta call my mum. Tell her I've been out tagging trains or something. Funny, usually I'm out tagging trains, and I have to make up a cover story for *that*."

Kyle picked up Nero's box. Nero regarded him with a look of abject reptilian disdain, but Kyle completely failed to pick up on the cue and said, "Best co-star I ever had, great work, Nero!" He turned to face everyone with an offensively bright smile. "So, I guess...we won? In my movies, when my character wins, someone gets thrown out of a helicopter or a space shuttle or into an inter-dimensional portal, then I do a big speech about good triumphing over evil, and then usually there's a sex scene or a cheering crowd?" He looked around the room at the mute, frozen bodies and his haggard companions eyeing him with weary confusion. "Well, okay, so I guess we don't do any of that, but...we *did* win, right?"

Darius shrugged and said, "We're all still alive. Sure, let's chalk it up as a win."

"Except for the fact that my best friend might never forgive me for putting her family in danger and Ray is dead and Oliver is in hospital and might never walk again and you and Darius are now unemployed and I killed a man with a belt and Riley stabbed Csaba with a ceremonial knife."

"*And* I almost definitely failed my chemistry exam," added Riley.

Lenore glared at her, shook her head, then held her arm out to Darius. He grabbed it and pulled her to her feet. She leaned into him, tired and defeated, and said, "We'd better leave this lot to their eternal nap time." She took one last look at the dewars. Her eyes drifted to one in the corner where a man roughly Quan's age and build slept, soundless and cold. For the second time that week, she imagined it was Quan lying in quiet cryonic slumber. She pictured herself flicking a switch, watching the frost fade, holding her breath as his eyelids flickered and his lungs filled with air, a disbelieving smile creeping across his face. But then she blinked, refocused her eyes, and the illusion was gone. The man in the dewar was just another dead body. Same as Quan.

Same as her mother.

Rena.

Claire.

Elliott.

Ray.

Ocky.

Csaba.

Same as Lenore herself would be someday. She fumbled amongst her robes for the security pass they'd stolen from Csaba, swiped it against the elevator's magnetic strip. They all climbed inside, and Riley announced, "Going up! Next stop: ladies' underwear, assault rifles, party supplies, and—"

Lenore touched her lightly on the shoulder and said, "Riley, may I ask a tiny favour?"

"Shoot."

"Would you kindly shut the fuck up, if it's not too much trouble?"

Riley shrugged. The doors slid closed, and the elevator carried them skyward.

The chamber was still and peaceful in their absence. The lights of the dewars glowed with a cold cerulean calm. The soft buzzing of their refrigeration mechanisms was almost meditative. Dozens of former rulers of empires— their thrones and board seats newly vacated— lay frozen and unmoving. In death, their faces were oddly indistinguishable. Beneath the blue lights and frosted glass windows, the hues of their skin and the shape of their features blurred and became uniform. In life, they had been CEOs, influencers, philanderers, innovators, politicians, thieves, entrepreneurs. In death, they were all equal — silent and serene.

III

SIXTH BARDO

45

AGATHOKAKOLOGICAL

Lenore sat in the church pew, studying the light coruscating through the stained-glass windows. The colours spilled over the small assembly as they dabbed at tears and quietly consoled each other. She listened to the piano notes tinkling towards the vaulted church ceiling. Although she'd only had time to procure a few basic items of clothing since the destruction of her apartment, she had gone out of her way to find the elegant black veil she was now wearing. She watched the world through a thin mesh of crisscrossing black lines, enjoying the partial obscurity it allowed her.

The funeral director finished his speech, then introduced Lenore, and gestured for her to come up to the stage. She studied the gentle taps of her feet on the wooden floor as she walked. She adjusted the microphone, placed her palm cards on the lectern in front of her, and spread her hands flat across its surface. She looked out at the familiar faces in the audience: Darius, Audrey and her girls, Oliver, Riley and her mum, Kyle and the latest in his long line of amorous acquaintances (Tiffany? Tina? Therese?)

She took a deep breath and began. "My father was not a perfect man. If he was here today, he'd be muttering criticisms about the decor, the food, my outfit. He'd be complaining that he was yet to meet his grandchildren, that my brother and I lacked respectable careers. Then he'd probably start smoking, bitterly sniping at any poor fool who had the gall to try and tell him that you can't smoke in church. 'What the hell does God care? He's already dead anyway!'" There was a quiet ripple of laughter from the audience.

"My dad was a good husband and a bad driver, a great father and an unreliable friend, a fantastic teacher and an awful gossip, a tremendous singer and a tragic cook; he was obsessive and irritable, cantankerous and kind, judgmental and jubilant. Like all of us, he was agathokakological; he contained both good and evil.

"For most of his life, he pored over an esoteric analysis of death and economics, claiming it would be his legacy, that it would change the world. It didn't. One local paper did call it 'oddly prescient' in light of the current global economic stasis. There was a small smattering of online discussion about it, so I'm glad he got some satisfaction from that before he passed away, even if he did spend his last days online yelling at his detractors who preferred to use terms like 'incoherent raving' and 'rambling pseudoscience.'

"Dad was obsessed with the idea of legacy, so much so that he sometimes forgot to dwell in the present. He didn't create the grand legacy he hoped for, but precious few of us do. Of all the souls who've ever lived, only a fraction manage to produce work of the calibre of Aristotle, Caravaggio, or John Lennon. But then again, Aristotle hated women, Caravaggio killed one of his rivals, and John Lennon used to beat his wife. In all of those regards, my father was vastly superior. So maybe Dad doesn't rank amongst the greatest geniuses who ever walked the earth, but he was more good than bad, and that in itself is a legacy of which he should be proud, and he will be missed." She paused, watched a tear slip from her cheek onto the palm card, corrupting the ink into a messy black ripple across the page.

"There's a Buddhist belief that states the process of death takes a total of forty-nine days. There are various bardos, or states of transition that a soul passes through over the course of its existence. In death, we move through the final three until the soul finds its new parents and is reborn." She paused, looked up. "But my father was no Buddhist. People always say, 'He died doing what he loved,' this was not entirely true in my father's case. He died in his sleep, and he *hated* sleeping. He once said to me: 'I'll sleep when I'm dead. Bury me in the earth; let me become food for the worms.

Even the sun will grow cold and die. Why should I be any more special?'
And I was only five at the time, so that should demonstrate how strongly he
felt about the issue." She turned to face her father's coffin and said, "Sleep
well, Dad. We'll miss you." She waved Darius up to the lectern, and as the
crowd moved their focus onto him, she walked over to her father's coffin,
leaned in, and said goodbye. Then she slipped the empty-clawed ring from
her finger and placed it in his suit pocket.

"Here. I think you need this more than I do."

46

THE WORLD'S MOST DEPRESSING SITCOM

Lenore wrapped Audrey in an awkward hug, somewhat encumbered by the two tiny humans who had enclosed themselves around her legs. "No robot legs today girls. I'm tired." The twins climbed off and mumbled complaints, then chased after a butterfly, squealing and laughing.

Audrey snorted a laugh, "God, I wish I could turn my emotional faucets on and off like that. It's crazy, isn't it? How they'll lose their shit for hours over not getting ice cream but straight after a funeral, they can frolic after butterflies like hysterical entomologists."

"I think you mean lepidopterists."

"Even at your dad's funeral, you're still pedantic."

Lenore shrugged. "You know I can't ever make up for what—"

"Shut it. We've been over this enough. I'm not going to stand here with your deceased father spitting distance away and squabble over this again. You're doing your best to atone, and that's all anyone can ever hope to do. And, you know, I'm not totally without blame myself. I still feel like a monster for not coming to Ray's funeral with you."

"I wouldn't have asked—"

"You shouldn't have had to ask. That's the whole point."

"I know. Thanks."

"You're welcome. That said if you ever put my girls in danger like that again? You'll be taking a permanent cryo nap alongside all those other creepy rich bastards."

"Understood."

Audrey swept her hair behind her eyes. "I should go, let you catch up with young Lazarus over there." She nodded at the slender solitary figure by the water's edge. "Rehearsal Thursday, yeah?"

"I'll be there."

Audrey scooped her girls up, hefted them over her shoulders like they were squirming, capricious sacks of flour, and walked off towards her car. Lenore walked over to Oliver, waving a gentle hello as she approached.

Oliver stared at the river, leaning on the cane that had quickly come to be as much a part of him as his own legs. It was a classic design: polished silver head, dark Birchwood body.

"That one of the fancy ones with a hidden sword inside?" Lenore asked.

"Of course," he replied. She laughed, and he looked at her solemnly, then slid the head back and revealed a slender blade that glinted resplendently in the sun.

"I was only joking!"

Oliver shrugged and slid it back in place. "Can't be too careful. Not as light and portable as a razor, but on the plus side, it's got a far more formidable reach so that certainly works in my...ah, you know..."

"Favour?"

"Yes," he grunted tersely. "It's hard to remember words sometimes. They feel foggy...indistinct. Like letters on an eye chart a little bit too far away."

"You're looking well, though."

"Am I?" he scoffed, turning to face her, revealing the cavernous scar on his other cheek.

"Well, you're not dead. So you've got that one up on my dad."

He looked at his feet and said nothing.

"Sorry. That was uncalled for. You've every right to be angry. It goes with your new look, in any case. I think it makes you look mysterious, enigmatic."

He grunted again. "Really? The other day, a kid pointed at me and said, 'Mummy, get the bad man away. He's going to eat me!'"

"Kids are dumb."

"It wasn't the child that bothered me. It was the mum who—instead of seizing a teachable moment and saying, 'actually, you shouldn't judge a person by their external appearance, he's probably suffered a lot of hardship, and we should show him kindness and empathy'— just glared at me, clutched her kid to her chest and whispered 'don't worry sweetheart, Mummy will protect you.'"

"Kids are dumb. Adults are monsters."

"Indeed."

"I'm glad you're back in the land of the living. Are you looking after yourself?"

"I have a good therapist. Things aren't exactly sunshine and seashells inside my skull, but I'm not delusional anymore. Most of the time. My parents have offered to pay for my treatment, which I appreciate. Therapy doesn't come cheap." He poked at the ground with his cane, stared at the water. "I'm not ready for a full-time job yet, but I've been doing a little bit of volunteer work at the youth shelter. Helping kids with homework, making sandwiches. The injuries make it hard, though. My head feels like it's filled with static. And I don't sleep well. Sometimes, even with all the drugs, the pain in my spine is just, ah…it's, um…"

"Excruciating?"

"I was going to say unbearable."

"Your parents are talking to you again, though?"

He nodded. "They've left the church. And to think all I had to do was attempt suicide, live in a graveyard in a state of psychotic delusion, and be permanently maimed by a violent criminal. They've been excommunicated. They did that for me. That's, ah, ah, s-s-s—"

"Something?"

"It's significant. I'm living in their rumpus room. It's like the world's most depressing sitcom. All we need now is a talking dog and a nosy neighbour." His phone bleeped. He took it out and smirked. "Speak of the devil. It's funny; they had no idea what I was up to or where I was for years, and now they need to check in on me if I'm out of the house for more than an hour."

The last of the funeral procession clambered out of the driveway. Audrey honked her horn and waved goodbye as she departed. "Are you and Audrey okay?" asked Oliver.

"'Okay' is a bit of a stretch. I had to promise six months of babysitting, which equates to approximately twenty billion dollars' worth of labour, in my estimate."

He laughed, then winced and held his ribs. "Sorry. Hurts when I laugh."

"You're a walking manifestation of the ridiculousness of the human condition."

He shot her a mock glare and said, "I hear you've left the exciting field of professional mourning?"

"Yes. After saying goodbye to Quan, and Ray, and now Dad, I've had enough death to last me a lifetime. I used my last paycheque to buy a new bass. Audrey, Darius, and I want to spend more time on the band. We've got a little regional festival and a couple of decent support slots coming up. Music is terrible money, obviously. But Kyle promised he could hook Darius and me up with PA work on his films whenever he shoots locally. It's not particularly glamorous, but he's a nice enough guy, and the money's decent."

"And I suppose you don't have to worry about rent anymore."

"The Brindle house doth provide, even if my current living arrangements are somewhat unorthodox. I should be able to get by for a while until I figure out what I want to do with myself. Job markets are all rather stale, what with the economic stasis. Who would've thought a bunch of snap-frozen CEOs intentionally plateauing the global financial market would impact my life choices so directly?"

"I read your dad's paper. Maybe prognostication runs in your family. It was strangely prophetic."

"Or just strange. Depending on your take."

"Perhaps." He adjusted his tie. Coughed. "You gave a beautiful eulogy. Much better than any of the eulogies at my funeral. Not that it's a competition."

"I ripped it off the internet. Check out movingeulogiesfordads.com if you're ever stuck for ideas."

"Very droll. You can be honest, you know. You don't have to always hide what you're feeling behind your literal and metaphorical veils."

She considered this, then pulled her veil off and threw it into the air. It carried gently on the breeze for a few feet, swooping and twirling like an intoxicated crow, then landed on the water and drifted away with the current. "It hurts. It hurts like my heart is being crushed and my soul is being stretched and my skin is burning and I can't sleep and a black hole is growing in my stomach."

He squeezed her into a hug. They pulled apart, watched the veil drifting out of view. "And I suppose we're going to ignore the fact that you've wantonly littered in a sacred place?"

"I was being symbolic!" she laughed and punched him in the arm.

Oliver doubled over in agony, gasping with pain.

"Sorry!"

He waved her apology away, drew himself back up. "It's fine. It's not like I'm covered in an array of obvious physical deformities to remind you of my fragility or anything." She commenced a stream of apologies, and he interrupted her and said, "I think you get a pass, given your current circumstance. And for the record, the only reason why I haven't said 'I'm sorry for your loss' or 'is there anything I can do?' is because I'm thoroughly familiar with your rant about funeral platitudes and clichés."

"Actually, I was going to ask you to do me a favour."

"Of course, anything."

"I need you to listen to what I'm about to say, very carefully. I don't want any confusion afterwards."

"After what?"

47

AN EPHEMERAL SNEEZE OF PROGNOSTICATION

I t was brief, gentle, and quiet. Afterwards, neither of them spoke for a while. Finally, Oliver turned to her and said, "Did it help?"

"A little. Thanks."

"You're welcome." He laughed and said, "That's the first time I've ever said 'you're welcome' after sex. Normally I'm the one who's grovelling and grateful."

Lenore turned to him with a half-smile. "Makes things a little less numb, at least for a while. I'm sorry about—"

"No, it's fine. I'm still getting used to reminding myself about the pain. I'll have to be more careful in future. It's not like I was ever any kind of sexual acrobat, but I might have to keep it simple from now on."

"Sexual acrobat? I'm using that as a song title at some point, for sure."

He sat up, looked around the bedroom, thick with the smell of fresh paint. "It's strange to be back in this house. You didn't think about selling it?"

"I did. I actually put it on the market briefly, but when I told Riley, she gave me these puppy dog eyes and—"

"Puppy dog eyes? *Riley?*"

"I know. It was like seeing the Pope flash metal horns. Anyway, I told Riley and her mum they could move in. The house should really be theirs

273

anyway."

"You're going to live with a social worker and a teenage girl?"

"Yes. They're moving in next week. I'm going to have a sitcom all of my own right here."

He smiled, darted his eyes upwards, and mumbled, "I know it's ungentle-manly to ask, but given the particular nature of your prognosticative ah ah ah—"

"Abilities?"

"Yes. Those. You can understand why I'd be curious if you, ah, arrived?"

"Yes."

"So…"

"I didn't."

"Oh."

"Yup."

Oliver stared back at the ceiling, then turned to her and said, "Breakfast?"

"Sure."

He turned to get out of bed, wincing as he stood up. She grabbed his hand and said, "I just want to be certain there's no misunderstanding here. This was me being selfish. You and I are friends. It's only a couple of months since Quan—"

"I get it."

"You get it, or you're just saying you get it?"

"No, I really get it. And, while we're being candid, there's this girl I've been working with at the shelter, Amy. She recently broke up with someone, and I'm not in any hurry, but I think there's something there. Chicks dig scars, right?"

Lenore smiled and ran her finger down the rivulets of scar tissue on his cheek. "Sure. Amy, huh? Alright, well, that breakfast won't make itself. I'm going to get up and have a shower. Close your eyes."

"But we just—"

"Yes, we did, and now I'm asking you to close your eyes." He complied, and she slipped on her robe, walked to the shower, and ran the water, listening to the sound of pots and pans clanging in the kitchen. The vision had been brief, more of a glimpse really, an ephemeral sneeze of prognostication. He'd been seventy, perhaps eighty. Wrinkles so deep they disguised the scars, hair thin and grey. He was in a hospital bed surrounded by children, grandchildren. A woman his age, maybe older, held his hand and wept as it happened. It was the best death that anyone could reasonably hope for.

The woman had been blurry, her skin ravaged by the caresses of time. Maybe it was Amy. Probably not. But it was someone. Another human form, another soul held in a body. Another complex composition of cells, proteins, bones, neurons, synapses existing in tenuous harmony for a cosmic blink of an eyelid, then returning to chaos, quiet, peace.

48

ECONOMICS IS TOTAL BULLSHIT

Riley dug the shovel into the ground, sweat trailing down her forehead, dirt staining her faded jeans. "*Ugh*. This stinks!"

"Dead bodies tend to smell, generally speaking."

"Yeah, obvs. It's not like I thought it'd smell like potpourri or whatever. But it's such a heavy smell. Like, it has *weight*."

"The quicker you dig, the sooner we don't have to breathe in the stench of formerly living flesh."

"Why do I have to do the fucking digging anyway?"

"Do we really have to go over the rules of 'heads or tails' again? If you'd been digging this whole time instead of talking, you'd be done by now."

Riley rolled her eyes and took a few more angry stabs at the ground. "God, you're like the annoying sister I never had." She planted the shovel, wiped her brow, and said, "That oughta do it. Refilling is your job."

Lenore pushed the body into the grave, then piled dirt on top.

"At least you didn't have to do this with Ocky and that dude you were nailing."

Lenore glared at her.

"Relax! Mum's inside listening to a podcast about fourth-wave feminism and macroeconomics or some shit. She can't hear us."

"I don't think you understand how guilty I feel. I *killed* a man."

"A man who was going to kill you."

"That doesn't make it alright."

"Doesn't it?"

Lenore said nothing as she finished refilling the hole, stamped it down with her boots. "Should we do, like, an epiphany or something?"

"You mean a eulogy?"

"Yeah."

"For a possum? I don't think so." She tilted her head at the planter box in the corner of the garden. "How're the strawberries going?"

"Managed to get rid of the aphids, but now they've got caterpillars, so I wouldn't eat them. They look pretty, though."

"Perfect. Shiny, pretty, inedible strawberries. Just like grandma used to grow."

"Your grandma grew strawberries?"

"No, I was being…never mind. Remind me to order that compost bin and the mushroom kit later. I keep forgetting."

"Already took care of it."

"With what money?"

"Kyle signed some stuff for me before he flew back to LA. I got 5k for some sneakers he scrawled on with a Nikko. *Five grand* for a pair of old kicks! Economics is total bullshit."

"A very astute observation." Lenore nodded towards the shed. "I'm going to clear some more junk out of there tomorrow. And we should probably build some better ventilation if you're going to be smoking weed in there all the time."

Riley froze, stared at her. "How did you—"

"I have five senses and a brain, Riley. No teenager in the history of humankind has gone into the garden 'to study' and re-emerged smelling like a deodorant factory for legitimate reasons."

"Don't tell Mum, okay? She's been on my back about my grades lately. And, I wanna do better, y'know, after all the shit I've put her through?"

"She said you're having trouble with your English essay. I'm about to go run some errands, but I can help you this afternoon if you like?"

"Yeah. Thanks, Len. That'd be cool. I want her to be proud of me, you know? Don't look at me like that. Shut up!"

Lenore laughed and opened the shed door, "You're really not half as terrible as you let on, are you?"

"Yeah, but don't go telling nobody, or I'll cut you." Riley jolted with a sudden realisation. "Hey, it's been more than forty-nine days since your dad passed away, right? That means his soul has found a new body or whatever?"

"If you believe in that kind of thing."

"And you don't?"

"I'd define myself as 'obdurately agnostic.'"

"I'd define you as 'annoying and psychotic.'" Riley shot back with a grin. She fumbled in her pocket, pulled out the fob watch Elliott had left her. "We better wrap this up. I'm going to go grab some water. You want?" She snapped it shut and put it away with an affected flourish.

"Yes. Please." Lenore watched Riley jog back inside and then close the shed door behind her, breathed in the musty scent of dust and cobwebs. The light flickered as a pair of moths slapped relentlessly against it, drunk with desire. Lenore swept her hand over Claire's former resting place, wondering how many times Elliott must've come out here, stood in this very spot, pressed his hand against this same surface, and wept.

She poked her head out the window. Riley was nowhere to be seen. The hinges of the dewar groaned as she prised the lid open. She climbed in and ran her fingers along the rusting metal. She reached into her pocket and took out Quan's phone, highlighted the hundreds of unanswered texts she'd sent him. Her finger hovered over the 'delete' button. She put it back in her pocket, stared at the ceiling. Then she took it out again and deleted them all.

Lenore put the phone away, closed her eyes, and listened to the perfect silence. Everything was as still as death, as quiet as oblivion.

Riley banged on the shed door. "Hey! You want this water or what?"

Lenore climbed out of the cryonic chamber, stared at it for a handful of heartbeats, then closed the lid.

49

NERO, ASCENDANT

Nero watched as the skinny female primate stood next to the grave, her lips moving as she spoke the hideous, discordant language of her species. Her arm was covered in a depiction of a raven, the upper part of it red and raw, covered in plastic. Over his two centuries on earth, Nero had been continuously confused by the human predilection for covering and adorning their perfectly functional forms with the skins of other animals, dangling rocks from their ears and necks, and placing ink under their skin. What a tremendously superficial species. He watched as she knelt on the ground and spoke in a low, sobbing voice. Tears fell from her freakish, spherical, single-lidded eyes. She removed a small wood and metal claw from her bag and dug a hole in the ground, then dropped in one of the flat, rectangular black stones that humans were always carrying around and talking into. She covered the hole back up, placed her fingers to her lips, and then pressed them against the engraved stone. Then she stood up and walked back over to Nero.

She looked at him and muttered more unintelligible garble. Nero ignored her, neither understanding nor caring what she had to say to him, until the point when his tiny glass tank began to tip, and he realised that she was delivering an emancipation speech. He trembled with excitement at the prospect of freedom as gravity carried him over the lip of the tank. He ignored her wave goodbye as he raced, charged, surged towards his newfound freedom. His nostrils filled with the scent of fresh grass, bugs, moss. His three eyes drank in glorious, radiant light.

He had lived for two hundred years, twice as long as a human, ten times as long as a lion, two hundred times longer than the average mouse. He had seen dozens of eclipses, hundreds of winters, thousands of full moons. He had felt the warming of the earth, watched great steel teeth fill the sky, heard metal birds roaring through the air. He had known joy and pain and hunger and satiation and ecstasy and freedom and captivity and yet, after all this time, the thrill of simply being was still intoxicating.

He felt effulgent with life, overflowing with it, drunk with its flavour. As Nero ran without destination or direction, running for the sheer thrill of movement, he felt as though he was actually lifting from the ground and flying. It took him a few moments to realise that this was quite literally the case. The wind rushed against his scales as he watched the world fall away beneath him. The humans became fleshy pink specks, the trees splotchy green clumps, the river a twisted blue serpent. Nero watched the earth fade like a distant memory as he embraced each tiny remaining moment of his life, his head roaring with the exhilaration of its fleeting remaining seconds. In a few flaps of the eagle's wings, he would be dead. But now? In this glorious, gravity-defying moment, he was alive, and he was *soaring*.

Acknowledgements

I released another book this year with three pages of acknowledgements, so I'll keep this one brief. Thank you to Shawn Simmons for your tireless work on so many aspects of this book including (but not limited to) editing and cover design. Thanks to my agent Cindy Bullard for helping to find a home for Lenore and the gang. L. E. Daniels was instrumental with her guidance on an earlier draft of this book. Matilda, you reminded me how important it is to stare at clouds, roar like a dinosaur, and dance like a monkey. Thank you always to all the readers who pick up these weird little word-babies I keep hurling out into the world, you all deserve promotions and puppies and jetpacks. All my love and gratitude to Hannah, who makes both the real and fictional worlds shine brighter.

About the Author

J.M. Donellan is an author, musician, poet, and podcaster. He was almost devoured by a tiger in the jungles of Malaysia, nearly died of a lung collapse in the Nepalese Himalayas, and once fended off a pack of rabid dogs with a guitar in the mountains of India. He has performed at the Sydney Writers' Festival, TEDxBrisbane, the Sydney Opera House, Brisbane Festival, and some very prestigious basements.

His previous works include the poetry collection *Stendhal Syndrome*, the Kirkus Prize-nominated novel *Killing Adonis*, and the podcast series *Six Cold Feet.* His children's poetry collection *19 ½ Spells Disguised As Poems* has been hailed as 'the worst recipe book of all time.' His most recent novel (besides the one you're looking at now) is *Rumors of Her Death.* He's won a bunch of awards but refuses to list them all here because no one likes a braggart.

SOCIAL MEDIA HANDLES:
@jmdonellan (twitter/Instagram/facebook/threads/substack)

Also by J.M. Donellan

A Beginner's Guide to Dying in India

Killing Adonis

Rumors of Her Death

For younger readers:
  Zeb and the Great Ruckus
  19 ½ Spells Disguised as Poems

Poetry: *Stendhal Syndrome*

Podcast series: *Six Cold Feet*